Emma

To dear Carol, my friend, writer buddy!
Joan

EMMA

Remembering my mother

Joan Grindley

iUniverse, Inc.
New York Lincoln Shanghai

Emma

Remembering my mother

Copyright © 2006 by Joan H. Grindley

All rights reserved. No part of this book may be used or reproduced by any means, graphic, electronic, or mechanical, including photocopying, recording, taping or by any information storage retrieval system without the written permission of the publisher except in the case of brief quotations embodied in critical articles and reviews.

iUniverse books may be ordered through booksellers or by contacting:

iUniverse
2021 Pine Lake Road, Suite 100
Lincoln, NE 68512
www.iuniverse.com
1-800-Authors (1-800-288-4677)

Names have been changed to protect privacy.

ISBN-13: 978-0-595-38320-7 (pbk)
ISBN-13: 978-0-595-82692-6 (ebk)
ISBN-10: 0-595-38320-3 (pbk)
ISBN-10: 0-595-82692-X (ebk)

Printed in the United States of America

I dedicate this book to the three women I love most in this world, my daughters. Now that they are grown women, I see the bits and pieces of both my mother and my grandmother in them, and it makes me proud. It also inspired me to write this second novel in the hoped-for trilogy representing their heritage.

Chapter 1

▼

The rain beat on the window pane. The glass rattled. The world outside was trying desperately to get into her bedroom. Seventeen year old Emma shuddered at the ferocity of the storm but bravely turned back to her journal and continued writing; ignoring the distraction Mother Nature was provoking.

He loves me. I know he loves me, but do I really love him? We've been dating for almost two years now—two years! I know Mama hates him—no, hate is too strong a word, but she certainly doesn't like him, not even a little bit. But then, why should she? He can be arrogant—I admit that; but I love him anyway. At least I think I do. He treats me like a queen and he makes me feel beautiful and clever and older than my years. He gives me things too, things I'd never get from the boys my own age.

She fingered the narrow silver bracelet on her right wrist. The tiny heart sparkled in the half light as it moved on the intricate silver chain.

When I think how lucky I was to meet him, a boy from Morningside Heights and me, a daughter of immigrants still living in Yorkville. I know Mama has her own business now, but we are certainly not in society like the Carneys.

When she remembered the day they met just two blocks away at Ginger's house, Emma still registered awe at her good fortune. Charles Carney was working as a meter reader for Con Edison on weekends while attending Columbia University School of Engineering.

"I'm not working for the money," he hastened to inform Emma, "but to get business experience and learn responsibility. That's what my father says is important."

Emma was at her friend Ginger's house studying and suddenly the lights went out. Ginger's father called Con Edison and twenty minutes later Charles Carney appeared at the door of the apartment. After a brief discussion with Ginger's dad, Charles excused himself and went down the stairs that led to the basement. As soon as he left, Ginger jumped up, grabbed a comb and began combing her long auburn hair and pinching her cheeks to increase their color. She wanted to impress the handsome young man when he returned from the basement.

Charles Carney came back up the stairs a few minutes later, smiling confidently. He strode into the center of the room and announced to Ginger's father, "It was the old penny trick, Sir."

"The old what?" was the response.

Charles hastened to explain.

"Some people put pennies in the fuse box to extend the power of the fuse above the amps it's designed to produce. This addition of copper to the wire causes the wire to overheat and even spark in some cases, and that shuts down the power source."

He looked around at his audience to see if his words had made the proper impact and then went on.

"It's an old trick." "My boss told me to be on the lookout for it and report it wherever I found it so they could catch the people doing it and charge them a fine for disrupting the power." He glanced at Ginger's father again and then shifted his gaze to Emma. He looked at her long and hard.

"Your daughter, sir?" He cast another sideways glance at Emma.

"No, the redhead's mine."

"Oh," said Charles, and pausing briefly, he continued. "I'm sure you didn't put the penny in there, sir. If you had, you would have retrieved it when the power went out and before you called Con Ed. Someone else on your floor must have done it and got the wrong box by mistake. Anyway, I fixed it and put a warning sign up above the box so maybe he'll think twice next time. I'll just report it as a loose wire, and then there won't be any trouble."

All this excitement had caused Emma to lose track of the time and she now realized she was late starting for home.

"I gotta get home now, Ginger. Mama will be wondering what happened to me and you know how she gets when I'm late. See you tomorrow."

"Ok, Emma, see you tomorrow."

Ginger tossed her red curls and turned to see if Charles Carney was watching. He is a beauty, she thought to herself. Before she could even begin to flirt with him, Charles had left the room.

As Emma turned to leave the apartment, Charles held the door for her and escorted her down the stairs to the front door. Emma thanked him and began walking up the street toward her house. Charles began to walk along beside her and then broke the silence with a question.

"What is your name, pretty lady?" he inquired softly.

"Emma. My name is Emma Pedesch," she stammered. "I live just down there a few blocks," she added, pointing down the street.

"Well, Emma Pedesch," Charles answered while taking hold of her arm, "You're about to be walked home by Charles Carney, a junior at Columbia University and a part time employee of Con Edison. What do you think about that?"

Emma was so overcome, she could not answer and they walked the last two blocks in companionable silence. When they reached the steps in front of Emma's house, she turned, thrust out her hand to attempt a handshake, and found herself enveloped in Charles Carney's embrace. Before she knew what was happening, Charles was kissing her—right there in broad daylight, in front of her very own apartment and in full view of any of her neighbors who might be looking out their windows. Emma was struck dumb but reacted quickly. She pulled away from Charles' arms and ran up the stairs of the apartment building as fast as she could. She did not look back. As she went through the front door, she heard Charles shout behind her.

"I'll be calling you, Emma Pedesch and soon. You can count on it."

As Emma entered the apartment, her head was spinning. Her cheeks were aflame and she felt like her heart was going to beat right out of her chest.

"How dare he kiss me like that? How dare he? Suppose Mama or Papa saw us or any of our neighbors. I could just die of shame right here and now. Just die."

Fortunately for Emma no one was at home to witness the incident. She went straight to her room and threw herself onto the bed. She turned over and stared at the ceiling and then began to smile. The more she thought about what had just happened, the more she smiled. She ran her fingers across her lips where Charles Carney had kissed her, and hugged herself.

It had taken Charles only a few days after that fateful kiss to call Emma and ask her out on their first real date. They had been dating almost every weekend since then, and Emma was feeling pretty comfortable with the young engineer. Everything had been going fine until this weekend. Emma was about to graduate from High School and Charles was already talking about marriage.

"I'm almost twenty three now, Emma, and have a good job with AT&T and I want to start my life with you as my wife. I'm going to tell your father and mother tonight."

"You will do no such thing, Charles Carney," Emma retorted. "After all, you didn't even officially ask me yet. I haven't even graduated from high school. Charles, please let me enjoy that moment first and then we will talk about getting married. If you say anything now to Mama or Papa it will spoil the whole celebration. Please, Charles, please don't say anything just yet. If you do, I will never speak to you again—I mean it, never."

Emma stopped to catch her breath and looked up at the tall, dark-haired young man beside her. Charles was speechless for once and she had to compose herself to keep from grinning.

"You will marry me, Emma. Of that I have no doubt, but I won't say anything to your parents until after the graduation if that's so important to you. Just remember that after the ceremony is over, I will speak to them. I don't want to wait any longer. I want us to be married, and as soon as possible."

Charles stalked off in mock anger. The subject hung in the air like an unsettled storm warning.

Chapter 2

Emma couldn't think of anything right now but her pending graduation. Not even Charles Carney's proposal of marriage could replace her anticipation and feeling of achievement as she contemplated walking down the aisle of the school auditorium in cap and gown to receive her diploma. Her parents were so proud of her. This day was as important to them as it was to Emma.

As a mother, Julia Pedesch had great dreams for her daughter and hoped that Emma would embark on a career before settling down to marriage, especially marriage to Charles Carney whom she despised. Emma had been modeling in her mother's salon this past year on Saturdays and had a taste of both the hard work and glamour of being a model. She liked the work and felt confident in the way she handled herself. Julia knew she was a natural and often told her so.

"God has gifted you with the most beautiful legs, Emma. Even though you are only five feet two, your legs are perfectly formed and when you wear a pair of silk stockings and designer heels, you are every bit a model."

To Emma's chagrin, however, she was built like a boy, flat on top with a small waist and hips. She wore her long honey-blond hair cut to the shoulder in a soft bob. Fortunately, the popular style of the day, commonly known as 'the flapper,' called for a flat bosom. Women who were well endowed could be seen binding their ample breasts to attempt to emulate this new trend and do justice to the many designer creations which featured the bosom-less silhouette. Emma's slender body was in perfect proportion so she could wear just about anything. This made her one of the most sought-after models in her mother's salon.

Julia's fashion house was known as American Chic, and her line featured flapper dresses as well as the sporty golf outfits for women, starring another new rage of the day—knickers. These were trousers constructed of soft worsted fabric that billowed, oh so gently, above the knees and then hugged the leg below with a soft band of knitted fabric. Contrasting hose up to the knee were tucked under the band. Silk blouses gently cut in varying gem tones were worn on top to complete the ensemble. These designs were a natural for Emma and resulted in a good many sales for the popular salon. Julia was very proud of Emma and enjoyed seeing her new creations shown to their best advantage on her own beautiful daughter.

Julia's biggest challenge right now was the creation of Emma's graduation dress. She wanted it to be totally original and above all, spectacular. Emma had chosen a bolt of ice green satin and Julia had just laid it out on her cutting table. She sat back to admire the shimmering fabric when Emma burst into the room. Eyeing the lush satin rolled out on the table like a puddle of mint ice cream, she rushed over and snatched it up. She wound it skillfully around her slender body and whooped with delight.

"Oh Mama, it is the most beautiful fabric I have ever seen. Have you come up with a design yet? Can we start working on the dress now?" Emma was bursting with enthusiasm.

"Of course we can," Julia answered. "I wanted it to be a surprise, but maybe your input into the design would be a good idea. Let's put our heads together right now and see what we can come up with."

Julia stood back and looked at the way the fabric was draped around Emma's slim body. She cocked her head to one side and began to walk around her daughter studying the drape of the fabric.

"I think you've done it, Emma. The way you have draped the fabric around yourself is the essence of the design—a soft gentle wrapping from your shoulders to your toes. The dress will be on one shoulder only and tucked in at the waist to gather in the folds. We'll widen it slightly from the hips so you will be able to walk comfortably. If I cut it on the bias, it will drop smoothly to the tips of your shoes. You'll look stunning, Emma, simply stunning. What do you think?"

"Oh, Mama, I think you are a genius. I love the idea of the one shoulder and I can't wait for you to start on it. Ginger will just die when she sees it. Thank you so much, Mama. Thank you for everything. I love you." Emma threw her arms around her mother and hugged her hard.

"I love you too, my dear, and I'm delighted you like my idea. I'm sure you will be the belle of the ball in this creation. I'll start the cutting room on it first thing tomorrow. With luck and a few fittings, it should be done in a week or so."

"I can't wait to tell Ginger." "May I run down the street and tell her my good news?

"Of course you can, and if Ginger needs help with a dress for graduation, I'd be glad to help her too. Please tell her that, Emma. I know her mother may not want me to; she's so possessive of her daughter and her wardrobe."

"I know what you mean about her mother, Mama, but I'll tell her anyway. I know she'd love to get her dress at American Chic, but I don't know if her mother will agree. I think she'll have to settle for ready-made. I'll go down there now and see her, and we'll both come back here for lunch. You're making noodles and pot cheeses today, aren't you Mama? That's Ginger's favorite, and mine too. See ya later."

Before Julia could answer, Emma was out the door. She made the two blocks to Ginger's house in record time. She bounded up the steps of the brownstone and knocked on the door.

"Coming," said a voice from within. The door opened and a blowsy woman with dyed red hair stood in the doorway.

"Hello Emma. Looking for Ginger are we?"

"Yes, Mrs. Rogers. Is she here? I want to tell her about my dress for graduation. My mother is making it special for me and it is so beautiful."

"Oh really," said Lorraine Rogers. Aren't you the lucky one. Ginger is in her room, dear. You can go on up if you want to."

"Thanks, Mrs. Rogers, I'll go right up. See ya later." Emma took the steps two at a time and knocked on Ginger's door.

"Come on in," her friend's voice came through the door. I'm just curling my hair." As Emma entered the small pink bedroom, Ginger turned from her dressing table. Emma burst out laughing at the sight of her friend.

"You look like a Negro pixie," Emma said between giggles. "What on earth are you doing to yourself, Ginger?"

"I'm making rag curls, silly. Haven't you ever seen these before? You tie rags at the ends of your damp hair and then roll them up to your scalp and tie them there. When your hair dries you take out the rags and *voila* you have curls. Pretty smooth, huh?

"You're too much, Ginger. Where did you learn about making rag curls?"

"Oh, I read it in a magazine, Emma. It's the latest beauty trick among the movie stars. You'd be amazed at what you can learn from those movie magazines. If I want to be a star one day, I have to keep up with all the tricks of the trade. Do you want to try it, Emma?"

"No thanks, Ginger. I'll just watch you. My hair is curly enough as it is. The reason I came over was to tell you about the graduation gown Mama is making for me. The fabric is so beautiful and we designed it ourselves. I can't wait for you to see it. Mama says to tell you that she'd design a dress for you, too, if you want. What do you think about that?"

"I don't know, Emma. I'd love to have your mother make a dress for me, but you know my mom. Her nose would be out of joint. We can't really afford salon prices, and you know she's going to insist on paying full price. She's used to going shopping with me at the department store. Tell your mother thanks for me though, will ya? I'll be down in about an hour and you can show me the fabric for your dress. I got some chores I gotta do first, ok?"

"Ok, but Mama is making our favorite lunch so don't take too long. I don't know about you, but I'm starving. See you at my house."

Emma left her friend and went down the stairs and out the front door. Ginger's mother was nowhere in sight so Emma closed the door behind her and began the short walk back to her house. She went up to her bedroom and pulled out her journal.

Poor Ginger. She and her mother are not close like Mama and I. I'm so lucky. I can tell Mama most anything. I think Ginger can talk to me or Mama easier than she can to her own mother. She can't talk to her dad either. They used to have fun together, before he got sick. That's what Ginger calls it. He doesn't go to work any more and mostly just stays home and drinks.

Being an only child doesn't help either. At least I have Jerry to talk to. Baby brothers aren't much good for advice, but he does listen and that makes me feel better sometimes. I'm glad I can be here for her though. She's my best friend in the whole world. I just hope she'll have a dress even half as pretty as mine. I can't believe we'll be graduating in a few weeks. I wonder what Ginger will do after graduation. Maybe we could model together—just until she gets discovered and becomes a big movie star, of course.

Chapter 3

Graduation day arrived. Julia finished Emma's dress two days before and had put it away covered with fresh tissue paper, awaiting the big event. Plans for the party at the Pedesch home were complete down to the last morsel of *polachinta* and George was making a special batch of wine for the occasion—for parents only of course. The graduation ceremony at the school was to begin promptly at 6:30 p.m. and the party afterward would begin around eight o'clock.

Julia prepared her special fruit punch. Their next door neighbor, Mrs. Glass, was busy putting together all the ingredients in two huge punch bowls in the dining room, leaving nothing to add but the ice rings. Julia had made these ahead of time and put them in the ice box to form. She was in the kitchen putting the final touches on the salads and homemade breads. The exquisite aroma of cabbage rolls filled the room and pots of all sizes and shapes were simmering on the big iron stove.

"Mama, you have totally outdone yourself for this party," said Emma, smacking her lips in anticipation of tasting her favorite foods. "I love you so much for going to all this trouble for me."

"It was no trouble, Emma. It was a pure joy. Don't you know how proud Papa and I are of you. This is one of the most important days of our lives. You are the first Pedesch to graduate from high school. It is a dream come true. I just hope everyone enjoys eating the food as much as I did preparing it."

Julia reached for her daughter and placed a kiss on her forehead. "I love you Emma. You have only to make the right choices and anything is possible for you. Just look at me—a simple, uneducated peasant girl from Hungary. And now I am the owner of a popular dress salon and making a good living—especially for a woman. I want that kind of success for you, and now you have the education to make that happen and far exceed my accomplishments. Anything you want is there for the taking, even college if that is what you decide. Papa and I will find a way to support you in whatever you want to do."

"I appreciate all you and Papa are doing for me. I will try to make good decisions but please be patient with me and please understand about Charles. I care for him so much, Mama, and I want him to be a part of my life. Just give him a chance."

She gave her mother a hug and went to her room to change for the graduation which was less than two hours away.

"Call me if you need any help with the cap and gown, Emma. Everything here is ready. I have all the neighbors on duty while Papa and I are at the ceremony."

The cap and gown were hanging on the door of her room. She pulled the hanger down and held the gown in front of her before the mirror. "A graduate, I'm going to be a graduate," she hummed to herself.

Emma came down the stairs wearing her cap and gown. As she reached the landing, she looked up to see her father staring at her from the bottom step. There were tears in his eyes. She hurried down the rest of the stairs and put her arms around him.

"Don't cry, Papa. I'm only graduating from high school; I'm not leaving home. You should be happy for me, not sad."

"I am happy, Emma. These are tears of joy, not sadness. It's just that I am so proud of you I think my heart will burst. How could I have such a smart wonderful daughter? After all, I had only two years in the seminary in the old country and here you are graduating high school—with a diploma yet."

Just then, Julia came around the corner. She stopped and eyed her husband and daughter with curiosity.

"And what are you up to? It's getting late you know. We must get going to the school now or we will be late for our daughter's big day."

"I'm ready, Mama. Papa looks so handsome in his suit, doesn't he? Where is Jerry? Is he dressed and ready to go?"

"He's been ready for an hour. I sent him downstairs to wait for us. I'll get the car now, and pick you and Papa up outside. Is Charles going to meet us there?"

"Yes, Mama. Charles will be there in plenty of time. He had to go uptown with his father this afternoon but he knows what time the ceremony is. I'm sure he won't be late."

The high school was only ten minutes away. When Julia parked the car she noticed that young people were entering the front door of the high school from all sides of the building. Young men and women dressed in caps and gowns were calling to each other across the grass. Emma jumped from the back seat and shouted greetings to several of her classmates. Just then, Ginger's family arrived. The two best friends hugged and linked arms. They led the parade into the main door of the building.

"See you later," both girls shouted over their shoulders as they ran ahead.

"Maybe our families can sit together," Emma said, looking expectantly at Ginger.

"I don't think so, Em. My dad likes to sit in the back so he can get out for a smoke if he needs to. You know how he is. You and I can sit together in the center while we wait for our names to be called. I'll need you there for moral support. I still can't believe I am going to get my diploma after all. It was a real close call for me, you know. If you hadn't tutored me in math, I never would have made it. You're a really good friend, Emma, in more ways than one."

The house lights dimmed and the school orchestra struck up the notes of Pomp and Circumstance. The Principal rose from his chair and announced, "let us now welcome the graduates of the class of 1924."

Tears welled up in Julia's eyes as she watched her daughter approach the stage. Emma carried her small frame tall and went up the stairs to the stage with the grace and ease of the model she was. George too was dabbing at his eyes with his handkerchief and both parents were mesmerized by the spectacle. All eyes were on the long line of gowned students slowly filling up the stage in preparation for the final event.

Ginger's father whistled and clapped loudly as his daughter came down the aisle. People turned to stare at the uncouth behavior. He dropped his hands into his lap and shrugged. His wife just shook her head. Ginger pretended not to notice, and with head held high, found her place on the stage. As the last student was seated, a hush came over the crowded hall. The Principal stood up and walked to the small speaker's platform at the center of the stage.

"As your name is called, please come up to the podium and accept our congratulations."

He called the names slowly and clearly. As each name was called, the student walked to the podium, shook the Principal's hand and took possession of his or her diploma. Family and friends cheered and clapped for each recipient. When Emma's name was called, Julia, George and Jerry, could hardly contain themselves. They all stood up and begin clapping. A loud 'yay Emma' could be heard from the rear of the auditorium. That must be Charles thought Julia to herself. I suppose he's proud of Emma, too, and wants her to know he's here for her big day.

"Edward Zinanski," called Principal Greenway.

"That's got to be the last one, George," Julia said. "Now there will be the speech by the Valedictorian and then the ceremony will be over." George muttered an acknowledgement and closed his eyes. He will probably sleep through the whole speech, Julia thought to herself.

While the Valedictorian was speaking, Jerry fidgeted in his seat, totally bored with the whole thing. His mind was on home and all the good things to eat there. Julia wished they could leave now before George disgraced her by snoring, but she knew they must wait for the end. Emma would expect them to meet her in the hall where all the graduates would greet their relatives and friends before leaving the school for the last time.

The applause filled the hall and the Valedictorian returned to his seat on the dais. The Principal thanked everyone for coming and the orchestra struck up the chords of Pomp and Circumstance again. Emma was being pushed and shoved by the mob in the hall but saw her parents struggling to reach her across the sea of celebrants. She forced her way toward them, and then out of the corner of her eye she saw Charles pressing through the crowd toward her. They all arrived at the same spot at the same time. Charles picked Emma up off the floor and hugged her before Julia or George could even reach her. When he put her back on her feet, she turned and reached for her mother. Julia hugged her soundly and then made room for George and Jerry to congratulate her too. The hall was a mob of people all hugging and kissing and wishing each other well.

"Can we leave now, Emma?" Julia asked. "I'd like to head home and get ready for the party. You have to change into your dress too, and the ceremony lasted a bit longer than we expected. Some of our friends will be at the house already, waiting for us."

"We can leave now, Mama. Charles can follow us home in his car with Ginger if her parents don't mind. She brought her dress to change at our house. Let's make our way toward the side door. That's closest to where you parked the car."

The Pedesch family moved together with Emma leading the way. Charles agreed to bring Ginger and so headed across the room to find her. The graduation was over, but now the real celebration would begin. Emma was euphoric. Her whole life was unfolding in front of her and she was more than ready to celebrate that fact. She pushed open the heavy wooden doors and breathed deeply of the unseasonably warm night air.

"C'mon Mama, let's go home so the party can begin."

Chapter 4

▼

As they turned the corner and approached the house, Emma could see several cars already parked in front. Julia pulled up to the end of the driveway, and before she could turn off the engine, Emma was out the door like a flash.

"I'm going right up to change into my party dress," she shouted over her shoulder. When Emma opened the door she was immediately besieged by several of their neighbors.

"Congratulations, Emma, We are so proud of you. Come and let me look at you now that you are a high school graduate." Mrs. Glass opened her arms wide to give her a warm hug.

Emma accepted the show of affection and murmured her thanks. "Please, Mrs. Glass, let me change into my party clothes and I'll be right back. I promise."

Emma side-stepped another neighbor and took the stairs two at a time.

Everyone clapped and cheered as she raced up the stairs. Just then Julia and George entered the foyer, followed by Charles leading Ginger with her dress over her arm.

"Excuse me, Mrs. Pedesch," said Ginger, "but I am going up to Emma's room to change, too, if that's okay."

Charles released Ginger and waded into the background. He wanted to catch the first glimpse of his beloved Emma when she came down the stairs. He had a beautiful bouquet of yellow roses in his arms that he was going to present to her before anyone else could favor her with anything. She was his girl and she was going to know that for sure before this evening was over. What Emma wanted was a proposal. Charles was convinced of that. Well, he was going to make her one tonight—one she wouldn't be able to resist. He smiled smugly to himself as he thought about what he was planning.

Moments later his head turned as Ginger descended the staircase, resplendent in a coral chiffon dress that complimented her beautiful red hair. It was strapless and showed off her ample bosom. She beamed as she was welcomed by the guests, wishing that her own parents were in the crowd, but knowing that they wouldn't come to the party.

Emma was right behind her. She paused at the top of the steps and looked over the crowd. She could hear the intake of breath from some of the women. She smiled as the applause exploded around her. When her eyes found Charles, she began slowly to descend the stairs. When she got to the bottom, he offered her the huge bouquet of roses.

"Oh, thank you, Charles, they are beautiful. They make me feel like a queen."

"You are a queen, Emma—my queen," was Charles's answer. He had all he could do to keep from kissing her right there in front of everyone, but he knew Julia Pedesch would not take kindly to this show of affection. He controlled himself and merely took her arm and led her through the crowd into the living room where Ginger was temporarily holding court. Both girls were stunning, but Emma's gown created ooh's and aah's from every woman in the room, and several of the men, too.

Charles took her aside for a moment with the pretense of getting her something to drink. "Emma, darling, you are ravishing. I have never seen you look more beautiful than you do tonight. May I take the roses into the kitchen for you and have one of the women put them in water?"

"Thank you Charles. That would be wonderful. I want them to last as long as possible." Emma turned and handed the bouquet to Charles.

Julia was on the other side of the door when Charles entered the kitchen. She took the roses from him without a word and reached for a slender crystal vase on the top shelf of the cupboard. Julia was tall but still had to strain to reach the top shelf so Charles wangled himself between her and the cupboard and retrieved the vase for her. She accepted it from his hand rather coolly.

"I could have managed, thank you," she announced.

Charles muttered a terse "you're welcome," and returned to the living room. By this time, Emma was surrounded by every eligible young man in the room. He seemed to be separated from her by a solid wall of people, most of them handsome young men. Ginger too had her share of admirerers, and was obviously enjoying the attention. Emma was so busy accepting compliments and congratulations that she was temporarily unaware of Charles's absence from her side.

Charles, though not pleased with the situation, decided it was wiser to take a back seat and allow Emma to enjoy her moment of glory. He began to circulate around the room to see if there was anyone else he could find that would be interesting to talk to. He scanned the periphery of the small living room and his eyes rested on a tall middle-aged man impeccably dressed in a tuxedo. He was strikingly handsome with strands of silver at his temples and Charles deduced that he must be someone of importance.

He made his way across the room and stood next to him. He looked rather like a movie star, Charles thought, except for a long scar down the right side of his face. The elegantly dressed man carried himself tall and with total confidence. He was speaking to a younger man, much smaller in stature and not nearly as elegantly dressed. As Charles came closer, he realized they were conversing in French, and rather animatedly.

The man with the scar looked up and seeing Charles staring at him, paused and put out a hand. *"Bonsoir, Monsieur,"* I am Louis Chatelaine, a friend and former business partner of Mrs. Pedesch."

"I am pleased to meet you, *Monsieur* Chatelaine," answered Charles in his best French accent. "I have heard Emma speak of you. I am Charles Carney—Emma's—uh—friend."

"Mais oui, Monsieur Carney. I have heard the lovely Emma speak of you also. May I introduce my good friend, Pierre Manot? He is an artist friend of mine and of Mrs. Pedesch also. Our roots go back to France where our families were close friends."

"A pleasure, sir," said Charles. "Then you are both originally from France, I presume."

"*Oui*," answered Pierre as he too extended his hand to the tall young man. "I had the privilege of coming to America shortly after Louis arrived. We have been friends a very long time. And how do you come to know our charming Emma, *Monsieur*?"

"Oh, I hope to be Emma's fiancé quite soon now that she has graduated from high school," responded Charles confidently. "We've been dating for the past two years now and I am very serious about her."

"I see," said Pierre. "And does Julia—I mean Mrs. Pedesch, know of your intentions, young man?"

"Well, not yet, *Monsieur* Manot, but I hope that she will very soon. Emma is well aware of my intentions toward her and I……….."

Louis interrupted. "Forgive me, Mr. Carney, but I advise you to slow down a bit in your pursuit of the lovely Emma or you will have a fiery Hungarian dragon to deal with. I happen to know that Julia Pedesch is very protective when it comes to her darling daughter. I believe she has some plans for Emma's future that perhaps do not include you. Are you aware of this?"

"Well, sir, I know that Emma has been modeling in her mother's salon, but I hardly think that suggests a career in modeling, do you?"

"I am forced to disagree with you, Mr. Carney," interjected Pierre. "I am the artist who painted the portraits of Julia displayed in *Monsieur* Chatelaine's salon. Emma takes after her mother and is already being sought after as a photographer's model. If my guess is right, she will soon be gracing the pages of many of our most prestigious fashion magazines. Do you really want to stand in the way of her having a successful career? As a Frenchman, I know how overwhelming love can be, but if you really love her, you wouldn't stand in her way, would you?"

Charles was speechless—prestigious fashion magazines? What was this Frenchman talking about? Emma had not said a thing to him about being a photographer's model. Modeling was just something she did after school and on Saturdays, or was there more to it than that? He vowed he would speak to her the first chance he got. He wanted answers and he wanted them now. He was going to marry Emma Pedesch and no modeling career was going to stop him. Suddenly he knew he had to find Emma, had to talk with her, be with her. He excused himself, turned from Louis and Pierre and without another word headed for the opposite side of the room where he could see Emma shimmering like a beacon in her ice green satin gown.

Emma was still surrounded by well-wishers. Charles forced his way through the crowd and made his way to Emma's side. He grasped her hand in his and held on. Before she knew what was happening, she was being led away from her friends and into the dining room by Charles.

"What's going on Charles? Why are you dragging me out of the room?" Emma wanted to know.

"Because I need to be with you. We haven't spent five minutes together since the party began. I want to share your graduation with you. I was feeling very left out. I don't think you care if I'm here or not," he added angrily.

"Of course I do, Charles. I am truly sorry. I've never graduated from high school before and this dress Mama made me makes me feel like a princess. I got carried away. Please don't be mad at me, please."

Emma stood on her tiptoes and kissed Charles on the cheek. He was immediately disarmed and all the angry thoughts disappeared. He kissed her back and led her out into the living room where several couples were dancing to the music of the phonograph. *Begin the Beguine* was playing and they blended together and swayed to the music. This song had always been one of their favorites and it seemed to wipe away any misunderstanding between them.

"I love you so much," Charles whispered.

Serious talk about the modeling will wait till tomorrow, he thought to himself. I'm not going to do anything to spoil tonight. Emma snuggled close to his chest, and no one watching them could doubt that this was indeed a serious young couple. Louis and Pierre watched from the sidelines and were glad that Julia was too busy in the kitchen just then to witness this overt display of affection.

Chapter 5

▼

The party was a huge success. Julia suddenly realized that she had spent little or no time with Emma. She looked around the room and tried to find her. Suddenly she spied her in a corner of the dining room with Charles Carney. They appeared to be deep in discussion and the look on Emma's face was somewhat agitated.

As Julia approached, she heard Emma say, "Not now, Charles, please. I'm just not ready to settle down yet. I haven't even begun to live my life. I'm too young to be a married woman."

Julia stopped in her tracks and took a deep breath. Is Charles Carney pressing Emma to marry him? That arrogant young upstart is apparently pushing her daughter to agree to marriage—a marriage Emma does not seem to want. How dare he do this without even discussing it with her?

She put her hand on Emma's arm to let her know she was there, and in the calmest voice she could muster, addressed her daughter.

"Emma, dear, some of our guests are leaving and they want to say goodbye to you. I'm sure Charles will excuse you. You don't want to be rude to our friends and neighbors, do you?"

Emma looked up, startled by her mother's words, and then recovered herself.

"Of course, Mama. I'll go with you at once. Charles, please excuse me. I must say good night to our guests."

Her face flushed and with her hands shaking slightly, Emma followed her mother to the front hall where several of the guests were gathered.

"It was such a lovely party, Julia," said a tall woman holding a baby," but as you can see the children are just exhausted by all the festivities. They are not used to being out in the evening with their parents. It was so kind of you to include them. Come now, father, let's get these children home to bed."

"Thank you for coming," Julia said as they went down the steps.

"Yes, thank you so much," Emma chimed in.

As the last guest was ushered out the door, Julia turned to survey the living room. Charles Carney was sitting in the corner, staring out the window. Louis and Pierre were finishing a last glass of wine with George. Julia took Emma's hand and together they walked across the living room and into the dining room. Charles rose from his chair as soon as he saw them.

"Emma, I need to talk to you," he said quietly.

"Not now, Charles. I want to spend a little time with Louis and Pierre. I have barely had a moment with them all evening."

Charles stopped where he was, and putting his hands on Emma's shoulders, he turned her around to face him. Emma looked directly into his eyes before she spoke.

"Charles, please don't spoil this wonderful evening with more serious talk. This is my graduation after all. Let's just enjoy what's left of it. We can talk tomorrow, but tonight is for celebrating and I don't want to think of anything else. Please, Charles."

Completely taken aback, Charles agreed. "All right Emma. We'll have one more glass of wine together and then I will head for home."

Emma smiled at Charles, took his hand and led him into the dining room.

"*Bon soir* once again, *monsieur*," said Pierre. "Louis and I are having our final glass of the evening in honor of *Mademoiselle* Emma. Will you join us?"

"Why thank you, *Monsieur* Manot. I would be pleased to join you and raise a glass to my dearest Emma."

"She is the belle of the ball this evening, would you not agree?" interjected Louis. Your gown is *absolutement magnifique*, my dear Emma. I understand from your delightful mother that you designed this creation together, *n'est pas?*"

"*Oui, Monsieur* Chatelaine," responded Emma in her best French. I love working with Mama at the salon, but this was my first time being part of the design of a gown. I think modeling is more where my talent lies, but it was fun to plan the dress together. I did pick out the fabric, but most of the rest was Mama's idea."

"Well you are quite a team, my dear—a mother and daughter to be reckoned with in the world of fashion."

"And worthy of my brush and palette, too," added Pierre. "I don't know of a more beautiful mother and daughter anywhere in New York. I would love to paint a portrait of Emma and Julia together if they would permit." He glanced at Julia for approval.

"That's a lovely idea, Pierre. We'll have to commission you to do that one day. But right now let's have a final toast to our beautiful graduate."

George immediately took the decanter and filled all the glasses. Even Emma was permitted a glass of wine on this momentous occasion. George raised his glass and in his best broken English announced, "Health, happiness and long life to my beloved Emma."

"Here, here," echoed the group and Emma smiled delightedly.

She stole a glance at Charles and was relieved to see that he was not going to add anything to the toast. He made an effort to behave himself in the presence of the two Frenchmen. Louis seems to intimidate the young man with his obvious wealth and sophistication and Emma was relieved at Charles's acquiescence.

After the last drop of wine disappeared from their glasses, Pierre and Louis bid goodnight to their hosts. They bestowed kisses on both of Emma's cheeks in elegant French fashion and took their leave. Being the only non-member of the family left, Charles graciously expressed his thanks and with a mere kiss to Emma's cheek, he bid the Pedesch family goodnight.

"I'll call you tomorrow, Emma. Get a good night's sleep."

"Good night, Charles, and thank you again for being here and for the beautiful roses. I will probably sleep a little late tomorrow, so we'll talk in the afternoon."

Charles smiled and went down the steps. Sleep well, Emma, he thought to himself. You will have much to think about tomorrow.

Chapter 6

The clock in the hall chimed eleven when Emma rolled over and pushed her covers aside. Her bedroom was flooded with sunlight. She threw her legs over the side, grabbed her robe and staggered sleepily to the bathroom. She stared at the rather disheveled young lady in the mirror.

"You look an absolute fright," she said to her reflection. "Can two glasses of wine and a little less sleep make such a difference? My head hurts, my mouth feels like it was stuffed with cotton and my eyes are barely functioning."

"Who are you talking to, Emma?" asked Jerry, knocking at the door.

"No one. I am talking to myself."

"I need to get in there Emmy. Please hurry."

"If you're in a hurry, use the extra wash room in the cellar. Papa won't mind. I'd like to take a shower so I can wake up. Please?"

"Ok, Emmy," came the sullen reply. "I guess you're still special this morning. I'll go down to the cellar."

Emma heard him shuffle off down the hall and bang his way down the stairs. Little brothers can be a nuisance, she thought, but he's really a good kid most of the time. As Emma finished drying her hair and was getting ready to vacate the bathroom, she heard Julia's voice.

"He's on the phone for Emma. Go and tell her please."

"Emmy, it's Charles," said Jerry. "He's on the phone and wants to talk to you right now. Are you coming or not?"

"Of course I'm coming. Tell him I'll be there in a minute."

O bother! I was hoping he wouldn't call until after I have some breakfast. I can think better on a full stomach. Julia was standing in the doorway with the phone in her hand and a worried look on her face.

"Good morning, Emma. Did you sleep well? Charles is on the phone," she added without waiting for an answer.

Emma gave her mother a peck on the cheek, took the phone from her outstretched hand and sighed.

"Hello, Charles," she said, trying to sound as cheerful as possible. "How are you this morning?"

"I'm fine, Emma, but I want to talk to you. When can I come over?" There was a pause.

"I just got up and need to have some breakfast and Mama and I have some cleaning up to do. What's the hurry?" Another pause ensued, but this time it was on Charles's end of the conversation.

"You know why I'm anxious to see you." His voice rose slightly in obvious irritation. "I want to talk about our getting married. You agreed we'd discuss it as soon as you graduated."

"I know I did, but I didn't think you meant first thing the next morning. Couldn't it wait until tomorrow, Charles?"

"No, it can't wait. I'm coming over this afternoon. I'll be there about four o'clock and we'll talk then." The phone went dead before Emma had a chance to say another word.

She looked at her mother and placed the phone back in its cradle. "He's coming over at four o'clock. He wouldn't take no for an answer. Please don't be angry, Mama. I'll help you clean up before he gets here. He just wants to talk to me."

"What's so important, he has to talk to you today? Does he have to see you every single day? You were up so late and you're still tired. Let me call him back and tell him you're exhausted. He can come tomorrow if it's so important."

"No, Mama. It will only make him angry and I'm in no mood for an argument. I'm sure he won't stay long. May I have my breakfast now?"

"Of course. What would you like me to fix for you, my beautiful graduate?"

Emma's face broke into a broad smile. "I'd almost forgotten, Mama. I am a graduate, an honest-to-goodness high school graduate. I'll never have to go to school again, will I?"

"Not if you don't want to, but you do have choices you know. You could go to college if you want to."

"I don't want to decide anything right now. I just want a big plate of your blueberry pancakes with lots of sour cream and a big cup of coffee. I'm going to concentrate on my appetite right now, not my future."

"That's all right with me. You have lots of time yet to make these decisions. I just don't want Charles Carney to influence you. I hope you will make your own choices. I never had the chance to make decisions when I was your age, but it's different for you. This is not Hungary. It's America. It's New York City and anything is possible here. I am a living example of that."

Emma interrupted. "Aren't they done yet, Mama? I'm starving."

"All done," answered Julia with a sigh. The plate barely touched the table before Emma dove in.

"One thing I know for sure," said Julia. "My daughter has a healthy appetite."

"I'll get dressed now, Mama, and come back down and help you clean up from last night. Just give me a few minutes, okay?"

"There's not much more to do, Emma, but you can help me put away the glasses and the good china. I treasure that china so much because Louis brought it back from France." Emma headed for the stairs and Julia turned her attention to the sink.

She was back in a few minutes dressed in a plain tan skirt and a white blouse with a small bow at the neck. Instead of her usual sensible brown shoes with laces she wore a pair of soft leather sandals, a concession Julia permitted in the summer time now that Emma was becoming a young lady.

"You look lovely, Emma. You always look nice. You have a natural flair for fashion. That's why you make such a good model. Your sense of style makes you feel comfortable in the clothes you wear. That is a gift, Emma—a gift."

"Well if it is, I come by it naturally" said Emma looking at her mother with obvious pride. "You wouldn't be where you are today if you didn't have style. Even Louis agrees with that."

Before Emma could finish putting away the beautiful French china, they heard a knock at the door. She looked at her mother and shrugged.

Charles Carney made his usual flamboyant entrance. "Emma, you look gorgeous," were his opening words. "I'm sorry if I'm a little early. I just couldn't wait to see you."

Emma looked up at the tall handsome young man. Charles was wearing grey slacks and his Columbia jacket and looked elegant. Nothing but the best for Charles Carney she noted. His father took him to his personal tailor on a regular basis. Lawrence Carney didn't believe in regular clothing stores; they were for the middle class.

"You look very nice yourself, Charles," Emma said sincerely, as she followed him into the living room. "Can I get you something to drink?"

"No, no thanks. I would like to talk with you in private if that's okay. Can we just sit on the couch?"

Emma walked across the room and settled herself on the big over-stuffed sofa. Charles followed right behind her and sat as close to her as he dared.

"Emma, I'd like to get right to the point. Please don't say anything until I finish." He looked at her and then knelt down. He raised himself up on one knee and took her hands in his.

"Emma Pedesch, will you marry me?"

Before Emma could react, Charles took a small black box out of his jacket pocket. He put the box in Emma's hand and waited. She looked at the box and then at Charles. He heard a deep intake of breath and then she raised the lid.

The blue-white diamond resting in a square of platinum captivated her and she couldn't speak. Charles stared at her and waited for some word, some sign. Nothing came. Finally, he took the ring from the box and attempted to place it on her finger.

She pulled her hand back. The ring slipped to the floor. Charles gasped and scrambled to pick it up.

"Emma, darling, please tell me what's wrong. You had to know that I wanted us to get engaged. I want to marry you. You know that. Say something—please."

Emma was ashen. "I'm sorry, Charles. Really I am. I just wasn't prepared for this. I know you wanted to talk about marriage but I had no idea you wanted to get engaged right away. I can't believe this is happening. I'm not ready to make this decision. I just graduated yesterday. I haven't had time to just be Emma Pedesch yet. I don't know what I want to do with the rest of my life. I care for you. I do, but it's too soon—too soon for talk of engagements."

Emma stood up. "I think you'd better go, Charles. I wouldn't want Mama to come in here and see you on your knees. Please put the ring away. I can't accept it—not now anyway. Please forgive me, Charles."

Tears welled up in her eyes, and for once in his life Charles Carney was rendered silent. He was totally unprepared for this outcome. In his mind this had all been a foregone conclusion. He wanted Emma Pedesch and he was going to have her. All he had to do was ask her and she would say yes. What had gone wrong? He rose to his feet, still staring at Emma in utter disbelief.

"I never thought you'd be upset. I thought you'd be thrilled. I guess I was wrong on both counts. I love you. I want to marry you. How can you be mad at me for that?"

"I'm not mad, Charles, just completely overwhelmed. I never expected…never thought you'd…. a ring like that. I just can't."

Emma turned and walked toward the stairs. Charles had no choice but to let himself out the door. His father had assured him that Emma would not be able to resist the beautiful diamond that had been his mother's. How would he make his father understand that he had been rejected? He didn't understand himself. He went down the steps, and then paused to look back at the house, fully expecting to see Emma at the door. It is all a mistake, she'd say—a terrible mistake. As he looked back, all he saw was the closed door. He crossed the street and didn't look back again.

CHAPTER 7

▼

Saturday arrived in glittering fashion—a sky so blue that clouds shimmered like sheep in the meadow. Emma stretched luxuriously and stared out the window. She yawned and turned to glance at the clock on her bedside table. Nine o'clock the numbers announced—time to get up and get down to the salon. Emma always modeled for her mother on Saturdays. *American Chic* didn't open till eleven o'clock so she still had time to get to work.

She grabbed her robe and ran down the stairs to the kitchen. Julia had already left for the shop but there was a note for her on the kitchen table along with breakfast.

How thoughtful you are, Mama, thought Emma as she peeked under the cover at the golden brown waffles. She decided to eat first and then get dressed.

Before Emma finished, the phone rang. Something told her it was Charles.

"Hello," she said sweetly into the receiver.

"Hello yourself," said Charles. "Did you just get up?"

"Yes, I'm having my breakfast and then I have to hurry down to the salon to work with Mama. It's Saturday, you know, and she needs me to model clothes for her special weekend customers."

"Oh," said Charles. "I guess I forgot. Can I see you tonight? Maybe we could take in a movie at the Rialto and then go for a snack after the show. Whaddya say?"

"That would be swell, Charles. There's a Mary Pickford movie playing that I've been dying to see. Can we go to that one?"

"Sure, Emma. Whatever you want. The show starts at seven so I'll pick you up about six thirty. Okay?"

"Okay, Charles. See you tonight."

Emma hung up the phone and went upstairs. She picked up her journal from the night table and began to write.

Charles just called and I guess he isn't mad at me any more. Maybe he won't bring up this engagement thing for a while. I hope not 'cause I'm just not ready to be tied down. I love him, I do, but I'm not ready to get engaged yet. I hope I can convince him that we should wait another year at least. I want to continue my modeling and now that Pierre has found me a contact to be a photographer's model, all sorts of things are possible. I just want to try my wings before I settle down to be someone's wife. The idea of modeling and having my picture in a fashion magazine is so exciting. Why can't Charles understand that and be proud of me? I better close now and get to work. Mama will be wondering what happened to me.

Saturday was a big shopping day for American Chic and Emma wanted to be there right in the thick of things. She loved the beautiful clothes and admired the well dressed customers who came to purchase her mother's designs. This wasn't work; it was fun.

She took the street car from the Hunts Point Station and arrived at the salon by ten thirty. She could see her mother through the window, dressing the mannequins and setting up some displays in the sitting area while, at the same time, talking to a handsome young man with a briefcase. She knocked on the door, which was always kept locked until the official opening at eleven.

Julia looked up and smiled when she saw her. She put down the fabric she was draping and came to open the door.

"Well hello, sleepy head. I wasn't sure if you were coming to work today. I am very glad that you did, however, because I would like you to meet someone—Stephen Lang. He is a friend of Pierre's and a freelance fashion photographer. His photos have been in all of the best magazines." Julia hugged Emma and then turned to the young man.

"Stephen, this is my daughter, Emma. She models for me here at the salon on the weekend. She just graduated from high school and is trying to decide what to do with her life."

Stephen Lang stepped forward and extended his hand. "I am very pleased to meet you, Emma. I've heard so much about you from Pierre, but now that I see you in person, I am even more pleased."

Emma blushed and shook Stephen's hand. "Thank you for the lovely compliment, Mr. Lang. I'm afraid Uncle Pierre is a bit prejudiced when it comes to me and Mama. It's very nice to meet you, too."

"Stephen, please," the young man answered. "Pierre Manot is like an uncle to me. He has been my mentor ever since my father died. They were old friends here in New York when both of them were struggling artists. I did not inherit his talent, however, except perhaps with a camera. Photography is my art form of choice and I certainly would like to express it with you as my subject." He looked at Julia for approval and continued. "Your mother agreed to let me photograph some of her new collection for *Fashion Monthly,* and so I am here to do just that."

Emma looked at her mother questioningly. "Do you want me to model some of your new designs, Mama? I've only done this for customers so it will feel a bit strange without potential buyers."

"I think this would be a nice change for you Emma. I have always suspected you would make a good photographer's model and now is a good opportunity to find out, don't you think?"

"Help yourself to some coffee, Stephen, while I go over today's schedule with Emma."

Julia took her daughter's hand and led her into the back room of the salon. There was a large rolling rack by the wall filled with her creations. Many of the new designs were the popular golf outfits of the day....soft tweed knickers with matching socks, topped with silk blouses in varied jeweled tones. Cloche hats to match the blouses were stacked on a hat rack nearby.

"Will you model my new line for Mr. Lang and launch yourself as a photographer's model?" Julia asked her daughter.

"I had no idea this would happen so soon, Mama. Now that it's here I'm really nervous. I've never been photographed professionally before. I may look absolutely ugly and then your designs will be wasted on me. I don't know how to be a photographer's model. I'm used to just walking around showing off the clothes to your customers."

"Silly girl," Julia interrupted. "That's all you have to do for Stephen—just walk around where he tells you and look beautiful and relaxed. If you do that my clothes will look wonderful, and the orders will come pouring in. Will you do it, Emma? Will you do it for me?"

"If that's what you want, of course I will. I'm just scared, but I'll do my best."

The two women returned to the main room and joined Stephen, who was drinking his coffee and looking over one of the mannequins.

"These new golf outfits are really something, Mrs. Pedesch. I can't wait to see Emma show them off. Has she agreed to model your line for me?"

"Yes, Stephen. We can't do it today, of course. Saturday is my biggest day here and I can't afford to lose the business. Would you mind doing it on Sunday? I'd be happy to open the shop in the early afternoon and we could do it then without any interruptions. I'll even include an invitation to dinner," Julia added. We go to mass in the morning, but Emma and I can be here at the salon by one o'clock and work through the afternoon, if that's agreeable. Then we can all have dinner together at our house. What do you say to that, Stephen?"

"I say yes, Mrs. Pedesch. I'd love to come. I don't often get a home-cooked meal."

Julia was obviously pleased with the arrangements. Looking at her watch, she realized that it was almost time to open the shop.

"Well then, Stephen, Emma and I will see you here tomorrow at one o'clock. How many ensembles do you think you want to shoot? This golf collection is about twelve pieces and the new ball gowns are eight. Our line of daywear is rather extensive. Maybe we should save that for another spread altogether—assuming, of course, that this one will be a hit."

"How about six golf outfits followed by four gowns," says Stephen. "The contrast will make a great layout, and as you say, we'll do the daywear another time. We don't want to give all the good stuff away in one swoop, now do we," he joked. "I'll see you ladies tomorrow at one."

Stephen grabbed his camera and briefcase and headed out the door just as the first customer was coming in. He was smiling all the way to the curb.

Chapter 8

The Pedesch family attended early mass at the Church of St. Constantine. Jerry complained when he found out his mother was not going to cook a big dinner right after mass.

"But we always eat Sunday dinner at one o'clock," he whined. "I'll die if I don't eat soon. Just see if I don't."

Julia laughed. "Today will be different, Jerry, but I don't think you will die from the change. We'll all have a big bowl of soup before Emma and I go to the salon. I have an icebox full of leftovers from the party and they will make a very special buffet dinner tonight. We are having a special guest to share dinner with us, so please behave yourself."

"Who's special?" inquired Jerry. "Who's so special we have to change dinner?" He looked at his mother with genuine concern.

"His name is Stephen Lang," said Julia, "and he's a friend of Uncle Pierre's. He's a photographer and is taking pictures of my designs for a fashion magazine. Besides that, Emma will be the model."

"You mean Emmy's gonna be in a magazine?"

"Yes, Jerry. Isn't that exciting? Isn't that worth changing our dinner for?"

"Well, I guess so, Mama. It isn't every day my sister gets in a magazine. Are you excited, Emmy?"

"I think so, Jerry, but I'm a little scared too. I've never modeled for anyone but Mama and her customers. Maybe I'll take awful pictures, and Mr. Lang won't want me to model after all. Anyway, Mama invited him home for dinner after we finish, so please be nice to him."

"I'll be good, Emmy. You don't have to worry. I'll just talk to him man-to-man and let him know what a good model you are."

Emma smiled at his bravado and patted Jerry on the head.

"Let's get the soup, Mama, and then we can leave for the salon. I'd like to have a little time to prepare before Mr. Lang arrives."

After they finished, Emma put the dishes in the sink and began washing. In a few minutes the kitchen was sparkling clean again and the two women were ready to leave.

George had already gone out to the porch where he could read his Hungarian newspaper in his favorite chair with the sunlight streaming in the window. He loved it out there where he could see his garden and the grape arbor, bent low with the weight of ripening fruit. It would soon be time for the harvest and a new season of wine making would begin.

Emma joined her mother in the car and they drove to the salon. Stephen Lang was parked outside, waiting for them when they arrived.

"Good afternoon, Stephen. I hope you haven't been waiting too long. I had to feed my two hungry men before I left or they would not have survived until dinner."

"It is I who should apologize, Mrs. Pedesch. I am rather early I'm afraid—a little over anxious I guess. I've been looking forward to this all day." He looked at Emma admiringly. She blushed and followed her mother into the shop.

"Well, now that we're all here, let's get to work. Emma, why don't you go in back and change. Let's start with the first golf outfit on the rack. Stephen can get set up while you're changing."

Julia looked at Stephen Lang for reassurance.

"Yes, yes, that would be fine. I'll just set my equipment up out here while Emma is getting ready. I want to hang a backdrop for the golf outfits. Is that all right, Mrs. Pedesch?"

"Of course, Stephen, and please call me Julia. There's no need to be so formal."

Stephen unpacked a stanchion and draped a large piece of fabric between the posts. The scene on the fabric resembled the fairway of a golf course.

"I have another backdrop with me too," he announced. "It looks like the backyard of a mansion where a formal party might be in progress. I thought that would be appropriate to use for photographing the ball gowns. Do you agree, Mrs. Ped....er ..I mean Julia?"

"That sounds perfect, Stephen. I'm sure you've done this sort of thing before, and I trust your judgment."

Before he could answer, Emma entered the room. She was wearing navy blue tweed knickers with a matching jacket slung casually over one shoulder. Her blouse was a brilliant teal blue silk and the socks were of the same hue. A navy tweed cap sat jauntily on her blond hair. She was a knockout. Stephen gasped.

"Emma, you are enchanting," is all he could muster.

"Yes, Emma, I agree," said Julia. "You look like you were born to the golf course. You certainly do justice to that outfit. You make me proud to be the designer."

"Thank you both," said Emma. "You make me feel much better. I was really nervous about doing this, but now I think I'll be fine. Just tell me what you want me to do, Mr. Lang."

"Stephen, please Emma. We can all be on a first-name basis here. Just walk over to the backdrop and pause near the center. Here's a golf club to hold. It will give you something to do and make you feel more at ease."

He handed Emma the club and showed her how to grasp it. He placed a golf ball on the carpet in front of her.

"It's what they call an iron, Emma. Just rest it on the ground in front of you as if you were lining up the ball and I'll do the rest. We'll vary the pose a bit with each outfit, but just relax and keep your face toward me. You can swing the club a bit if you want and I'll get the shot at just the right time."

Emma did as he suggested, and before she knew it, she had posed in all six outfits and Stephen was changing the backdrop and preparing to shoot the ball gowns.

"Ok, Emma, whenever you're ready," he announced. "Come out in the first gown and stand in front of the new backdrop." He placed the camera on a tripod and stepped behind it. Emma came in clad in the ice green satin gown her mother had designed for her graduation.

"Wow," said Stephen. "That gown is a real beauty and so is the woman wearing it."

Emma blushed to the roots of her hair. A woman….. he called me a woman, she thought to herself. Julia was beaming. Emma certainly does look like a real model.

"Thank you, Stephen. That is the gown Emma and I designed together for her graduation party last week. I'm so pleased that you like it. The one-shoulder effect was her idea. It makes the dress, don't you think?"

"I don't know much about design, Julia. I'm only a photographer, but I do know what beautiful is….and she, I mean the gown certainly is." He stared at Emma, the admiration evident on his face.

"Well now, ladies, let's get on with it. We have three more gowns to photograph. I've brought a few props, Emma. Tell me which ones you feel comfortable with in each case. There's a small bench, a parasol, a stuffed dog and a bouquet of flowers. You can choose what you want to include in each shot and I'll try to accommodate it."

They worked for the next hour and soon all four gowns had been photographed and Emma was exhausted.

"Are we finished yet, Stephen?"

He could detect the weariness in her voice.

"Yes, Emma, this is a wrap, as they say. We're done for today and you did a great job. This layout is going to be super. I can guarantee it. As soon as I pack up my equipment we can all leave. I'm looking forward to that home cooked meal, I can tell you."

"I'll be right out then. I'll just change back into my street clothes."

"I'm so pleased with the way it went," said Julia, "but poor Emma is worn out, I think. A good dinner will give us all a second wind. Just follow us home, Stephen, and I'll have dinner on the table before you know it. I hope you don't mind leftovers buffet style."

"Not at all, Julia, and I'm looking forward to meeting the rest of your family."

"Let's go then. C'mon Emma. We're all ready out here," she called. "Let's go home and celebrate a job well done."

Chapter 9

Stephen had never been to Hunts Point before, so he drove close behind Julia. He was surprised to see this large piece of wooded land just outside the bustling city. He was even more surprised to find that theirs was the only house on the Point—the only building in fact, except for the old brick iron works, no longer in operation.

"I feel like I am in a strange new country," said Stephen as they walked up the steps to the house. "I had no idea there was so much open land out here so close to the city."

"It is quite unusual," agreed Julia, "but it is one reason why we love it so much. It reminds me a bit of the old country and there are a few Hungarian families living on the other side of the woods. We get together in the summer and have old-fashioned *Magyar* picnics," she added with some enthusiasm.

"Delightful," said Stephen.

Jerry opened the door when he heard the cars pull up. "I'm starving, Mama. When can we eat?"

"Patience, my dear; we just got home. It will take only a few minutes to warm up the food. Come meet our guest and say hello."

"Stephen, this is my son, Jerry."

Stephen put out his hand and shook Jerry's firmly. "How are you this evening, young man?"

"I'm hungry, sir," was Jerry's reply. "I've been waiting and waiting for Mama to come home and fix our Sunday dinner. We usually eat our big dinner right after church, but today she made us wait 'cause you were coming."

Julia interrupted. "That will be enough, young man. Go call your father and tell him to bring us some wine for dinner."

Jerry looked a bit chagrined but scampered away to find his father and relay the message.

"Please come in and make yourself comfortable, Stephen. My husband should be here in a moment and we will have a glass of wine before dinner. George makes his own, you know. We grow the grapes in the arbor over the driveway. He is very proud of his wine."

Just then George arrived at the top of the cellar stairs carrying a large jug of white wine. He put the jug down on the counter and walked into the living room to greet their guest. He extended his hand. Stephen grabbed it instantly and said, "I am pleased to meet you, sir."

At his full height George was not much taller than Emma, who was barely five feet two inches tall. That made him at least five inches shorter than Julia. He was stocky of build but with not an extra bit of fat on his body. The hand he proffered Stephen was very large for his size and the skin was tan and course, evidence of hours spent outside. Stephen studied the sturdy man. He looks like a miniature Paul Bunyan, he thought to himself.

"I am pleased to meet you, also," George said in his best English. "Julia has told me about your pictures. Did you take pictures of my Emma today?"

"Yes sir, I did and a beautiful subject she is too. You must be very proud of her."

"Oh yes, I am. Can I offer you some wine, Mr. Lang.?"

"Yes, but please call me Stephen. It was so nice of Julia to invite me to dinner and allow me to meet the rest of the family."

George nodded and poured glasses all around. Stephen picked up his glass and stood to propose a toast.

"Here's to a wonderful new partnership with American Chic and a successful new career for Emma." He raised his glass. Julia answered his toast and even passed a small glass of wine to Emma. "This is a big day for you, too, my dear. I think you can join in this toast to your future."

Emma raised her glass. She felt so grown up and was very excited about the prospect of her new career.

"Can we eat now, Mama? Can we?" Jerry looked earnestly at his mother.

"Of course, Jerry, and we'll have one more toast and you can join in too. Come now, Emma. Help me get the food on the table before your brother expires from a lack of sustenance." The two women returned within minutes, platters of food in each hand.

"Come and sit down, gentlemen," Julia's voice called from the dining room. "All we have to do is say grace and we can begin."

"Hooray," yelled Jerry. "Pass the potatoes, 'cause here I come."

When they were all seated, Julia said a brief prayer and a welcome to Stephen Lang as a guest in their home. Jerry picked up his glass and said, "Here, here." Everyone laughed and the plates of food began making their way around the table.

An hour and a half later they were sitting over their second cup of coffee and talking amiably like old friends. Julia could see that George was beginning to fade and Jerry had already been excused to go to his room. Stephen sensed that the evening had indeed come to an end and stood. He graciously thanked his hostess for the lovely meal and made his exit. Emma retrieved his coat and walked with him to the front door.

The young man looked down on Emma with admiration apparent on his face.

"Thank you for a lovely evening. I think you will be a very successful model, and I hope we will see each other again soon. Goodnight."

"Goodnight, Steven, and thank you for today. It was such a wonderful experience. I hope the photographs turn out well. It's such a great opportunity for Mama—and for me, too, of course." She smiled up at him.

"Here's to bigger and better photo shoots," he responded as he headed for the front door. "I'll call as soon as I have your next assignment."

Emma closed the door against the evening chill and hugged herself.

"What a magical beginning to my new career. I am a real professional model," she said out loud, to be sure she wasn't dreaming.

Chapter 10

▼

Emma hurried to the corner to make the next trolley out of Hunts Point Station. She was still thinking about yesterday and the exciting photo shoot with Stephen Lang. Her mind was so preoccupied that she almost missed her stop. She looked out the window of the trolley and realized she was only one block from her mother's salon. She pulled the chord and the trolley drew up to the curb.

As Emma walked up the block toward American Chic, she remembered that Julia had told her to stop at the furrier. She glanced at her watch and knew she still had time before Mrs. Wiesel, her mother's best customer, would be at the salon. Emma looked up at the various shop marquees, searching for the one marked Furrier. She spotted it almost at once and headed for the door. She peered inside, and seeing no one in the front room, proceeded to knock. She remembered Julia telling her that furriers and jewelers always keep their doors locked, opening them only when business was imminent. She knocked again and saw a rather rotund man walking toward the door with a big grin on his pudgy face.

"Good afternoon, *dahlink*," cooed the voice in a thick Yiddish accent. "And *vhat* is so beautiful a *goyem* doing at *mine* front door?"

"Good afternoon, Mr. Rosenbloom," said Emma politely. "I am Emma Pedesch. My mother said you wanted to speak to me. She owns American Chic just a few doors down from here so I thought I'd stop in on my way to her salon."

"*Oyvay*, you mean Julia, *mine* dear friend. So you are her daughter, Emma. *Vat* a lovely *goil* you are. I am so pleased to make your *acvaintance*. Come inside and sit down please."

Emma entered the furrier's shop and immediately noticed a huge rack of beautiful fur coats being pushed across the room by a tall, thin young man. The young man stared hard, and when she met his gaze she found it difficult to turn away. Mr. Rosenbloom broke the tension and yelled to the young man.

"Hey, Eddie, roll *dat* rack into *da* storeroom and start bagging *dem* coats *vhile* I talk to Emma here, and *vatch* out for *da* silver foxes. *Dey* are very special and need careful handling."

He turned back to Emma and pointed to a small loveseat against the wall. Emma sat down and waited.

"Emma *dahlink*, I am a wholesaler, and I need a model to show off *mine* coats to the retail buyers. I really need two models but I *vill* settle for *von*, especially *vhen* she looks as good as you," he added grinning. "*Vould* you be interested?"

"Oh yes, Mr. Rosenbloom, and I have a very pretty friend who would be interested also if you really need two models. Her name is Ginger, and she has beautiful red hair and has done some modeling before."

"*Vhat* luck *dhat* I found you, d*ahlink*, and *mit* a friend, besides. *Vhen* can *da* two of you start?"

"I'll call my friend tonight and let you know tomorrow, Mr. Rosenbloom. As for me, I'll have to check with Mama. She is signing a contract for me today to be a photographer's model so I will have to see when my first assignment is. I know she said you needed help right away—tomorrow in fact. Is that right?"

"*Zat is da trute*, Emma. I need you to model *dose* new fox coats *vhat* just came in. Do you *tink* you can do *zhat*?"

"I think so, Mr. Rosenbloom, but I have to check with Mama. I'll stop back later after I talk to her and let you know. I might even be able to get hold of Ginger by then too. Right now I'd better get to American Chic. Mama has a special customer waiting for me to model the new line. I'll talk to you later, okay?"

"*Hokay*, Emma *sveetheart*. Run along now. You shouldn't keep your mama *vaiting*. But call me soon please," he added.

Emma walked out the door and waved at the over-sized proprietor as she hurried up the street. As she approached the glass door of American Chic, she could see that Mrs. Wiesel was already there. She was an elegantly dressed woman with perfectly coiffed dark brunette hair styled in a French twist and held in place with a lovely tortoise shell comb. She sat on the sofa with her long legs crossed at the ankles. Her shoes were of the finest leather and were always a perfect match to every outfit. Emma never failed to check that out every time she saw her.

"I can't imagine being rich enough to have shoes to match every outfit," Emma remarked to Julia on several occasions when modeling for Mrs. Wiesel.

"That seems to be her one weakness," was Julia's response.

Emma pushed open the big glass door. "Hello, Mama. Good afternoon, Mrs. Wiesel. I hope I'm not late." Emma looked at her mother questioningly.

"No, Emma," answered Julia. "Mrs. Wiesel came in a bit early today. We had a few matters to discuss before she looks at the new line. Were you at the furrier?"

"Yes, Mama, and I'll tell you about that later. What outfits would you like me to begin with?"

"I believe several of the afternoon frocks would be appropriate, Emma, and two of the gowns. I have put the designs I had in mind aside on a rack in the back. If Mrs. Wiesel is ready, we will begin immediately."

Mrs. Wiesel nodded in agreement and settled back on the sofa. Emma walked to the back to change into the first outfit.

It took only an hour and a half for Emma to model the outfits her mother had put aside for this discerning customer. As usual, she ordered them all, and Julia was very pleased. As soon as Mrs. Wiesel left the salon, Emma began to tell her mother about the meeting with Mr. Rosenbloom. Before she could finish, however, the door of the salon opened and in came Stephen Lang.

"Well, Ladies, are we ready to do business?" he inquired.

"Yes, we are," both women answered at once. Julia smiled at her daughter, walked to the back and called out.

"Rose, please come out and cover the floor." A robust young woman came out from the rear of the salon. She walked straight up to Julia and stopped.

"There are some fabric samples you can set up for me while I am in the office with Mr. Lang," Julia said and pointed to the pile of fabric swatches stacked in the corner.

"I'll take care of it, Madame," said Rose, and she walked over to the pile and began sorting. Julia led Emma and Stephen into the small back room she used as an office. As soon as he got inside, Stephen began rummaging in his briefcase.

"Here's the contract for you to look over, Julia. I think you'll find everything in order, but if you have any questions, please don't hesitate to ask me. It keeps Emma under contract to us for the next eighteen months. That is the usual time for a beginner. She will have at least one assignment a month and maybe two. Her hourly pay is also stipulated, but that could go up after six months if the client base increases, and I think it will. She can only work so many hours a day, due to her age, and all assignments will be approved by you as her parental agent. Read it over. Take your time. While you're perusing the contract, I'd like to take some stills of Emma if that's alright. We'll need them for her portfolio—you know, to show potential clients."

Stephen led Emma back out to the main floor. There was a white screen there and he had her pose both sitting and standing in front of the screen. They worked together for about fifteen minutes before Julia appeared—contract in hand.

"I've read it over, Stephen, and I'm ready to sign. I don't see anything that needs to be changed. I find it to be fair and equitable and will be to Emma's benefit as well as yours."

"That's good news, Julia. Just sign here on the dotted line—both copies please. I'll have my boss sign them also and return one copy to you for your records."

"Absolutely," said Julia smiling. "It's been a pleasure, Stephen, a real pleasure."

"For me, too," said Stephen. "I'll call you tomorrow after my boss signs and I'll be back with your copy. I'll probably have Emma's first assignment with me too." He smiled at Emma. "All ready to be famous, Emma?" he asked. Emma grinned back and found she was blushing. "I don't really want to be famous, Stephen. I just want to do a good job and have fun doing it."

"That you will, my dear. I think we'll make a great team. Bye now—until tomorrow."

No sooner was he out the door than Emma started pacing up and down. "I can't believe it, Mama. I'm going to be a real live model—not just for you but for a genuine agency. Can you believe it? I am so excited."

Emma ran over and hugged her mother. "Thank you, Mama, for making this happen. And now, let me tell you about Mr. Rosenbloom."

Emma related the conversation between herself and the furrier. "He needs Ginger and I both tomorrow," she said. "May I call Ginger now and give her the good news? And can we start tomorrow?"

"It's fine with me, Emma, but you'd better call Ginger right away. I doubt if Stephen's assignment for you will be as soon as tomorrow."

Emma dialed Ginger's number. It rang several times before Ginger answered.

"Where were you? I've got great news. Mama sent me in to see Mr. Rosenbloom, the furrier and he needs two people to model fur coats for the retail buyers. I told him about you and he said he'd hire both of us—if you're interested that is. How 'bout it, Ginger? Wanna be models together?"

"Wow, that's great Emma, but what about your contract? Didn't you sign yet? Won't that interfere with your photo modeling?"

"I'll work for Mr. Rosenbloom between assignments, Ginger. I'm still gonna work for Mama too. It won't be a problem. What about it? Can I tell him okay? He needs us tomorrow so I hope you can make it."

"Tell him I'll be there, Emma. My mom will be thrilled for me. I can't wait to tell her. Between the furrier and American Chic, I'll really be able to save some money for Hollywood. Thanks again Emma. You are the best friend ever."

"You're welcome. See you tomorrow at ten, okay? I'm going down to Mr. Rosenbloom's now to tell him the good news. Bye for now."

Chapter 11

▼

"Goodbye, Mama. I'll see you at home," shouted Emma. "Ginger is sure her mom will say yes so I want to tell Mr. Rosenbloom right away."

Emma ran the short distance to the furrier and entered the shop, breathing hard. Mr. Rosenbloom was nowhere in sight. The young man she had seen earlier was unloading another rack of coats and Emma went over to look at them.

"What kind of fur is this?" she asked. "It's so soft and such a beautiful brown color."

He looked at her thoughtfully and then answered. "Mink, miss. These are mink coats. Haven't you ever seen one before?"

"No, I haven't," answered Emma. "But it sure is beautiful. It's about the prettiest fur I've ever seen. I don't think I could ever afford a coat like that."

The young man studied her before answering. "Models make lots of money," he said. "I bet you'll have one like this before you know it."

"Oh not for quite a while anyway. I'm just starting out as a model. It will take a long time to make that much money I'm sure." She patted one of the coats. The fur felt like velvet under her fingers. She put her cheek down to the soft pelt and closed her eyes. When she opened her eyes, he was watching her. His eyes were dark blue, almost black and his fine dark hair curled down on his forehead. He was dressed in twill pants and a sweater which showed his muscles—a fact that did not escape Emma's notice.

"My name is Eddie," he said. "What's yours?"

"I'm Emma," she answered. "My mother owns American Chic just a few doors down. Will you give Mr. Rosenbloom a message for me? Tell him Emma and Ginger will both be here tomorrow at ten o'clock. We're both going to be models here."

Eddie grinned. "That sure is good news. I'll be happy to pass on your message to the boss. He'll be relieved. He's got a bunch of buyers coming in here tomorrow."

"Well, thank you and goodbye then, Eddie. I guess I'll see you tomorrow."

Emma fairly floated down the street to the trolley station. Visions of beautiful fur coats filled her thoughts and she felt very grownup, excited and happy. Her feet barely touched the ground as she waved at the conductor and boarded the trolley for home. As soon as she got home she ran up the stairs to her room and closed the door. Emma threw herself on her bed and got out her journal.

Today is the best day of my life. Mrs. Wiesel bought every outfit I modeled for her at the salon today. Mama signed my contract with Stephen and I got a job for Ginger and I as models for Mr. Rosenbloom, the furrier. So much is happening to me. I can't believe it. I feel like my life is really beginning, and it's going to get more wonderful every day. I can't wait to tell Charles. I'm sure he will be happy for me, too, and will forget about us getting married. That's the last thing I want right now—some day, but not now. Now I want to be somebody in my own name, not somebody else's. I pray Charles can understand.

Emma put down her pen and considered her last words. She hadn't seen Charles since their movie date on Saturday night. It had been a pleasant evening and they had enjoyed the Mary Pickford movie Emma had been so anxious to see. Charles had not mentioned one word about getting engaged and Emma had just relaxed and enjoyed herself. They went for ice cream afterward and she was home by eleven. Charles had kissed her goodnight on her steps and had left without any further incident. He had called on Sunday, but Jerry answered and told him they had company for dinner and Emma couldn't come to the phone. Now here it was Monday and she still hadn't talked to him. She picked up her pen again and turned the page.

I'd better call Charles this afternoon or he will be really upset. He'll think I'm ignoring him and I don't want him to think that. It's just that so much has been happening so fast I haven't had time to catch my breath. I haven't even thought about Charles since Sunday. I guess I should be ashamed of myself, but I'm not—I'm just too excited and happy. I want to tell Charles all about it though, and I want him to be as happy for me as I am.

Emma put the pen down again and closed her journal. She went downstairs to use the phone in the hall. George was out in the garden and Jerry was still in school so the house was quiet and Emma had the phone to herself. She dialed Charles's number. The phone rang about four times and then Maude Carney's voice came on the line.

"Hello, who's calling please?"

"Hello, Mrs. Carney. It's Emma. Is Charles at home by any chance? I'm very anxious to talk to him."

"Why hello, Emma dear. He's not working today, but he's downtown at present visiting his father at his office. He did call you earlier today but there was no answer he said. I'll tell him you called and I'm sure he'll call you as soon as he gets home. Don't be a stranger, dear. Do come and visit us soon, won't you?"

"Thank you, Mrs. Carney. I surely will. Please tell Charles I called."

Emma put the receiver back on its hook and walked slowly back up the stairs to her room. The journal was still open on her bed. She began to write.

He's not home just now so I haven't been able to tell him my good news. I just know he will be proud of me—a photographer's model and all. And now I'll be modeling fur coats just like his mama wears. Ginger and I will have a swell time at the furrier's. Stephen said he may have my first photographic assignment tomorrow. I can't wait to see myself in a real magazine.

The ringing of the phone broke the silence again. Emma put down the pen and hurried down the stairs to take the call. She snatched the receiver from the hook and before she could say a word, Ginger yelled.

"We're gonna be real live fur models, Emma. I can't believe it. Mama did say yes, so I am ready whenever Mr. Rosenbloom wants me. Do we start right away? Tomorrow? What do I wear and when do we go there?"

"Slow down, Ginger. We're all set. Mr. Rosenbloom says he needs us right away so that means tomorrow. He opens at ten so we better be there a little before to find out exactly what we're supposed to do. I've never modeled for anyone but my mother before, so this is all new to me too. Are you as excited as I am? Wait till you see the minks and the fox coats. They are so gorgeous. You're gonna feel like a movie star when you put one on. Eddie says all the big movie stars wear them."

"Eddie? Eddie who?" asked Ginger.

"Oh, he's the guy who works for Mr. Rosenbloom. He's real cute, too, Ginger. I'm sure you'll like him."

"Wow, a job and a possible new boyfriend," said Ginger. "I can't wait to start this job. I'll be at the trolley station by nine, Emma, so we can go together in the morning. See ya."

"See ya, Ginger. I'm sure glad your mother said yes. It's gonna to be swell working together."

Emma no sooner put the receiver back on the hook than the phone rang again.

"Hi Emma, who were you talking to?"

"Oh, hi, Charles. I was talking to Ginger. We start work together tomorrow and we had to set up a time to meet at the trolley station."

"Work? What work? Modeling for your mother, you mean?"

"No, silly. We're going to be fur models for Mr. Rosenbloom the wholesale furrier a few doors down from Mama's shop. Oh, Charles, I have so much to tell you. You just won't believe what's happened to me today."

Emma took a deep breath and began explaining to Charles all the exciting developments of the day—her mother's customer, the contract with Stephen and last but not least, the job with the furrier. Charles was flabbergasted.

"All this happened today, Emma? I can't believe it. No wonder you're so excited. I didn't know I was dating a professional model. I certainly am impressed. I hope you're going to be able to find time for me, Emma. Now that you're out of school I thought we could spend some real quality time together."

There was a pause at the other end of the line.

"Emma, are you there?" There was anxiety in Charles's voice.

"Yes, Charles, of course I'm here. I want to spend time with you too. I'll be working during the day, and you'll be working too. We'll have some evenings and a Sunday afternoon or two. It'll work out, Charles. I know it will. Aren't you proud of me?"

"Of course I'm proud of you, Emma. May I come over? We can take a walk and you can tell me all the details."

"Okay, Charles. Come over now and we'll have lots of time to talk."

"I'll be there in a jiffy," said Charles as he hung up the phone.

Chapter 12

Emma heard Charles's car pull up in front of the house. She opened the front door and waited for him to come up the walk.

"You must have flown here, Charles. We just hung up the phone less than half an hour ago."

"Yes I did Emma. I was in such a hurry to see you."

He came inside and without another word pulled her close to him.

"Emma, I missed you so much and I want you to know how proud I am of you."

"But Charles, we only saw each other on Saturday night."

"But this is Monday, Emma. It seems like an eternity since we've been together and so much has happened to you. I want to be a part of everything in your life, Emma. Don't you know that? After all, you are going to be my wife, aren't you?"

"Well, Charles, I think so but that's something we have to talk about. Let's go sit on the porch."

Charles looked a bit downcast but followed Emma obediently onto the back porch.

"What do you want to talk about? I've tried not to pressure you, but I have to admit our getting married is uppermost in my mind."

"I know that, Charles, and that's why I want to talk to you. You can certainly understand after today how important my new modeling career is to me. I want a chance to follow through and prove myself. Stephen and Mama seem to think I am a natural at modeling and so I want to pursue it as my career. Mama just signed a contract for me with Stephen for the next eighteen months and Mr.

Rosenbloom, the furrier, has promised that Ginger and I will have all the work we want over the next year. On top of that there is still American Chic on the weekends. So you see, Charles, I won't have time for much else in the near future—certainly not marriage."

There was a dead silence. Charles looked at Emma and for a few minutes he said nothing. Emma stared back. Charles leaned over and took her hands. He hesitated and then spoke.

"Emma, I love you and I want you to be my wife. I didn't know you wanted a career, but now that I do know, that changes things. I can see that. I just want you to be happy and if a career is what you want right now then I won't try to talk you out of it. Actually, I am very proud of what you have accomplished, but I also don't want to lose you. Could we at least get engaged for a year or two and then talk about marriage?"

Emma smiled. "You mustn't be afraid of losing me, Charles. I love you too, I really do. I think because you're five years older than me you forget sometimes that I'm barely eighteen and I haven't seen anything of the world yet. I want so desperately to try my wings and be somebody on my own before I am anyone's wife. Let's wait a year and if we still feel the same way about each other, then we can get engaged. I'm still your girl whether I wear a ring on my finger or not. Please say you understand and agree with me."

Charles stood up. "I do understand, but I don't agree about the engagement. I don't see what harm it can do for you to wear my ring."

"It's just that it will make Mama and Papa much happier and I want to please them too. They both feel I am too young to become engaged and I want to honor their wishes. I owe them that much."

"Okay, Emma, I don't want to come between you and your parents. I'll go along with this if you'll agree that we can talk about it again in six months. That's not too much to ask, is it?"

"Agreed," said Emma, and she stood up and threw her arms around Charles and kissed him. He kissed her back and held her close. "You see, Emma, there isn't anything I wouldn't do for you. You are going to be my wife one day, but until then, you're going to be my best girl and the best model ever."

Just then Julia arrived home. Having seen Charles's car in the driveway, she walked through the house to the back porch looking for the couple. She saw them on the porch lost in an embrace and anger made the blood roar in her veins. Before she could utter a word, however, Emma broke from Charles's embrace and ran to meet her.

"Hi, Mama. I've just been telling Charles all about my day and he is so happy for me. He says I'll be the best model ever. What do you think about that?"

Julia was taken aback. She gathered her wits about her, took a deep breath, and enclosed her daughter in her arms.

"I agree with Charles whole-heartedly," she said. "You have a wonderful career ahead of you, Emma, and I know you will succeed beyond your wildest dreams. Why don't we have a little celebration—just the three of us? Come into the kitchen and I'll make a pitcher of lemonade and we'll have some of that fruit stolen you like so much."

Emma looked at Charles. He immediately took her hand and led her into the kitchen behind her mother.

They were sitting happily at the kitchen table when George came in from the garden. He was wearing dirty overalls and had a long streak of mud on his cheek.

"Am I missing a party?" he asked smiling at his wife and daughter.

"Yes, Papa," answered Emma. "We are celebrating the fact that I am going to be a model. Today is the beginning of my new career and I am so happy. Please come and join us so I can share my good news with you, too."

George grinned and walked over to the sink. Julia handed him the strong brown soap she kept just for him when he had been gardening. "Wash up good, Papa," she said. "I'll cut you a piece of stolen to go with your lemonade. Our daughter has much to tell you, and I think you will be pleased."

George joined the intimate group at the kitchen table and Emma proceeded to tell him all the news.

"So you see, Papa, I have made several decisions about my future. I am not going to go to college but will pursue a career instead—a modeling career, and I am so excited. Charles thinks it's a good idea too." She glanced at Charles with a knowing look.

"Yes, Mr. Pedesch, I think it's a wonderful decision. Emma will make an outstanding model and we will all be proud of her." He sat back, pleased with his contribution to the conversation.

George nodded and turned his attention to his daughter. "If being a model makes you happy, Emma, then I am all for it. All I ever wanted is your happiness."

"Thank you, Papa." Emma went to her father and gave him a big hug.

"Let's have a toast to the new model," Julia said, raising her glass in salute. They all raised their glasses and shouted, "To Emma, our model. Hip, hip, hooray."

Emma basked in their admiration and even Charles seemed pleased. Just as Julia refilled the glasses all around, the phone rang.

"I'll get it," said Emma, running into the hall.

"Hello, Emma, It's me, Stephen," came the voice on the other end. "I have your first assignment already. It's for *American Fashion Monthly* and we will be shooting on Thursday. Is that okay with you? The clothes will be from a new French designer and will include a lot of fancy stockings and evening shoes. I think it will be fun for you. The shoot will be downtown at another one of the photo studios near Madison. Can you find it on your own, or do you want me to meet you at the trolley station?"

"Oh, would you, Stephen? I'm still a little unsure about finding my way around Manhattan. I'll take the trolley across town and up to Madison and meet you at the station, if that's okay with you. After I've done it a few times, I'm sure I'll be able to find my way alone, but I would appreciate a little help in the beginning."

"No problem, Emma. I'll be at the station with my car at ten o'clock on Thursday. See you then."

Emma hung up the phone and raced back to the kitchen. "That was Stephen, Mama. I start work on Thursday doing a photo layout for *American Fashion Weekly*."

"That's wonderful, Emma, but when do you start at Mr. Rosenbloom's?" I thought he needed you and Ginger right away, didn't he?"

"Yes, we go there tomorrow, Mama, and probably Wednesday and Friday too. All his buyers are coming to town this week he said. I guess I'm going to be a very busy girl now that I have officially started my new career. But, I'll still come to work for you at American Chic on Saturday like always," Emma added. "After all, that's where I got my start." She grinned at her mother and Julia responded by giving her daughter a huge hug.

"Well, I guess I'd better be going," Charles said. Emma realized she had almost forgotten he was there.

"I didn't mean to neglect you, Charles. I just got carried away thinking about my next professional photo shoot. I'll talk to you tomorrow and tell you all about Ginger's and my first day as fur models."

"Okay, Emma. That'll be swell. I'll call you tomorrow after I get home from work. Maybe we can do something, if you're not too tired. Break a leg!"

Julia looked up at this remark and groaned.

"Oh, I'm sorry, Mrs. Pedesch," Charles stuttered. "That's just a remark that theater people make when they start a new show. My father told me it really means good luck. I was just wishing Emma good luck, you see."

"Thank you for the explanation, Charles. I had never heard that saying before. Let's hope it will bring good luck. Goodbye now."

Charles knew when his welcome was over in the Pedesch house and with a smile he walked toward the front door. Emma walked with him and kissed him on the cheek before she hustled him outside and returned to her parents.

"I'm going upstairs and rest awhile," said Emma, dreamily. "It's been such an exciting day. I just want time to digest it all."

She threw herself on her bed and grabbed her journal. The words come pouring out as soon as her pen hit the paper.

I am full of joy. All my prayers have been answered. I am going to be a model—a real, honest-to-goodness model. Even Charles is happy for me. Ginger and I start tomorrow at Mr. Rosenbloom's and then on Thursday, I do my first real photo shoot with Stephen—and for a French designer too. I better practice up on my French—ha, ha. I better call Ginger now and tell her and also make sure she is ready for tomorrow. Goodnight for now.

Chapter 13

Tuesday morning came early. Emma found herself awake at six o'clock, raring to go. She had slept fitfully—filled with the anticipation of her first day modeling for Mr. Rosenbloom. She wondered if Ginger was awake too.

She tiptoed to the bathroom and began her morning routine. By seven thirty she was washed, dressed and ready for work. She had selected a street-length dress of voile to wear and hoped it would be cool enough under the fur coats she would be asked to take on and off for the multitude of buyers Mr. Rosenbloom was expecting. She glanced at the clock and realized she had not had any breakfast yet and the morning was progressing rapidly. She headed for the kitchen where she found Julia preparing the first meal of the day.

"Good morning, Emma. Are you ready for your modeling adventure today?"

"Oh yes, Mama. I can't wait to get started. I was just going to grab a bite and then head out the door to meet Ginger."

"Can I give you two a ride into work? I'll be leaving shortly myself."

"Thanks, Mama, but we want to be on our own today if you don't mind. I'm not sure how long we will be at Mr. Rosenbloom's, so if we get through early, we can just come on home by ourselves on the trolley."

"That's fine, Emma. I'll see you tonight at dinner. Have a wonderful day at work."

Emma crossed the room and gave her mother a hug. She grabbed her sweater and moved toward the door.

Ginger was already at the trolley station when Emma arrived. She rushed up to greet her. Emma could see that Ginger was as excited about the new modeling job as she was.

"Hi, Ginger. You look really nice today—and so mature. I love the way you did your hair, piled up on top of your head that way with those tendrils hanging down. Mr. Rosenbloom will be so happy when he sees you. You look like a real professional model already."

"Thanks, Emma. You look nice, too. I hope he likes me 'cause I really want this job.

Just then the trolley came around the corner. The two girls hopped on board and got a seat near the front. Before they knew it, they had arrived at their destination. The lights were blazing inside the furrier, and Eddie opened the door as soon as Emma knocked. Mr. Rosenbloom was nowhere in sight, but several men and a woman were milling around a coffee pot on a table in the corner.

"C'mon in," said Eddie. "The boss is in the back lining up the coat tricks."

"Coat tricks?" Emma looked at Eddie for clarification. He smiled knowingly.

"That's trade talk for the lineup—the order he wants to show the coats in. You'll catch on soon, Emma. Don't worry about the lingo. I'll fill you in on what you don't understand. Just rely on me," said Eddie with as much bravado as he could muster. "So who's your friend?"

"Oh, I'm sorry, Eddie. This is my best friend, Ginger. Ginger, this is Eddie."

"Pleased to meet you, I'm sure," said Ginger in her most professional voice. She smiled up at the handsome young man. "I think I'm gonna like working here."

Just then the corpulent proprietor came out from the back, sweat dripping from his pudgy forehead. "Start lining up *da* racks, Eddie. *Ve'll* be ready to roll as soon as *da* rest of *da* buyers get here." He stopped talking as soon as he spotted Emma and Ginger.

"Hello, *dahlink*," he shouted exuberantly. "I'm so glad you're on time for your *foist* day. And *dis* lovely creature must be your goil friend. I am pleased to make your *acvaintance*, Red. You *don* mind if I call you Red, do you?" he grinned.

"No, of course not, Mr. Rosenbloom. Thank you so much for giving me this chance to model for you. I'll work real hard, I promise."

"You two *goils* are *da* best lookin' models in town," said Mr. Rosenbloom. "You *vill* be an asset to *mine* business. Now come *qvik* in back and let's get you ready to sell coats."

Emma and Ginger followed the big man into the back of the store. The first thing they saw was half a dozen racks filled with coats. One rack was filled with fox jackets and three-quarter length coats in a variety of colors—from silver gray to a tawny russet brown. Matching turban-style hats were on a separate rack above the coats. Another rack had a mix of full-length sable and mink coats and a third displayed leopard and other exotic furs that Emma did not recognize. The girls exchanged glances and then began to caress the beautiful coats as if they were live animals waiting to be adopted.

"Wow," said Ginger. "I think I died and went to heaven. Have you ever seen so many gorgeous furs in your life, Emma? And just think, we're gonna get paid to wear 'em."

"I hope he let's me wear the mink," said Emma. "Wearing that fur makes me feel like a queen."

"I don't care what I wear," said Ginger. "They're all lush in my book. When I'm a movie star I'm gonna have one for each day of the week."

"Get *da goils* set up, Eddie," Rosenbloom shouted. "I'm going out to schmooz up the buyers. I'll give a holler *vhen ve're* ready to roll."

"Gotcha, Mr. R. We'll be ready when you are," Eddie assured him. He wheeled the racks out closer to the door and lined them up in single file.

"We're gonna start with the foxes," said Eddie. "That's you, Ginger, and then Emma will alternate with the minks and the sables. When they're done, you can take turns with the exotics. After that you'll put on only the ones requested specifically by the buyers. That's when the fun begins and the boss starts taking orders. Just take your time and don't get rattled. If you're not sure which coat they want, just look at me and I'll point it out for you. Ok?"

"Roll 'em," yelled Rosenbloom. Eddie grinned and Ginger put on the first silver fox. She sauntered out into the front room and strolled across the makeshift runway in front of the buyers. Oohs and aahs could be heard from some of the men, but Ginger just kept on walking. As she headed back up the runway, Emma was starting down in a deep chestnut brown full-length mink. One of the women buyers squealed. "My kind a coat, Mr. R. Be sure to put that one aside for me."

Ginger and Emma continued taking turns up and down the runway. Everything seemed to be going well and both girls were caught up in the exuberance of the buyers as they commented on the various coats and shouted cracks at one another and at Rosenbloom. Eddie remained in the wings to be sure the girls took the coats in the right order. Soon it was time for the exotics.

"Let's take a short break now and give my *goils* a rest. Then *ve'll* bring out *ze* exotics and any items you *vant* to see again," said Rosenbloom matter-of-factly.

Emma and Ginger collapsed on the tiny loveseat behind the coat racks and threw off their shoes.

"My feet are killing me," said Ginger, rubbing her toes with both hands.

"Mine too," said Emma. "That runway is hard on the insteps. I'm used to modeling on carpet like at Mama's. We may have to give more thought to what shoes we wear from now on.

"You can say that again. I'm ready for bedroom slippers about now." The girls grinned at each other and both padded barefoot over to the water fountain to get a drink.

"Ok girls. It's time to get back to work," said Eddie.

"Are you kidding?" said Ginger. "We haven't had a chance to catch our breath and you're ready to go again. What are you—a slave driver?"

"Not me, Red, but the boss is. When the buyers are here, it's all work and no play. I'm gonna roll out the exotic rack now. Ginger, you start with that leopard number and Emma follow with the monkey fur cape. Then alternate the rest until we show them all. Break a leg," he added, grinning.

Ginger saluted and reached for the leopard coat. Emma followed behind her with the black monkey fur cape and a matching cloche hat. They giggled as they passed each other on the runway. Twenty minutes later they were wearing the last of the beautiful furs and perspiration was hovering on both their upper lips.

"I'm pooped," said Ginger. "Are we done yet?"

Before Emma could answer, Mr. Rosenbloom came through the door. He swept them both into his ample embrace and hugged them till they thought they would never breathe again.

"*Dahlinks*, you *ver vonderful*," he bellowed. "Positively *vunderful*. The buyers loved you and they loved *mine* coats. *Ve* have a few special requests now so you should please come outside a minute. I'll tell you *vhich* coats to put on. Skip the runway *dis* time, just come into *da* carpeted area and show *dem* to *da* buyer who *vants* a second look. *Dis* is *vhere da* big sales come in. Hurry now, *dey're vaiting* for us."

Ginger came out first, and a tall gentleman in the front row asked her to wear the red fox three quarter length coat that almost matched her hair. Then the man next to him called to Emma and requested a black sable full-length to be followed by the monkey fur cape. Pretty soon they were running back and forth, filling requests from almost all of the buyers. When the last request had been filled, both girls collapsed once more, utterly exhausted. Eddie came back and was smiling from ear to ear.

"You chicks did real good. Sales ain't never been this good. Mr. R is real pleased. I think you're here to stay. Congratulations!"

Ginger let out a hoop of joy and Emma chimed in.

"We're models," Emma said—"honest-to-goodness professional models."

The girls collapsed on the loveseat and hugged each other.

"I can't wait to get home and tell Mama. Can we leave now, Eddie, or should we wait for Mr. Rosenbloom?"

"Better wait, Emma. He'll want to tell you when to come in again."

Just then Mr. Rosenbloom burst into the room, a wide grin covering his round sweaty face. "You are *mine* lucky charms," he yelled. "Business *vas* never better. Be back here tomorrow at ten o'clock and tell your mama *tank* you for sending me such angels."

The exuberant furrier left the room as quickly as he entered it, waving his order pad in a salute to the startled young models.

Chapter 14

▼

Emma and Ginger were at the furrier's by nine o'clock the next morning. Five minutes after they got there, the buyers started to arrive. Mr. Rosenbloom was already hard at work arranging coats on the racks in the back. Eddie was rushing back and forth with armfuls of furs, perspiration beading on his brow.

"Hi girls. Mr. R wants to see you in the back room. Better hurry it up. We're expecting a big crowd today."

The girls exchanged glances and headed for the rear of the salon.

"Ah here are *mine* jewels," muttered Mr. Rosenbloom. "Are you ready for another busy show? Today is special. All *mine* mid-*vest* buyers are here, plus two from *da vest* coast. *Ve* gotta make a good impression. I'm *dependingk* on you."

"We're ready for anything," said Ginger with a shake of her slender hips.

"Absolutely," added Emma with a confidence she wasn't sure she felt. "Where do we begin?"

"*Ve* start *mit de* exotics today, *dahlinks*, and *voik* backwards. I *vill* point out *da vest* coast guys and you can concentrate on *dem*. *Vhen ve* get to *da* minks, pay special attention to *da* mid-*vest* guys. *Dey* are big for mink—especially in Chicago. Eddie *vill* roll out *da* racks in *de* order I *vant* and *den* it's up to you." He grinned confidently and hurried out to the front to greet the buyers that were rapidly assembling. Eddie had plugged in the coffee pot as usual, and several men and women were vying for cups.

Emma and Ginger changed their shoes and positioned themselves in readiness for Eddie's signal to begin. Within fifteen minutes, the marathon began again. They took a break after an hour and both girls were glad for a chance to rest and regroup. Ginger headed for the water fountain and as she brought her head up, water dripping from her chin, she found herself face to face with Eddie.

"You sure are somethin'," he said. "You look like a million bucks in that leopard number, Ginger."

"Well thanks, Eddie. Glad you appreciate a good thing when you see one," she said with a giggle.

"I sure do and I'd like to show my appreciation too. How 'bout a date Saturday night? Rosenbloom closes early on Saturday and goes to temple so I'm free early. How about dinner and some dancin'? I got a friend who runs a club downtown. The food's pretty good and the dancin' is great. You do like to dance, don't you?"

"I'd rather dance than eat, Eddie. That's what I want to be some day in Hollywood—a dancer—in the movies."

"Well, then that settles it, gorgeous." I'll pick you up at five. Just give me directions."

"I'll write 'em down for you before I leave," she said and then stood on her tiptoes and kissed Eddie right on the mouth. Before he could react further, Ginger turned and walked toward the back room. Eddie watched her go, a grin spreading across his handsome face.

"Eddie," called Rosenbloom. "*Vhere* are you? *Ve* are ready for *da nex* round."

"Right here, boss," was the response, as he rolled out the first rack and the show began again.

"Where did you go, Ginger?" asked Emma, as she struggled into an extra long mink coat.

"Just for water, Em, but I got more than that. I'll tell you later. Let's get to work. She pulled on the sable at the end of the rack, and tossing her red curls defiantly, she positioned herself behind Emma.

"Let 'er roll," Eddie murmured from behind the curtain.

Emma sauntered out first, followed by Ginger, and soon they were crisscrossing the room like a pair of pros amid oohs and aahs from the audience. Rosenbloom was beaming.

As Emma slid the last coat off and returned it to the rack, she looked around for Ginger. She spotted her in the corner, deep in conversation with Eddie and a notepad and pencil in her hand. As she was taking off her shoes and getting ready to leave, Mr. Rosenbloom came around the corner.

"Emma, *dahlink*, you *ver* sent by God—you and Red. *Vhat* a day! *Ve* took more orders in *da* past two days *dan* I took in *da* last *tree mons*. *Ve vill* need a *veek* just to fill *de* orders. And *vhere* is *da* redhead?" he asked looking around.

"Oh, she's coming," Emma assured him, glancing toward the corner of the room. "When do you think you will need us again, Mr. Rosenbloom?"

"Yes, when indeed?" asked Ginger, coming across the room with the last coat she had modeled slung casually over one shoulder.

"I haven't been this pumped up in an age. I could keep this up all week."

"*Vell, dahlink*, I *von't* need you for *anoder veek* or two. Eddie and I *vill* have to *vork* overtime just to get *da* orders filled. *Zen ve haf* a charity show for *da* Ladies League. Can you help us out *vit dat von*?"

"Just tell us where and when, Mr. R, and we'll be ready to go to work." She grinned.

"Right, Emma?"

"Of course. Just give me a little warning so it won't conflict with any of my other modeling assignments. I'm a photographer's model now too, you know. Mama signed my contract last week and I start work officially tomorrow."

"*Vell*, congratulations, Emma. You are a real professional now and I *vish* you lots of luck. Plan on *comingk* in two *veeks* from today, okay? If *anyting* changes, I'll leave *vord* at your mama's. Goodbye *goils* and *tanks* again." He handed them each an envelope while depositing a wet kiss on each cheek.

"Thanks, Mr. Rosenbloom," they chorused and headed for the door. Ginger waved at Eddie and they began the walk to the trolley station. As soon as they were seated in the trolley, both girls opened their envelopes. Ginger gasped.

"It's a hundred dollars, Emma. That's fifty dollars a day. We're rich; we're rich. Can you believe it?"

"Wow," said Emma. "I've never seen that much money in my life."

"And that's only the beginning, Emma. Mark my words, there's a lot more where that came from. And you're gonna start your first photo assignment tomorrow with Stephen. You'll be rolling in it soon."

Emma became quiet. "This is all too much," she said finally. "Won't our parents be surprised. I still can't believe it. I can't wait to tell Charles. He won't believe it either."

"He will when you show him the cash," Ginger joked. "Now let me tell you my other news. I have a date with Eddie on Saturday night and he's taking me out for dinner and dancing. What do you think of that?"

"That's super. Maybe we could double date some time, huh?"

"Well, I don't know about that. After all Charles is pretty uptown and Eddie is more from the old neighborhood. He's really into dancing, too. Does Charles like to dance, Emma?"

"I'm not sure, but I can certainly ask him. I think that would be fun, don't you, Red?" she added jokingly. "I think you've got a new nickname as a model, Ginger. Do you mind?"

"I don't care what they call me if they keep paying this kind of money," she answered.

The trolley rounded the corner near Hunts Point and both girls rose to get off.

"I'm going straight home to give Mom the good news," said Ginger. "Good luck tomorrow and let me know how it went, okay?"

"Okay. I'll call you tomorrow after the shoot with Stephen. I'm still a little scared, so say a prayer for me, will ya? Tomorrow will be different than being photographed at Mama's salon. These will all be total strangers."

"You'll be fine, Em. After today, I think you can handle anything. Besides, from what you told me, Stephen will be watching out for you. Break a leg, as they say in the theatre."

"Thanks, Ginger. Talk to you tomorrow."

As Ginger continued up the street, Emma crossed over and walked the short distance to the Point. Julia was in the living room when Emma walked in. She stood up immediately and rushed to greet her daughter.

"Welcome home, Miss Model," she said smiling. "How did it go today?" Before Emma could answer, she added, "Stephen just called to confirm the time he will meet you tomorrow for your first assignment. But now, tell me everything."

Emma gave her mother a recap of the last two days and ended her soliloquy by shoving the envelope containing the money into her hand. "Look at this, Mama. Ginger and I each made a hundred dollars—just for modeling coats. Can you believe it?"

"Well, yes I can, Emma. Remember, I just signed your contract with Stephen and you will be making that and more working for him. Modeling is fast becoming a very lucrative business. Pretty soon, I'll have to pay you myself," she said with a laugh.

"Oh, no, Mama, never. I will always work for you for nothing," she answered with a serious face. "Saturdays are for American Chic as long as you want me."

"Well that's mighty generous of you, daughter. I'll remember that when you are rich and famous," Julia quipped. "Now let's see about getting some dinner on the table for the men in this family."

Before Emma could answer, the phone interrupted. She went to answer it.

"Hi, Emma. How was your day at Rosenbloom's?"

"Oh, Charles, it was so exciting. We did more business than yesterday, and Mr. Rosenbloom was so happy. He paid us one hundred dollars, Charles. Can you believe it—just for modeling coats?"

"Wow, one hundred dollars. That's a lot, Emma. I didn't know modeling paid so well. That's half as much as I make in a month at Con Ed." His voice dropped to a whisper. "When can I see you, Emma? It's been three days you know."

"I know, Charles, but I have my first photo shoot tomorrow with Stephen and I need to get some rest. I am just exhausted after these two days at the furrier, and I want to look my best tomorrow. You understand, don't you?"

"Sure I do, Emma, but I miss you. Can we get together Friday? Can I come over to the house after dinner? Then you can tell me all about your first day as a photographer's model."

"Ok, Charles. Come over about seven on Friday. We can take a walk and have some time alone. I miss you, too," she added fighting off a yawn. "Goodnight for now." She hung up the phone and returned to the kitchen where Julia was already preparing the evening meal.

"What a day, Mama. I'm bushed. I'm just gonna take a hot bath and turn in right after dinner if that's okay. This modeling is harder work than I realized."

Julia smiled at her daughter across the room. "And so your career begins, my dear. I was never able to choose mine—it just sort of found me. I pray you will find joy on this path you have chosen."

Chapter 15

▼

Emma checked her image in the hall mirror, and then rushed out of the house. She walked briskly to the trolley station where she was to meet Stephen at ten o'clock. As she rounded the corner, she saw his car parked at the curb. As she approached, Stephen jumped out and opened the passenger door for her to get in. He was dressed more casually than usual today Emma noted. A deep maroon sweater over a pair of soft grey slacks made him look like a young college boy. His blond hair was a bit more tousled than usual, and he seemed very relaxed.

"Good morning, Emma. I'm so glad to see you. Are you all ready for today's shoot?"

"I'm ready," she answered and climbed into the front seat. "It's so nice of you to take me to the shoot, Stephen."

"Well, we both have to be at the same place at the same time, and I want you to feel comfortable your first day on the job, so it seemed the logical thing to do. You'll have to travel on your own to other shoots later on, but by then you'll have met a lot of the people involved and so will feel more relaxed. This shoot is uptown on Madison so we'd better get going. There may be a little traffic getting across town."

Stephen revved the engine and pulled away from the curb. The drive uptown was a bit tenuous on this busy Thursday morning, but Emma was unaware. She was too busy enjoying the sights around her. She stole a glance at Stephen and elicited a grin from him when he realized she was watching him.

"I hope my driving doesn't scare you, Emma. I'm very careful on the road, especially when I have such valuable cargo on board." He grinned at her.

"Oh Stephen, I'm not afraid with you at the wheel. I'm used to driving with my mother, as you know, and you are as careful as she is. I'm just excited about today and I love seeing all the activity of the city going on around us. Madison Avenue is such a prestigious address. I hope I'll be good enough for this client."

"No need to worry about that, Emma. You are already good enough for any client. They will be thrilled to have someone as lovely and photogenic as you are. Take my word for it. You have nothing to worry about—nothing. Just sit back and relax. We'll be there before you know it. And by the way, you're looking especially radiant this morning, I must say."

Emma blushed and managed a thank you. Stephen reached over and patted her hand. She smiled up at him and settled back in the seat.

"Here we are," announced Stephen, guiding the car into a space against the curb. Emma looked out the window. Huge bronze doors flanked by two large show windows met her gaze. Beautiful clothes were displayed in both windows and several women were ogling their contents from vantage points on the sidewalk. Emma looked at Stephen questioningly.

"This is the place, Emma. The studio is upstairs over this couture showroom. Those clothes you're seeing were dreamed up by some of the biggest designers in New York. C'mon, I'll give you a closer look."

Stephen came around to open the door for Emma. She got out without hesitation, stepped up on the sidewalk and walked toward the window. She saw her reflection in the glass and frowned.

"What's wrong, Emma?"

"I just got a glimpse of myself in the window, Stephen, and I can't even hold a candle to the mannequins wearing those gorgeous creations. I'm sure the client is going to be disappointed."

"Well, why don't you just wait and see about that?" he answered with a shrug.

Stephen took Emma's elbow and steered her toward the big bronze door. As soon as they got inside he pointed to the stairs. A metal sign on the wall indicated a studio on the upper level. Emma began to climb the stairs and soon found herself facing another door. Bold black letters on the glass announced Fontaine Fashion Studio. She looked at Stephen. He nodded and with his free hand, pushed open the door.

Emma looked around and saw cameras and lighting equipment everywhere. Her hands felt clammy and perspiration was forming under the collar of her blouse. She could feel it trickling down between her breasts. She took a deep breath. I sure wish Mama were here, she thought to herself. Stephen interrupted her thoughts.

"C'mon Emma. Let me introduce you to the powers that be."

He led her over to a group of men standing around a very large camera on a platform.

"Mr. Caine, I would like you to meet Emma Pedesch, your model for this layout."

A tall middle-aged man with a shock of pure white hair looked up and without hesitation extended his hand. Emma stepped forward to take it and looked up into the bluest eyes she had ever seen. He shook her hand and turned to face her. Emma was mesmerized by his masculine beauty. Daniel Caine was a commanding presence, exuding an animal magnetism that was undeniable.

"Pleased to meet you, Miss Pedesch. All set to go to work?"

Emma hesitated for a moment, still captivated by this beautiful man, and then answered with a note of false confidence.

"I certainly am, Mr. Caine. Just tell me what you want me to do."

"Dutiful as well as beautiful, eh Stephen? I like that in a model. Stephen will show you what to wear and where to stand, but if you don't mind, I'd rather call you Emma, if that's alright. My name is Dan, and I hope that's what you'll call me." He paused and waited for a reply.

Emma nodded. "Dan it is," she said, "and Emma's fine with me too."

"Okay then. That's settled. Now, Stephen, let's put this little lady to work."

Daniel Caine walked toward the back of the room and Stephen stepped forward and steered Emma toward a rack of clothes that had been rolled in front of a make-shift dressing room.

"Ok, Emma, this is it. The clothes on this rack are arranged in a certain order—kinda like we did at your mother's salon. Do you remember? Just start with the first one and continue down the rack. Before you know it, we will have shot them all, and we'll be done for the day."

"You make it sound so easy, Stephen."

"It is easy. All you have to do is change into the outfit, walk across the front of the platform where the cameras are and stop in front of that backdrop. Just relax and be yourself. Daniel will tell you which way to turn and whether to smile or not. He's a pro so if you just follow his instructions, you'll be fine. I'll be right close by on that camera to the far left, so if you get nervous, just look at me."

"Are we ready, Stephen?" came Daniel's voice from behind the big central camera.

"Yes sir; just give Emma a minute to change. Go on, Emma, put on the first outfit and let's get this show on the road."

Emma almost ran into the dressing room, grabbing the first outfit off the rack, as she hurried in to change. The selection was a two-piece aqua silk dress with dolman sleeves and a wide scooped neck. It fit Emma like it had been made for her, and as she glanced in the mirror while she buttoned the last button on the neck, she felt like Cinderella. She stepped into the matching aqua heels that were in a cotton bag hanging from the hangar and walked toward the doorway. Before she could clear the door, a short, buxom woman rounded the corner and almost collided with Emma.

"Ooops. sorry, dearie. I'm your dresser and I got caught in traffic and so am a bit late. Let me check you out before you go on."

Just then a voice could be heard from the bowels of the studio.

"What's holding up the parade? Where's our model? Stephen, what's going on back there? Time is money, you know."

"Sorry, Daniel. I'll check right away." Stephen rushed toward the dressing room and immediately realized what the problem was. It looked like Emma was being frisked by a fat little troll. Mrs. Blume, the dresser, was going over her with a fine tooth comb while attempting to adorn her neck with a delicate lapis necklace. Emma was frozen to the spot, not knowing what to do under the scrutiny of this tiny woman with three pair of hands. Stephen had all he can do not to laugh out loud.

"Okay, Mrs. Blume," said Stephen gently. "That's enough. Daniel is waiting for Emma. Send her out now with your blessing, ok?" He turned and went back into the studio.

"It's ok, Dan," Mrs. Blume showed up a little late, and you know how these dressers are. She's all set now and Emma is ready to go."

Emma extricated herself from the dresser, took a deep breath, and walked out into the studio. It was like walking into a black cave and for a moment she couldn't see where the platform with the backdrop was. In a minute or two her eyes adjusted to the bright lights and she spotted the platform. Emma paused, straightened up to her full height and strolled over to the platform. She paused before the backdrop and fingered the lapis necklace at her throat. She looked toward the cameras trying to find Stephen but saw only the face and head of shocking white hair belonging to Daniel Caine.

"Turn toward me," Caine commanded. "Leave your hand at your throat. That's a lovely gesture. It goes with the dress. Now turn slowly away and walk back toward the dressing room."

Emma did as she was told, but was still shaking inside when she returned to the safety of the dressing room. Mrs. Blume was already armed with the next dress and began disrobing Emma before she knew what was happening.

"Step out of those shoes, dearie," she ordered. She dropped a green velvet dress over Emma's head. "Slip into this while I get the matching shoes."

She was back in a few seconds with green velvet shoes, the exact color of the dress. Emma was struggling with the buttons in the back and she came to her aid immediately. Before she could say another word, Emma was being maneuvered toward the door and gently pushed out onto the studio floor once more. This time her eyes adjusted to the lights more readily. She did not hesitate, but walked toward the fateful platform with dignity and confidence.

"Good work, Emma. A quick change—that's what we like. No time wasted. Now walk straight toward me and just before you reach me, turn and walk back toward the platform. When you get there look over your shoulder right at me and hold it till I tell you to move."

Emma did exactly as Daniel directed her. She looked straight into those blue eyes. His eyes seem to be luminous, and she felt like she was being hypnotized.

"Move, Emma, move away now," the voice directed.

Like a robot responding to its operator, Emma moved away from the voice and the piercing blue eyes.

"Turn once more," the voice commanded.

She did, and then the voice yelled, "It's a wrap."

As Emma approached the dressing room she felt a bit like a sleep-walker, but the bustling Mrs. Blume soon had her out of one dress and into another before she knew what hit her. And so the morning progressed, and after Emma changed her clothes more than a dozen times, she was feeling exhilarated more than exhausted. Stephen was waiting for her outside the dressing room door when she came out after the last shot.

"Oh, Emma, you were wonderful," he said. Everyone says so. Daniel is so pleased and the client will be thrilled when they see this layout in *Couture Magazine* next month. I am so proud of you."

Before she could answer, Stephen caught her in a bear hug and swung her around. As her feet hit the ground she found herself looking once more into those blue, blue eyes. She struggled for breath as her feet touched the carpet.

"Emma, you were great," said the voice behind the blue eyes.

"Thank you, Mr. Ca….. I mean Dan. I hope I did everything you wanted."

"You did that and more, Emma. You are a natural at this modeling, and I hope we will get a chance to work together again."

"I hope so, too," said Emma dreamily.

"Emma has another assignment with us next week, Daniel," interrupted Stephen. "Maybe we'll see you then. C'mon now, Emma, let's get you home."

Stephen led Emma out of the studio. As they reach the bottom of the stairs, he turned to her. "I know you're tired, Emma, but how about a little supper? I'd like to have a little time with you away from the cameras and the lights. We can talk about your next assignment. How 'bout it?"

Before she could answer, he opened the car door and helped her in. She settled back into the front seat and stifled a yawn while Stephen came around and climbed into the driver's seat.

"I don't know, Stephen. Mama is probably waiting dinner for me and I really am tired." She yawned again. "Could we please do it another time?"

"Sure," said Stephen, realizing how tired she really was. "How about tomorrow? Friday night is a special night at the Crab House down by the river. It's one of my favorite places. "Oh, that sounds wonderful, Stephen. I love seafood and a restaurant by the river would be really special. Thank you for being so understanding."

"That's swell, Emma. I'll pick you up at your house at seven, if that's okay."

"Seven would be perfect," she answered as another yawn escaped. "Boy, I really am tired. I'm not sure I even want any dinner. I may just go right to bed."

As they rounded the corner and pulled up in front of Emma's house, Stephen leaned over. "You were great today, Emma. You really were. It takes a lot to please Daniel Caine and you did just that. Sleep well, and I'll see you tomorrow."

Stephen got out and came around the car to open the door for Emma. He took her arm and walked her to her front door. Before she could say another word, he leaned down and kissed her on the cheek. Emma was speechless. Stephen Lang strode to his car without a backward glance. He got in and gave the horn a significant toot before pulling away from the curb.

Chapter 16

▼

Emma woke early to the shrill ringing of the telephone coming from downstairs. She heard Julia answer it and somehow knew immediately that it was Charles. She grabbed her robe and hurried to the stairs.

"I'm up Mama. Is that call for me?"

Julia looked up and shrugged. She put the receiver down on the hall table and returned to the kitchen. Emma picked up the phone.

"Hello."

"Emma, it's me—Charles. I'm sorry if I woke you up. I just wanted to check on what time to pick you up tonight."

There was a long pause. Emma suddenly realized that she had forgotten about the date with Charles when she told Stephen she would have dinner with him that evening. What was she going to say now?

"But I thought you said Saturday night, Charles," she heard herself say. "I can't make it tonight. Did you forget?"

"Forget? Forget what?" Charles answered, his voice rising. "I said Friday night, Emma. I know I did. It's you that's confused and forgot. What do you mean you can't make it tonight? Where are you going to be?"

"I have a business appointment with Mr. Lang," Emma responded. "I'm really sorry, Charles. I guess I did forget. Please forgive me. Can we make it Saturday night? I'll do anything you want to do, honest. Please say you're not angry and that we can go out on Saturday. Please!"

"Emma, I don't understand you at all. Since you became a model you don't seem to care about me at all. Maybe I just shouldn't call you anymore." There was an even longer pause and then Emma spoke.

"You're right, Charles. It's all my fault. I've been so excited about my new career that I haven't thought of anything else. I've been very selfish and I wouldn't blame you if you never spoke to me again." She sniffled into the phone.

"Well," Charles said softly, "you have a right to be excited, Emma. Everything has happened so fast, I guess I can understand how you could forget, and get your days mixed up. Just tell me you still care for me, please. I love you so much, Emma, and I can't help getting jealous when I don't get to see you as often as I'd like—especially when you're going out with another guy." He waited for her to say something, and when she didn't, he went on. "Do you like this Stephen person? Do you plan on dating him? I thought we were practically engaged."

"Of course I'm not dating him, Charles—it's just business. He only invited me out to discuss some future shoots. Please don't be jealous. There's no reason to be, honest."

"Well, okay, Emma, if you're sure, but, please, don't do this to me again. I'll pick you up on Saturday instead and we'll go out to dinner at that little Italian place you like near the movie theatre."

"That sounds swell, Charles. And could we go dancing afterward? We hardly ever get to dance together and I'd really like that. There must be someplace we could go after dinner to dance, don't you think? Ginger might know of one. I could ask her."

"I'm sure there is, Emma, but I'll ask my father. He knows all the places in the City and there must be one not too far from Hunts Point. I'll find out and then it will be a surprise. So put on your dancing shoes on Saturday and we'll have a good ole time. I love you, Emma. Don't forget that. I'll see you Saturday night about six."

"I'll be ready, Charles, and I won't forget—I promise."

Emma put down the phone and drew a deep sigh of relief. She ran back up the stairs to her bedroom. Her journal was lying on the table next to the bed. She opened it and the words rushed forth.

Whew, that was a close one. What could I have been thinking when I said yes to Stephen for Friday night. I guess I wasn't thinking at all—that's the answer to that. I hated to lie to Charles, but I didn't know what else to do. I've never done anything like that before, but I've never had a career or been a model before. I just got so carried away and Stephen was so complimentary. He's very good looking and so nice and I really do want to go out with him. But I'd rather be with Charles—that's the bottom line. As nice as Stephen is, I'm still in love with Charles Carney and I don't want to do anything to jeopardize that. I know Mama doesn't like Charles, but she wouldn't want me to lie to him either. I'm really ashamed of myself. I'll never, ever, do anything like this again.

Emma closed the cover and put the journal away in a dresser drawer. Her stomach began to growl and so she went downstairs to the kitchen where she knew her mother was preparing breakfast.

"Good morning, Mama. What are you making for breakfast? I'm starved," said Emma, giving her mother a peck on the cheek.

"Bacon and eggs," was the terse answer. "What did Charles want?"

"Just to confirm what time to pick me up tomorrow night," answered Emma. "Can I have one of your blueberry muffins with my eggs, Mama?"

"Sit down, Emma. Your eggs are about done. The muffins are in the tin box. Help yourself."

Julia put a plate in front of Emma and then sat across from her daughter. "What are your plans for this evening?" she inquired.

"Oh nothing much, Mama. Stephen is taking me out to dinner to discuss some of the shoots we'll be doing in the future. He's picking me up at seven. I hope that's okay."

"Of course, it's okay. How did you explain that to Charles?"

"There was nothing to explain, Mama. I told Charles that this was just a business meeting to discuss future shoots. It's not like it's a date or anything." Emma looked down at her plate and begins spooning in the scrambled eggs. She did not look at her mother, but kept on eating.

"So it's not a date, huh? It's just a business meeting? Somehow I don't think Stephen Lang thinks of it that way, Emma." She tried to make eye contact with her daughter, but Emma was having none of it. She kept her eyes cast down and continued scooping the eggs into her mouth.

Finally Emma looked up. Julia was sitting back in her chair looking intently at her.

"Well, maybe he does," said Emma, sulking a little. "But I intend to make it perfectly clear that it isn't a date—it's just business. Charles Carney is the only boy I'm dating, and furthermore, he's the only one I want to date. After all, I'm going to be his wife some day, Mama, you know that. I just want to enjoy my career for a while, that's all."

Emma pushed her chair back and stood up. It was evident to Julia that the conversation was at an end. She decided to say nothing further and picked up her coffee cup in silence.

"I have to go now, Mama. This is our last day at Mr. Rosenbloom's for a while. I have to meet Ginger at the trolley station. He's got two or three west coast buyers coming in today for a special showing of the exotics. He says they are very important buyers, so we better not be late."

Emma leaned down and gave her mother a kiss and then turned and went up the stairs. She was still feeling guilty about her deception when she went out the front door, but turned her mind to the fur coats she would be modeling today. Ginger was already at the trolley station, dressed in what was becoming her signature color—ruby red. In contrast to the thick auburn hair, which today was piled on top of her head with a few wispy curls escaping, the outfit was positively startling.

"Wow, Ginger, you look amazing," said Emma. "Where did you get that red suit?"

"My cousin, Adrienne came over yesterday, Emma. You know the one who's the same size as me. She's moving down south and so is cleaning out her closet and getting rid of lots of her winter things and bringing them over to our house. This is one of the outfits she brought over. Whaddya think? Is it me or what?"

"It certainly is you. Mr. Rosenbloom is going to flip—and so is Eddie. I can guarantee that."

Ginger grinned appreciatively. "I sure hope so. I really got a thing for that kid, and I hope it's mutual." She patted her red curls and stepped up on the trolley steps.

"C'mon, Emma, let's get our gorgeous selves to work, whaddya say?"

Emma grinned and followed her friend into the trolley.

"Mr. Rosenbloom, here we come," she giggled.

As expected, Mr. Rosenbloom did a double take when he saw Ginger, and Eddie was rendered speechless. Ginger was drinking in the admiration like a nomad at her first oasis. The showing went off without a hitch and the buyers completed their orders by early afternoon. As the girls were getting ready to leave, Ginger tapped Emma on the shoulder and said, "I won't be going home with you, Em. Eddie and I are going to spend the afternoon together in the City and then he's taking me to dinner tonight. I didn't think you'd mind going home by yourself. You don't, do you?"

"Of course not, Ginger. Have a great time and tell me all about it. Charles and I are going dancing Saturday night. If it works out, maybe next time we can double date with you and Eddie. I'll talk to you over the weekend."

Emma went toward the back room to get her things and say goodbye to Mr. Rosenbloom.

"*Dahlink, you ver vunderful* as usual. I *vont* need you *goils* for a few *veeks*, but I *vill* call you next time *mine* buyers come to town. You *vill vork* for me again, *v'ont* you?" he asked grinning broadly and handing her a white envelope.

"We sure will, Mr. Rosenbloom. Just call me or leave word at Mama's. I'd love to model for you again and so would Ginger. Well, goodbye for now and thanks."

Emma walked slowly to the trolley station, savoring the soft breeze and the sunny afternoon. Suddenly she was aware of the aroma of fresh baked bread and the spicy smell of sausages cooking. Her mouth was watering as she turned the corner and walked right into the middle of a street fair. There were vendors on the corner cooking the sausages that smelled so good along with meat balls and piles of green peppers and onions. Huge loaves of homemade bread were hanging from hooks along with small whole roasted chickens and strings of garlic. What a feast for the eyes and the palate thought Emma. Since lunch was the next item on her agenda, Emma decided to have it here at the street fair. She wandered down to the end of the block where several young children were gathered around an old man who was dipping apples into a boiling pot of bright red sugar mixture. The residue of this sticky mixture was evident on several of the children's faces. Emma smiled and thought how Jerry would enjoy one of these treats. She decided right there and then that she would bring one home to her brother. *But first I must attend to my own stomach,* she vowed. Emma took in all the culinary sights around her and finally opted for the sausage. She walked up to the man cooking the shiny, fat links.

"One sausage plate with onions and peppers on the side, please," said Emma, digging in her purse for the right change. "Does it come with bread too?" she inquired.

"Sure does, pretty lady," answered the cook, perspiration running down his face. "You must decide between dark or light though." He grinned, waiting for her decision.

"Oh, dark please," said Emma. "That is my absolute favorite. My mama makes dark bread too. I wonder if this will be as good."

"I guarantee it," said the cook. "My mother makes it for me and she made this batch too. Take a bite and tell me what you think."

Emma took a bite of the big piece of thick black bread, but before she could answer, a light went off in her face. She jumped, almost dumping her plate of food. She looked up and there to her amazement was Stephen, doubled up with laughter.

"What are you doing here and what was that flash?" Emma asked, staring up at him.

"I was in the neighborhood and spotted the fair. It's lunch time so I thought I'd take advantage of all this good food. I always have a camera with me wherever I go, so when I saw you out of the corner of my eye, I couldn't resist. You looked so funny trying to get your mouth around that big hunk of bread. I just had to take a picture. I hope you don't mind."

"You really took me by surprise, Stephen, but now that I know it's you, I feel better. I just didn't expect to see you down here. I just finished at the furrier and, like you, was drawn to the fair by the delicious smell of sausages cooking. So here I am."

"As long as we're both here, Emma, can I take a few more shots? This would make a great pictorial and you are a natural choice for the model. Besides you're here already." Stephen smiled and, before she could answer, he began taking more candid shots of what was going on around them.

"I want to get a candy apple for Jerry," said Emma. "C'mon down to the end of the block where the vendor is. He is a character himself and there are quite a few kids hanging around him. You can get some great human interest shots."

"You've got a natural eye for this stuff," said Stephen. 'You make your purchase and I'll just step back and take a few photos. Just forget I'm here, Emma. Do what you would naturally do and I'll take the pictures as I see them."

He moved back from the apple stall and Emma walked up and placed her order. There were two young urchins in front of her taking turns biting one big red apple. In their exuberance, one boy turned suddenly to push the other one out of the way, and the apple fell to the street. The boys looked down at the smashed remains of their apple and were immediately devastated. Emma was filled with pity for the youngsters.

"Two apples please," she asked the vendor. "Wrap one, please and I'll take the other one myself."

The old man handed her the wrapped apple and then the second one. Emma turned and handed it to the smaller of the two boys.

"Now share it gently," she said. "Remember what happened to the last one. Take turns taking your bites on each side so it won't get lopsided and fall into the street again."

The two urchins looked up at Emma in total disbelief. The taller one took off his grubby woolen cap and doffed it at Emma.

"Thanks, maam," he said.

"Me brother and me both thanks ye."

"You're quite welcome, I'm sure," answered Emma as she turned to find Stephen filming the whole incident. Embarrassed, she started walking back up the street in the direction of the trolley station. Stephen followed behind, still snapping photos as they progressed to the other end of the street.

"What a great shot that was," said Stephen. "Talk about human interest—you were great, Emma, really great."

"Well, I just felt sorry for the boys," said Emma. "They probably paid for that apple with their last pennies. I couldn't bear to see them looking so dejected. It was a small price to pay to see them smile. Now I better get this one home to Jerry before it turns to stone," she added. "Ill see you at the house tonight, Stephen."

Emma waved and ran the last few steps to the trolley station. A car was just pulling in as she got there and she climbed aboard with a last wave to Stephen, who she noticed, was once again snapping her picture.

Chapter 17

Stephen rang the bell at the Pedesch home precisely at six o'clock.

"I'll get it, Mama," Emma shouted from upstairs. She opened the door and greeted Stephen, standing nonchalantly on the other side.

"Hi, Emma. Hope I'm not early, but I was really anxious to see you and show you how good the photos turned out—you know, the ones I took this afternoon. They're really great. I can't wait to show them to David at the agency. He really likes this human interest stuff."

"C'mon in, Stephen. Can we show them to Mama, too?

"Of course we can. Where is Madame Julia?"

"I'm right here," came the answer. "So now I'm Madame, eh Stephen?"

"Well, you do run a popular fashion salon, Julia. I didn't mean any disrespect—quite the contrary."

"Don't worry, Stephen. Actually, I rather like the sound of it, but please just call me Julia. What is this I hear about photos today? I thought Emma was working at the furrier. Were you doing a shoot there as well?"

"No, no, Julia. We met quite by accident."

Stephen told Julia all about meeting Emma at the street fair and how he took the series of photos. As he spoke, he laid out the photos on the kitchen table. Emma picked up the first few and broke into a smile.

"These are wonderful, Stephen, just wonderful—not because I'm in them but because they are so real. You got some wonderful shots of the children, especially these two boys with the candy apples. I'm sure David will be thrilled with them."

"Why, Stephen, I didn't know you were interested in anything but fashion shoots," said Julia, holding two of the photos up to the light. "These are so different from what you usually do. You really have a feel for the people."

Julia put down the last of the photos. "Your work reminds me of the kind of photos Pierre used to take during the war—full of human emotion and pathos. He would have been very proud if he could see this work."

"That's high praise, Julia. I admired Uncle Pierre's work very much and to even be compared to him in the slightest way is overwhelming. Thank you for that. And now, before I get a swell head, I am going to take your daughter out of here. We have a reservation for dinner, and I don't want us to be late."

"By all means." "Goodnight, you two, and have a lovely evening."

"Goodnight, Mama," said Emma with less than her usual enthusiasm. She walked down the steps ahead of Stephen and waited at the car for him to catch up to her.

"Is something wrong, Emma? You look a bit disturbed. Did you mind that I showed your mother my photos?"

"Oh no, of course not, Stephen. It's just that I'm afraid she thinks this is a date."

"And is that such a bad thing?"

"No, not bad exactly, but not true either. Remember I told you about Charles. We've been going together for quite awhile. He graduated from Columbia. I told him about tonight, but I said it was a business meeting about future shoots—definitely not a date. Madame Julia, as you call her, doesn't care much for Charles. If she had her way, I would never see him again, so my going out with you gives her hope that her fondest wish might come true. I adore my mother, Stephen, but when it comes to Charles we just don't see eye to eye. I wouldn't want you to get in the middle of this. After all, we are friends I think, as well as business associates. Mama should understand that I could be just friends with a man. After all, she was friends with both Pierre and Louis. I just don't want her to get her hopes up about Charles. I am going to be Mrs. Charles Carney one day—just not right now. I am having too much fun being a model and I want to be just me for a while longer. Can you understand that, Stephen?

"I do understand, Emma. I must admit though that I am disappointed that we can be nothing more than friends. I did have hopes in that regard, but I appreciate your honesty. I like you, Emma Pedesch, and you are going to be a pleasure to work with so let's call tonight a celebration of our union—our business union that is. We'll have a wonderful dinner and talk about our future in the world of photos and fashion. What do you say to that?"

"I say let's do it and thanks for being so understanding, Stephen. I like you, too—very much and I hope we will be working together for a long time."

Emma squeezed Stephen's arm and settled back in the passenger seat. They arrived at the Café Epicure, where Stephen had reservations, and were greeted by the valet parking attendant. Stephen got out and went around to help Emma. She was a bit nervous, never having been anywhere where the car was valet-parked before. She was quiet as they entered the dimly lit foyer of the rather elegant restaurant.

"Am I properly dressed?" Emma whispered to Stephen, holding his arm as they entered.

"Most certainly, Emma. You look positively chic. I will be the envy of every man in the room."

He grinned as he followed the maitre de into the softly lit dining room. Emma drank in the room which was unlike anywhere she had ever been. It was like a burgundy palace with plush carpeting and beautiful draperies all in the same deep wine tones. Even the tablecloths were wine colored with napkins of a slightly softer hue. Candles on every table surrounded a fresh gardenia floating in a shallow crystal bowl. The silverware gleamed as if it had just been polished and the china was ivory porcelain with a delicate burgundy rim. The *maitre de* pulled out Emma's chair and waited for her to be seated. No sooner was Stephen seated than a waiter came, and with a flourish, placed their napkins in their laps. Emma remained silent. As the waiter handed her the menu she looked at it and then at Stephen. She lowered her head.

"Stephen," she whispered, "I'm not sure I know how to act in a place like this. Why just look; there are four forks at my place—two next to the plate and two above it. I don't even know what they're for. There is even one so small it could barely hold a bite of anything," she added, looking almost woeful.

Stephen smiled. "Emma dear, please don't be upset. Just relax and enjoy yourself. Don't worry about the silverware and which fork to use. Just follow my lead and if you are still unsure, you can ask me. My mother was an excellent teacher in matters of etiquette and I was one of her star pupils, so you're in good hands."

Stephen ordered for both of them and the meal was a culinary celebration. He chose escargot for an appetizer and ended the meal with crème brulee for dessert. Emma had never tasted food like this, having been brought up on good Hungarian peasant fare. The delicacy of French cooking with its special sauces and exquisite desserts was truly an experience. The strangest experience for Emma, however, was managing the escargot.

"Now you know what that strange little fork is for," chuckled Stephen as he demonstrated how to scoop up a snail.

"I don't know if I can do that as gracefully as you, Stephen, but I'll try." Emma picked up the tiny fork and aimed it carefully at the slippery shell. She felt the fork make contact with the snail and slowly brought it to her mouth. Stephen watched, smiling.

"Oh, it's delicious," said Emma. "I've never tasted anything quite like it." She aimed at the next snail and made another transition from plate to mouth.

"Mama would be so proud of me. I wonder if she's ever eaten escargot before. I would think Louis or Uncle Pierre may have introduced her to it, but she's never said anything. I can't wait to tell her about this elegant meal and how delicious it is. I feel like a sophisticated woman of the world, Stephen. Thank you for this exciting experience. I bet my friend Ginger would be impressed if she were here. She's going to be a movie star one day, you know. I guess she'll get to eat lots of escargot in Hollywood when she's famous."

Stephen basked in Emma's pleasure and then added, "I guess Ginger has evenings like this to look forward to then. You'll both have to get used to eating in elegant restaurants and using several forks. You certainly seem to come by it naturally, Emma. You look and act like you belong here, believe me."

Emma smiled at his compliment. Stephen folded his napkin, placed it on the table and pushed back his chair. "Is there anything else you would like, Emma?'

"No, nothing more, Stephen. I'm so full I probably won't eat for a week. We've had so much fun eating this wonderful dinner; we haven't even talked about work. Do you know when my next assignment will be?"

"I'm not certain, Emma, but I think we will be doing another layout for David next week. I'll call you as soon as I know. He's been preparing for a huge hosiery layout for a new client. He already mentioned to me that you have the most beautiful legs of any model we have, so there's a good chance he'll ask you to do that job. I'll let you know as soon as I check with him and firm up the schedule. Now let's get you home before Madame Julie sends the dogs out after us."

Stephen gestured to the waiter to bring the check and within a few moments they were out on the sidewalk enjoying the warm night air. The valet brought the car around and Emma settled comfortably in the front seat. She was still reliving the evening in her mind when the car pulled up in front of her house. Stephen got out and came around to help her and walked her slowly to the front door.

"Thank you for tonight, Emma. I hope you enjoyed it half as much as I did."

"Oh, yes, Stephen. It was one of the most exciting evenings of my life."

She stood on tiptoe and placed a kiss on his cheek. "You're a dear man, Stephen, and I hope we will always be friends."

Before Stephen could answer, Emma was up the walk and inside the front door.

"If only I had met you before Charles Carney," Stephen intoned, and turned to his car to head back home.

Chapter 18

▼

The weeks and months ahead were busy ones for Emma. By the spring of 1925 she and Ginger had more modeling work than they could handle. In the fall of that year Emma, now almost twenty stopped working for Mr. Rosenbloom and spent more of her time working with Stephen Lang. What began with a glamorous layout featuring the newest style in silk stockings and the latest designer shoes ended on a high note with a four-page spread in *Vogue* featuring Emma in Chanel suits.

"Only last year *Vogue* did a spread with the Marquise de Paris and two of her friends wearing Chanel suits," Emma told Ginger one afternoon. "And this year it's me, Emma Pedesch, wearing Chanel's glamorous creations. Can you believe it?"

"It's so exciting, and I'll bet Charles is beside himself with all your celebrity. He'll be proposing again any day now—just wait and see if he doesn't."

"He better not," Emma retorted. "I'm not ready to become a housewife just yet."

"Me neither, Em, and I think it's time for me to make the break. Eddie is a sweet kid, but there's no future for me with him. One of Rosenbloom's buyers said he could get me a screen test in Hollywood. I've been trying to break it to Ma all week. I want to quit Rosenbloom and go to Hollywood. Whaddya think?"

"I think you should follow your instincts, I hate to lose you, but if Hollywood is what you really want, then you should try your luck now while you're still young. You're beautiful and talented. You'll be a smash and I can say I knew you when. Just promise me one thing."

"What's that Em?"

"You'll come back to New York and stand up for me when I do marry Charles. I'll give you plenty of warning. I promise. I couldn't get married without you. Will you promise?"

"Oh Emma, of course. You don't think I'd let you go down the aisle without me, do you?"

"Thanks. I knew I could count on you. When are you planning to leave? Have you told Mr. Rosenbloom yet?"

"Yeah I told him yesterday. He wasn't too happy about losing me but he wished me luck and he even gave me a bonus. He's a sweetheart."

"And what about Eddie? Is he mad at you for leaving?"

"Not really. He says he will follow me out there as soon as he has a few more bucks saved up. He wants to be a dancer too, you know. Maybe we'll make a movie together some day. Wouldn't that be something?"

"I sure will miss you. You will write to me and let me know how you are and what you're doing, won't you?"

"You bet I will, Em, and you'll write back and tell me about your work and Charles and all your news. I'm gonna miss you too—something awful. You've been my best friend all through high school."

The two girls hugged and tears gathered in Emma's eyes.

"I better get home now," said Ginger. "Now that you've helped me make up my mind, I can soften the blow to Ma. She treats me like a girl friend until I say I am leaving and then you'd think I was five years old again. Pop isn't much company for her, especially when he's drinkin' so I know she's gonna miss me a lot. I thought of bringing her with me, but it's no use. She'd never leave her big lug, as she calls him. Bye for now, Em. I'll call you tomorrow and let you know how I made out."

Emma closed the door on her friend, went upstairs to her bedroom, and began to write.

It looks like my life is going to change again—Ginger is leaving and going to Hollywood to be a dancer in the movies. I sure will miss her. I know she is happy for me and all the success I've had these past few months but I think she realizes that time is passing her by and she's still modeling at Rosenbloom's. The only dancing she is doing is when she's out with Eddie on weekends at one of his clubs. They really are great dancers though. I even got Charles to take me there one night to watch them. We danced a little, but spent most of the evening just watching the dancers. There were a lot of good ones, but Eddie and Ginger were the best couple on the floor. Even Charles was impressed.

Speaking of Charles being impressed, he still can't get over my last layout in Vogue. *He keeps calling me his little celebrity. He doesn't like it that I spend so much time with Stephen but I think I've convinced him that it's only for work. Stephen and I are just good friends, even though I know he would like to be more.*

Here it is, the spring of 1926 and I have already been in two major fashion magazines. Charles is so proud of my success. He brags to all his friends about me and when we go to his house, his mom and dad are always complimenting me. I am lucky to have such a great boy friend. His father is swell too. He wears spats and carries a silver-headed cane and knows lots of people on Broadway. He told me in confidence that in some circles his dad is known as Blond Al. He's a gambler too and owns a big chemical company in downtown Manhattan. I guess Charles has always been rich, but he doesn't seem to mind that we're not. I know he makes Mama feel uncomfortable, but I think she's getting more used to having him around. He's picking me up in an hour so I'd better start getting ready. We're going to dinner some place special tonight. Maybe I'll order escargot again—Charles doesn't know I ever had fancy food like that before. Won't he be surprised? Bye for now.

Emma opened her closet and perused the rack. She scanned several hangers and then selected a soft blue silk dress with a matching cape. Standing before her full-length mirror, she held the dress up to her. She turned from side to side allowing the soft fabric to swish around her calves. This was the perfect choice.

As Emma slid her stockings up over her legs and adjusted the garters she examined her legs. She could still hear Stephen saying, "those legs of yours are the key to your success, Emma." She wondered if he was right. Should she concentrate on being a stocking model as Stephen suggested, and what would Mama think of that? She decided to put that thought out of her mind for now and just concentrate on making herself presentable. She glanced at the clock and realized he would be picking her up in less than twenty minutes. She finished her makeup and dropped the blue silk over her head. A tiny pair of pearl earrings—a gift from Charles on her birthday—completed the ensemble, and she was ready to go downstairs.

Before her feet touched the last step, the doorbell rang. "I'll get it," said Emma as she opened the door.

"You're a vision in blue, Emma," said Charles, appreciation evident in his eyes.

"Come in, Charles, and thanks for the lovely compliment. Come and say hello to Mama and then we can leave."

Emma led him by the hand into the kitchen. Julia looked up from her chair at the kitchen table where she was rolling pastry.

"Good evening, Charles," she said curtly.

"Good evening, Mrs. Pedesch. I hope you are well."

"Thank you for asking, Charles. I'm quite well, thank you. Where are you and Emma off to this evening, if I may ask?"

"I'm taking Emma to the Epicure Café, Mrs. Pedesch." He paused, waiting for a reaction. When none came he continued. "It is one of the most elegant restaurants in town right now. My father recommended it, and nothing is too good for my Emma."

"Your Emma?" said Julia. Emma jumped in to head off any confrontation between Charles and her mother.

"How exciting, Charles. I always wanted to go to the Epicure. Let's go right now. I can't wait to see it. Goodnight, Mama. We won't be late."

She took Charles's arm and steered him toward the door.

"Well uh, goodnight, Mrs. Pedesch," mumbled Charles as Emma rushed him outside. Emma drew a sigh of relief. It seems like any room that Charles and Mama were in together became a potential war zone. She didn't want anything to spoil her evening with Charles. She smiled to herself as she realized she was going to the Epicure Café where Stephen had taken her and she first learned to eat escargot with a special fork. She vowed not to let on to Charles that she had ever been there before. This was his big surprise and she was not going to spoil it for him.

The waiter came to their table almost immediately and presented them with large, elegant menus, written entirely in French. Charles opened his menu and studied it carefully for a minute or two.

"What would you like to start with, Emma?" he asked.

"I think I'd like to try the escargot," said Emma.

Charles was surprised and impressed that she knew what it was but did not question her further.

"May I order the entrees for us, Emma, or do you have something in mind you'd like to choose?

"Oh no, Charles. Go right ahead. Escargot is the only word I can pronounce on the menu. That's because Louis told me about eating snails in Paris and he speaks French so perfectly. I just mimicked him."

Charles smiled and looked confident. He ordered Chateaubriand for two with salad Nicoise.

They ate in companionable silence for a few minutes. Emma was concentrating on the escargots and watching Charles out of the corner of her eye. He handled the slippery morsels elegantly and she was determined to do the same. By the time the main course arrived, she was feeling more confident. She looked up and noticed that Charles was staring at her across the table.

"What is it, Charles? Is something wrong?"

"No, Emma. What could be wrong? Everything is perfect. You're perfect. The evening is perfect. I was just thinking that you're almost twenty one—your birthday is next month, and I was wondering if we could talk about getting engaged on your birthday. It's been almost two years since we talked about it, and I think it's time." He looked up at her lovingly and took both her hands in his.

"You're right, Charles. It's been awhile since we talked about getting engaged."

"You haven't changed your mind about marrying me, have you, Emma?" Charles interjected before she could say another word.

"Of course not. I've just been so busy with my career this past year that I haven't really thought about anything else. I still want to be Mrs. Charles Carney one day."

"Well, that's a relief. I was beginning to wonder now that you are a big-time fashion model. So, can we get engaged on your birthday next month?"

Emma looked up at her handsome young dinner companion and smiled, hesitantly.

"May I talk to Mama about this, Charles, before I give you my answer? If it was just up to me, I'd say yes right away, but I want to be sure it's okay with Mama and Papa too. Please be patient just a little bit longer. I'm sure they will agree that it's fine now that I am going to be twenty-one and my career is pretty much established. I'll talk to her first thing tomorrow and then I'll call you."

"Okay, Emma. I guess I can wait one more day, but please tell her you want to get engaged now—please. I've been holding your ring all this time, and now I want to see it sparkling on your finger. I want everyone to know that you're mine."

"I'll do my best to convince her, Charles—really I will."

Charles leaned down and kissed her fingers.

"That's good enough for me."

Chapter 19

"Good morning, Mama." Emma came down the stairs rubbing the sleep from her eyes. "Where's Papa? Is he out in the garden already?"

"Yes, Emma. He's pruning the grapevine and watering the canna on the side yard. He had his breakfast an hour ago. May I fix you something, sleepy head?"

"Thanks, Mama. I can fix it, but would you join me for a cup of coffee? I'd like to talk if you have the time."

Emma cracked two eggs into a pan and put a slice of bread into the toaster. She poured two cups of coffee and turned to her mother.

"Aren't you going to the salon today?"

"Not till noon, and what about you? No assignment today?"

"I have to meet Stephen at *Vogue* this afternoon, but I have the whole morning off for a change. This can be our special time, Mama, so let's enjoy it."

Julia sat down across from her daughter and took a long sip from the mug. Emma raised her fork and pointed it at the plate. She began shoveling the eggs into her mouth so fast that Julia began to laugh.

"You'd think you were starving. Didn't Charles let you eat anything last night when you went out to dinner?"

Emma grinned. "Speaking of Charles, he proposed to me again last night, Mama. He wants us to get engaged on my birthday next month. After all I will be twenty-one then, and my career is going along well. If we just get engaged now, I think he won't mind waiting a year or so for us to be married. What do you think, Mama?"

Emma sat back and studied her empty plate. Julia, too, was silent, staring down at the tablecloth. She looked up and took her daughter's hands in hers.

"I've given this a lot of thought lately, Emma, and if this is what you really want, then you have my blessing. You know I have fought this relationship from the beginning but it has done me no good. I just want to be sure that you really do love this boy as much as he obviously loves you. I only want you to be happy. You know that, don't you?"

"Of course I do, Mama. I love Charles, but I still want my career too—for a while longer anyway. I'm lucky to have a boyfriend that loves me as much as he does. Thank you for giving me your blessing. Will you speak to Papa for me? I don't want him to think he was left out of this decision."

"Of course I will, Emma. As long as he knows I approve, he will do likewise. We'll tell him together before I leave for work. I think it would mean more coming from both of us. You know how your father adores you. He would feel so much better if he heard it from you."

"Alright, Mama. I'm going upstairs now to get dressed for my meeting with Stephen. By that time Papa will be coming in for his midmorning coffee, and I'll talk to him then."

Emma raced up the stairs, rejuvenated by her breakfast and her talk with her mother. She flopped on her bed and began to write in her journal.

Mama said yes!! I still have to talk to Papa but he will agree if Mama has. Now all I have to do is tell Charles it's okay, and we can get engaged on my birthday. It's so exciting—another chapter has begun in my life. I will soon be engaged to be married to Charles Carney. Just think, in a year or two I will be a married lady with a home and life of my own. I'll call him tonight and give him the good news. He'll be so happy. I can't wait to call Ginger and tell her too. She'll be excited for me. Got to close now and get dressed to meet Stephen.

Emma slid the journal into a drawer and turned her attention to her closet. As she finished dressing, she heard her father's voice downstairs. She finished hurriedly and ran down the stairs to find him. George was in the kitchen washing his hands while Julia was pouring him a cup of coffee accompanied by a large piece of apple strudel.

"Good morning, Papa," said Emma, throwing her arms around him and planting a kiss on his sunburned forehead. "Has Mama told you the good news?"

"What good news? It must be something special to have you so excited. I haven't had a hug like that from you in quite a while." He looked up at his only daughter and waited for an explanation.

"Well, Papa, it's just that Charles and I want to get engaged on my birthday next month, and we would like to have your blessing. I already told Mama and she says it's okay with her, but I want you to be happy for us also."

Emma paused and waited for her father to speak.

George put down his coffee mug and returned the piece of strudel he was about to enjoy to his plate.

"Get engaged next month," he mumbled. "Does that mean you are going to marry soon, Emma?"

"No, Papa. I don't expect to get married for at least another year or two. We just feel that now that I will be twenty-one and we do plan to marry each other, we should at least announce our engagement. We hope you will agree and give us your blessing. Will you?"

George got up from the table and gathered his daughter in a bear hug.

"My baby girl," he muttered into her hair. "How can you be old enough to marry? You are still my *Emmushkam*, my dear little one."

Emma hugged him back and wiped the tears beginning to slide down her cheeks. "Oh, Papa, I will always be your *Emmushkam*, even when I am an old married lady. I just want your blessing so much. Please tell me it's alright with you that I get engaged, please."

"All right, my dear one. I give you my blessing."

George looked up at his wife for confirmation. Julia smiled back at him, and walked over to Emma.

"Then it's settled," she said with a sigh. "Would you like to plan a small party to celebrate the occasion?"

"Oh, I don't know, Mama. Let me speak to Charles about that first. Now I'm going to call Ginger and give her the good news."

Emma went into the hall to call her friend, but before she could pick up the receiver, the phone rang.

"Hi, Emma, it's me, Stephen. I had a meeting not far from you and so am in the neighborhood. May I pick you up for our meeting at *Vogue*? No sense in you taking the trolley if I am so close by."

"That would be swell, Stephen. I would appreciate a ride downtown. I have some really exciting news to tell you, too. What time will you be here?"

"I should be there in about fifteen minutes. What's the news?"

"Not now, Stephen. I'll tell you when you get here. See you soon."

Emma hung up the phone and quickly dialed Ginger's number. Ginger answered after the second ring, sounding a bit breathless.

"I just made my reservations, Em. I'm flying to California on Friday. Can you believe it?"

"Wow that is exciting. You sure didn't waste any time after you made your decision, did you? Well, Ginger, I've got some news too. Charles and I are getting engaged on my birthday. I just told Mama and Papa and they gave me their blessings. I am so relieved. I won't be able to tell Charles till tonight after he gets home from work, so you're the first to know. Looks like we're both starting out on a new phase of our lives. I only wish we were still going to be together. I sure am going to miss you, but I hope you have all the success you've dreamed of. Just please keep in touch. Don't forget me. We've been through too much together. You'll always be my best friend. I've gotta run now, Ginger. Stephen is picking me up for a meeting downtown. Can we get together before you leave? Call me tonight and we'll make plans. Bye now."

As she hung up the phone, Emma heard Stephen's car pulling up in front of the house. She ran upstairs to get her purse and was back down before he got up the steps to the front door.

"Hi Stephen. I'm all ready to go," she greeted him. "Come in and say hello to Mama and Papa and then we can leave."

Stephen Lang stepped into the hall and headed for the kitchen, a familiar destination for him after this past year.

"Hello, Julia. Hello, George. It's so good to see both of you. I guess you're pretty proud of Emma, aren't you? That last spread in *Vogue* was really something, wasn't it?"

Emma's parents greeted Stephen enthusiastically and Julia planted a kiss on his cheek.

"You've been too much of a stranger lately, Stephen. We have missed you. We are both pleased about Emma's work. She has been very lucky indeed, and we know we have you to thank for that. Please don't be such a stranger."

"Yes, we miss you," added George. "You have been a good friend to my wife and my daughter, and I am very grateful, Stephen."

"It's not just me, George. Your daughter has a lot of talent. Maybe she will take pity on me and invite me for dinner again one night soon." He looked over at Emma and grinned.

"C'mon, Stephen. We'll be late if we don't get out of here soon."

The two young people headed out the door and were soon on their way. Before Stephen could say anything, Emma blurted out her news.

"Charles and I are getting engaged on my birthday."

Silence pervaded the car. Stephen looked over at his passenger and shook his head numbly. "Is that your big news, Emma? Is that what you couldn't wait to tell me?"

"Yes, Stephen. Aren't you happy for me? I haven't even told Charles yet. He asked me last night and Mama and Papa just gave me their blessing this morning. We won't be getting married for at least another year, April 1929 probably, but we will be officially engaged and I will be wearing his ring. He's been waiting a long time you know, and I don't think he should have to wait any longer."

Emma paused and waited for Stephen to comment. He said nothing and she had difficulty hiding her disappointment.

"Say something, Stephen. Don't just sit there. Say something—anything."

"I know you want me to be happy for you, Emma, and in a way I am. It's just that I kept hoping maybe you would change your mind about Charles. You know how I feel about you, Emma. Don't tell me you don't. It's hard for me to be happy about you getting engaged to someone else when what I really wish is that it could be me."

"I guess I thought you knew that I had not changed my mind about Charles. I am so fond of you, Stephen. You are one of my dearest friends and I hope you always will be, but I am in love with Charles Carney. I have been since I was sixteen and nothing has happened to change that. Please understand and be happy for me. We'll still be working together and I want to feel that you are still my friend. You are, aren't you?"

Stephen turned to Emma and ran his finger down her cheek. "Of course I'm you're friend, Emma, and God willing, I always will be, but you must know that I have much deeper feelings for you and have had for some time. Are you sure you know what you're doing? Isn't this awfully sudden?"

Emma did not answer and Stephen knew instinctively that she was disappointed that he was questioning her decision. He spoke again.

"You're going to have to give me some time to adjust to this engagement, Emma; I can't put away my feelings just like that."

He leaned down and pressed a kiss to her cheek. Before she could react, he put his fingers on her lips and said, "but for now, let's concentrate on our meeting with *Vogue*. Have you given any thought to doing another stocking layout? That's what they want to talk about today, I think."

"Okay, Stephen, we'll only talk about business now. I haven't given much thought to a stocking layout, but I will listen to whatever they propose, and if you think that is the way I should go, I will take your advice. When it comes to my career, I trust you implicitly. I always have and I always will."

Stephen parked the car in front of the now-familiar building and with a sidelong glance at his passenger, got out and came around to open the door for her. "Onward and upward," he said. "You're still one of the top models in our agency, Emma Pedesch, and Vogue is lucky to have you. Their rating on the stock market has never been better and it's only the last quarter of 1928. Let's go in now and do some business."

Chapter 20

▼

The meeting room at *Vogue* was filled with people. The head of the hosiery company made his presence felt at once. He announced to all attendees that he wanted to meet the lady with the extraordinary legs. Stephen introduced him to Emma and it was obvious to all onlookers that he was immediately captivated by her. Roger Milliken had a stocky build and sweat covered his brow. His lacquered black hair stuck to his head like a cap. He sported a pin striped suit and held the stump of a cigar between his teeth. Emma shuddered.

"You are more beautiful than they led me to believe, Miss Pedesch," he gushed. "I'm proud to have you associated with my hosiery ads."

He stepped back a few paces and studied Emma from head to toe, lingering on her lovely long legs. Although small of stature, Emma's height was all in her legs and they made her appear taller than her five feet two inches. She squirmed uncomfortably, and looked at Stephen. Realizing her discomfort, but not wanting to antagonize the potential client, Stephen stepped forward and addressed the client.

"Emma certainly does have beautiful legs that would show off your hosiery to its very best advantage, but Chanel has also asked her to do another spread two months down the road."

Stephen was interrupted before he could continue.

"Mr. Lang, let me assure you I will match any offer made by Chanel but will insist on an exclusive contract for at least twelve months. Would you and your client find that satisfactory?"

Stephen looked sideways at Emma and responded to the executive. "I'd like to talk this over with Emma, and get back to you tomorrow."

"I can live with that," said Milliken with a smile, "but don't keep me waiting any longer than that. Remember, Stephen, those aren't the only legs in New York." He chuckled, motioned to his entourage, and walked toward the door. "Nice to have met you Miss Pedesch and I look forward to a long and happy relationship. Take care of those gams of yours—they are the dollar signs of your future." He waved as he went out the door.

Stephen put his hands on Emma's shoulders in an effort to soothe her. "Don't be upset, Emma. He's what they call a diamond in the rough. He's made a lot of money real fast and is the big cheese in the hosiery business. It's just that there's a lot of money to be made as a hosiery model, and why not you?"

"Let's discuss this, Stephen, just you and me and then I'll decide. Will I still be able to do the Chanel layout if I accept Mr. Milliken's offer?"

"Let me confirm that before we leave."

The man who was second in command was still seated at the board room table. Stephen went over and sat down across from him. He was about thirty-two, with dark hair, olive skin and a cocky persona. He looked up at Stephen.

"How's it going, Lang?" he sneered.

"Fine, but I want to confirm something, Frank. Can Emma accept Milliken's offer and still do the Chanel layout in two months?"

"Not a chance." was the answer. "With Milliken, it's all or nothing. If he says twelve months, he means exclusively—no other layouts while she's representing us. Got it?"

"Got it," said Stephen. "Thanks for straightening me out."

He returned to Emma and told her what Frank had said. She looked a bit disappointed but all she said was, "Can we leave now?"

"Of course." He guided Emma out the door.

She slid into the passenger seat and waited for Stephen. "Where can we talk?" she asked.

"Let's grab some lunch at the coffee shop down the street. I think we can talk there without being interrupted. I'd like to settle this thing once and for all before I take you home. Is that okay with you?"

"Yes, I want to settle this as soon as possible, too."

She fell silent until they got to the coffee shop. No sooner were they seated in a booth, than Emma exploded.

"What a rude man," she spat. "I don't like him one bit, even though he is the big cheese of the hosiery business. Working for him would be like going into slavery. Heaven knows what kind of layout he would want me to do."

"Whoa, Emma, take it easy now. He's not a crook, you know. He just likes to throw his weight around, especially with the ladies. He just wants to sell a lot of stockings and your legs will help him do that. You could never make that kind of money even with Chanel. Hosiery is big business today. Remember, every woman wears a pair of stockings under every outfit—whether it's Chanel or Woolworth."

A tall, skinny waitress arrived at the table, pencil and paper poised in the air. "Are you guys ready to order?" she asked.

Stephen looked up and then glanced at Emma. "Give us a minute, will ya?"

He opened the menu and scanned the selections. Emma followed his lead and did likewise.

"I'll just have soup and a salad," she said, handing the waitress her menu.

"Soup and a BLT for me," said Stephen, giving up his menu also. "Now, Emma....."

"I know you're right, Stephen, and you only want the best for me. It's just that I don't want to be thought of as sleazy—you know—just showing off my legs. I'm sure you know what I mean."

"Of course I do, but remember what I said about every woman wearing stockings. And don't forget, this could lead to shoe accounts also. There's no reason why you can't show off both items at the same time, now is there?"

The waitress returned with two bowls of soup. "Your salad and BLT will be here in a minute," she announced. "Want crackers with the soup?"

"No thanks," they chorused and turned back to each other.

"I hate to say this, Emma, but you must realize that the flapper style isn't going to last forever. It's 1929 after all, and bigger-busted women are customers too. Pretty soon models built like them are going to be in demand. When that happens, the boyish look is going to be a thing of the past, but stockings on beautiful legs ending in gorgeous shoes will be with us forever. Just think about that."

Emma looked desolate. "You mean I won't be able to be a model anymore?"

"No, Emma, but your kind of clothes modeling may be on the way out. That's the way fashion is. Today it's flat on top with a short skirt and tomorrow it's low cut with the emphasis on cleavage and a skirt below the knees. It changes every year or so. It has to or the designers and clothing companies couldn't make any money. You understand that, don't you?"

"I just never thought about it before. I suppose I thought I'd be modeling flapper clothes forever. I've been working with my mother long enough to know better—her styles change every year, too. This flapper rage has lasted longer than most, I guess. You must think I'm a real self-absorbed dummy." Emma looked up to find the waitress staring at her.

"Can I get you folks anything else? We've got home-made apple pie today."

"No thanks," said Emma. "Me neither," said Stephen. "Just bring us the bill please." The waitress shrugged and assured them she'd be right back.

Stephen turned back to Emma. "I don't think anything of the kind, Emma. You've been modeling since you were sixteen and this style has been with us most of that time, but the handwriting's on the wall. Just look at some of the silent movie stars—Mary Pickford and Vilma Banky. They're not exactly built like boys, you know. Now they're talking about movies with sound—talking pictures they call them. And there are new stars coming up like Margit Symo and Barbara Stanwyck—fuller figured ladies."

Stephen grinned, a bit embarrassed, and even Emma began to smile.

"You're right as usual. I just saw an ad for *The Noose*, starring Barbara Stanwyck, and she is what Mama would call zaftig. So I do understand, and I will sign the contract with Mr. Milliken even though I can't stand him."

Stephen smiled and looked up to see the waitress eyeing them with interest.

"You were so deep in conversation, I didn't want to interrupt," she said. She placed the check on the table in front of Stephen and walked away.

Chapter 21

▼

Emma's career soared into 1929 as she became the foremost model for Milliken Hosiery. She found it funny that no one knew her by sight because she was only photographed from the waist down for most shoots.

"No pretty face should outshine the stockings," said Milliken, and Emma didn't argue the point. She was perfectly happy being anonymous. She got all the notoriety she needed being engaged to Charles Carney.

She and Charles had been attending theatre parties and concerts in the company of his parents, as well as alone, and their names were often found in the social column of the *New York Times*. This was the year that the Times broke the story about the first radio photo transmitted from London to 43rd Street.

"It shows a dinner honoring the retiring Viceroy of India and ran at the top of page one," announced Charles with authority. "Isn't that exciting, Emma? Why, some day one of your magazine layouts could be sent from here to London. Just imagine."

Only the year before *The Times* had lauded the introduction of the 35 millimeter Leica camera which, over the next generation, would revolutionize photo-journalism. Stephen had been more excited about that than the mention of Emma attending a party where Charles Lindbergh was present, Emma remembered.

Her contract with Milliken had been extended long past the original twelve-month commitment and was now enjoying its second year. Charles, though thrilled with her success, was beginning to get impatient and was more determined than ever to get Emma to the altar.

"I want you to give up modeling, Emma, and be Mrs. Charles Carney. I want to set the date for our wedding," he pleaded. "It's almost the spring of 1929 and we've been engaged since 1927. It's time, Emma. It's past time for us to be married. I've been patient long enough."

"Yes, Charles, you're right. It is time and you have been more than patient with me. My contract is up for renewal this month. I'll tell Stephen I don't want to renew it. We'll set a date for our wedding."

Charles was awestruck. "Oh, Emma, I'm so glad you see it my way. Let's set the date now—right now before you change your mind."

"But what about our parents? Shouldn't they be consulted first?"

"Parents be damned, Emma. This is our wedding. We'll pick the date and they will just have to go along with it. Please, don't let's wait another minute. Pick the day."

"Well….alright, Charles," Emma hesitated. "I always envisioned an April wedding. Let's pick a Saturday in April next year."

Charles was beside himself. He fumbled for a small calendar he always kept in his pocket. When he found it he looked at April and announced. The twelfth, Emma. Let's get married on April 12, 1929." He looked at his bride-to-be and paused for her reaction.

"Well, Charles, the bride's family is in charge of the wedding, you know, so I will have to talk it over with Mama before I can agree."

Charles looked down at Emma sheepishly and said, "I know that is traditional, my dear, but my folks would love to be able to provide for some of the festivities. Any date we pick will be alright with them. We'll check with your mother, of course, but I'm sure this is far enough in advance that she will have no problem with it. Let's go and talk to her right now."

Reluctantly, Emma agreed and Charles headed the car toward Hunts Point. Julia was in the kitchen when they arrived. After a few basic amenities, Emma blurted out the reason for their visit.

"Charles and I want to set the wedding date, Mama, and we hope you will agree with our choice—Saturday, April 12th next year."

Emma pulled herself up to her full height, took a deep breath, and waited. Julia appeared stunned into silence. Momentarily, she gathered her wits about her and then responded.

"That gives us only nine months to prepare. I'm not certain that will be enough time."

Charles intervened. "My parents will be more than happy to help with the plans." Julia looked at him in amazement.

"That is the job of the bride's parents. Do your parents agree with the date you have chosen?"

"Well, we haven't exactly told them yet," answered Charles, "but I know they will agree with any date we choose. My mother assured me of that when we got engaged."

"How nice," said Julia trying to control her angst. "Did you select the date, Emma, or did Charles?"

"I did, Mama, but Charles agreed with it, too."

Julia closed her eyes and took a deep breath.

"Well then, Papa and I will agree, also."

Emma looked at Charles in amazement and they both smiled. He took a step closer to Emma and casually put his arm around her. Julia scowled. Emma placed a brief kiss on Charles's cheek and turned to her mother.

"Thank you, Mama. I'm so happy you agree. I want to be married in St. Constantine's, of course, and walk down that long center aisle."

"I'm so glad you feel that way. I can't imagine you being married anywhere else."

Charles grinned. "I'm sure my mother will be pleased. That is such an elegant church. It looks almost like a cathedral."

"Well then, it's settled," said Julia. "I'll tell Papa and speak to the priest tomorrow."

"I'll have my mother call you, Mrs. Pedesch," said Charles. "Then you two can decide about the details. She has a wonderful caterer as well as connections with a great florist—but she'll tell you all that when you speak to her. Right now, I'd better get home and give my parents the good news. They have been waiting for this a long time."

"Caterer....florist, what do you mean, Charles? You will have a traditional Hungarian wedding—I will prepare the food as the mother of the bride."

Julia looked at Emma for support, but she was busy saying goodbye to her fiancée. As the front door closed and Emma returned to the kitchen, Julia knew at once that this was not to be the usual Hungarian wedding.

"What did Charles mean about a caterer, Emma? You know that I will be providing the food just as I did for your graduation. You can help select the menu of course, but......"

Emma interrupted before she could finish.

"Sit down, Mama. I think we need to talk."

"But, Emma, I only........"

"Now, Mama, please," said Emma, gently guiding her mother to the sofa in the living room.

"I know how much you want to handle all the wedding preparations—and especially the food, and I appreciate that very much. I really do. But this is 1929, Mama. Things are more sophisticated now and Charles's family is in New York society. We can't have what you call a traditional Hungarian wedding. The Carneys would be very uncomfortable. We are going to have to strike a happy medium. Just listen to Mrs. Carney when she calls. She just wants to help, Mama, and you may be surprised and like some of her ideas. It will all work out."

Julia paused and switched the rosary beads she had been holding to her other hand as she wiped her brow with her handkerchief. She looked over at Emma and shrugged helplessly.

"Alright," she said with a deep sigh, "I will agree to whatever you want, Emma. Louis told me long ago that if I am to be an American I must act like an American. Sometimes this means giving up some of the old ways—not all, but some of them. I guess this is where I am to begin in earnest. I will do my best to be a modern mother, but there is one thing I do insist upon, Emma. I will design and make your wedding dress and the only input into that dress will be from you and me. Is that agreeable?"

Emma leaned over and hugged her mother, tears streaming now. "Oh, Mama, of course you will make my dress. I wouldn't want it any other way." In the midst of this display of affection and tears, George came in.

"What's going on here? What's wrong? You are both crying."

"Nothing's wrong, George. We're crying for joy. Emma is getting married in April and we are planning the wedding."

"Married? My little girl is getting married?"

"Papa, I will be twenty two when I get married. I'm a grown woman. Can't you see?"

George walked over to Emma, took her by the shoulders and stared hard into her face.

"My God," he muttered. "You are right. You grew up right before my eyes, and I didn't even notice. You are a beautiful young woman and will make a beautiful bride. I hope Charles knows how lucky he is to get such a beauty. I give you my blessing, Emma, and may God bless your union."

"Thank you, Papa. Charles is a wonderful man and he loves me very much. We will have a happy life together."

Just then the last member of the family arrived. Jerry walked in on the tears and hugs and looked totally bewildered. Before he could speak, Emma ran to her brother and hugged him.

"I'm getting married, Jerry, and guess what? You're going to be the best man!"

Chapter 22

▼

Today was to be my wedding day, Emma wrote in her journal dated April 12, 1929. *Instead it is the saddest day of my life.*

Charles called a week ago with the news. His father had a heart attack and died. He thinks it's a result of the recent stock market crash. Mr. Carney lost all his money and the pressure of his debts and loss of wealth caused it, they say. I don't understand much about the stock market, but apparently, Charles and his mother are now even poorer than we are—broke in fact, according to Charles. Mrs. Carney is having a nervous breakdown and won't see or talk to anyone but Charles. The funeral was the day before yesterday and I haven't seen Charles since.

Naturally, our wedding is postponed. I don't know when it will be until I talk to Charles again, but I have a feeling it won't be until next year unless a miracle happens. Mama went to the funeral with me and is trying to be supportive. I think she's actually relieved that the wedding is called off, but she would never let on.

I can't believe this is happening to me. I guess it's a good thing Ginger couldn't make it, 'cause now there's nothing for her to miss. I'll have to call and tell her what happened, if I can reach her. She's filming her first movie out in Hollywood. I guess she's going to be a star after all. Part of me is so happy for her but the other part misses her something awful. She's the only person who could always make me laugh no matter how bad things got. I'm sure not laughing now. Even Stephen is no comfort. I think he is relieved that my wedding is postponed too.

The ringing of the phone interrupted Emma's writing. She pushed the journal aside and hurried into the hall. She could hear Julia on the phone downstairs and waited to see if the call was for her. Julia's voice rose up the stairwell.

"Emma, there's a call for you—it's Charles."

"I hear you, Mama. I'm coming right away."

Emma reached the landing in a matter of seconds and snatched the phone from the table. Julia patted her hand and backed off, returning to the kitchen.

"Hello, Charles," Emma gasped into the receiver. "I'm so glad you called. I've been so worried about you."

"I'm sorry I didn't call you sooner, Emma, but I've been so busy with my mother. She has taken to her bed and will not talk to anyone but me or the doctor. She's still in shock and the doctor has her on some kind of medication that makes her sleep most of the time. He told me not to leave her alone so I have not been able to leave the house all week. I wanted to hire a nurse to stay with her, but we really can't afford that now. Father's lawyer was here today and it is even worse than I thought. We've lost everything, Emma—everything. I am going to be the only support for the family now, and that really worries me."

My mother's sister is coming in today from Connecticut to stay for a little while. As soon as she gets here, I want to come over and talk to you. Can I do that, Emma? I really need to talk to you."

"Of course you can, Charles. I want to talk to you too. Just phone me when your aunt arrives and I'll be waiting. Please don't worry. Everything will turn out alright. I love you, Charles. We'll get through this together. Please believe that."

Emma hung up the phone and walked into the kitchen. Julia looked up as she entered and waited for her to speak. Emma reiterated what Charles had said about his aunt coming to visit.

"I can't wait to talk to him, Mama." Tears began to trickle down her cheeks again and Julia folded her into her arms and tried to comfort her.

"Don't cry, Emma. I'm sure you and Charles can re-schedule your wedding for the not-too-distant future."

"I hope you're right, Mama. Now that I am ready to be Mrs. Charles Carney, it seems to be an impossible goal. I hope his mother will recover from the shock and agree to let us go ahead with the wedding. I'm going to try to call Ginger out in California, if that's okay, Mama. I desperately need to talk to my best friend."

Emma walked into the hall and picked up the telephone. She was amazed when she heard Ginger's voice on the other end of the line.

"Why are you calling me, dear girl? Aren't you on your honeymoon? Did you forget everything I told you?" A giggle bubbled from the receiver.

Emma swallowed hard and proceeded to tell Ginger what had transpired. Silence came from the other end of the line.

"Are you there, Ginger?" Emma called into the phone.

"Yes, Em, I'm here. I'm just so shocked, I don't know what to say. Here I thought you were an old married lady already. What will you do now? Will you and Charles still be getting married?"

"I'm sure we will, but I just don't know when, Ginger. Charles is coming over this afternoon to talk to me and maybe we can make some decisions then. A lot has to do with his mother, you know. She isn't taking her husband's death very well. She was always so dependent on him. She doesn't seem to be able to function without him. Now she leans on Charles for everything. If his aunt didn't come to visit today, he wouldn't be able to leave his mother to be with me. I sure wish you were here, Ginger. I could really use a friend about now."

There was a pause on the other end. "I'm so sorry I'm not there for you, Em. You know I would be if I could. We won't be finished filming for another three months, or I'd take the next plane outa here. I hope you know that."

"I do, but it doesn't make it any easier. Thanks for listening though. I can't keep calling you—it's too expensive; but I'll write to you after I talk to Charles and let you know what we decide. Be happy out there and say a prayer for me. I miss you. Bye."

"Bye, Em. I'll write back as soon as I hear from you. I'll give you a call later in the month so we can catch up. I miss you too."

Emma stood in the hall with the dead receiver in her hand and tears trickled down her cheeks. She replaced the receiver and walked toward the stairs.

"Please call me when Charles gets here, Mama. I'm going up to my room for awhile. I've got a lot of thinking to do."

Emma must have dozed off, because she was awakened by the sound of the doorbell. She sat up in bed and ran her fingers through her hair and straightened her chemise.

Her mother's voice called to her from the hall below. "Emma, Charles is here to see you."

"I'll be right down, Mama. Just give me a minute."

She ran a comb through her blond locks, tucked a clean blouse into a brown skirt, shoved her feet into her shoes and ran down the stairs. Charles was sitting at the kitchen table talking quietly to Julia. He stood up as Emma entered and walked over to her. He gently enfolded Emma into his arms and they stood together for a few minutes in complete silence. Julia, uncomfortable with the situation, excused herself and went upstairs, leaving the couple alone. Emma remained in Charles's embrace as he lifted her chin and kissed her tenderly. She returned his kiss and then moved out of his arms. No one spoke for a moment, and then Charles took both her hands in his.

"Emma darling, I know how awful this has been for you, but I'll make it up to you. I promise. We'll be married just as we planned, but we'll have to be a little patient."

"It's alright, Charles. Sit here by me and let's talk. I know your mother is devastated and that your father left you with tremendous debts and no money, but it isn't the end of the world. You still have a good job with AT&T and a bright future. I can still work as a model and between the two of us we can make a life for ourselves. I know we can".

She looked at Charles for support. When he provided none, she went on.

"Your mother can live with us, Charles. I know that's not the ideal way to begin married life, but I don't see that we have a choice. We can start looking for an apartment right away and maybe by this time next year we can get married."

"This time…next year?" groaned Charles. "That sounds like an eternity."

"It's not that far away," said Emma, "but we need to set a date so we have something to work toward. Let's do it. Let's plan on April 14, 1930. We'll make it simple this time—a small wedding in St. Constantine with a reception in the church hall just for family and close friends. Mama wanted to do the cooking anyway. So now she and our neighbors will be the caterer. I will carry flowers from our garden—Papa will be so proud and I already have my dress. There, you see, it's settled already. Now let's tell Mama," she added gleefully.

"Emma, you're incredible. Any other girl would be moaning and groaning and making excuses but not you. You have the problem solved already. I know Mother won't be thrilled to hear she'll be living with us, but she has no idea how huge the debts are that Father left behind. She also has no idea that he left us no money to pay the debts or to live on after his death. It will take me several years to pay them all off. According to the lawyer, there are some things we can sell, including the townhouse, but we won't get anywhere near what they're worth. No one has money to spend now that the stock market has crashed. He is going to try and find some west coast investor who didn't take such a big hit in the crash. There are still a few of them around, I'm told."

As for my mother, I'm afraid she has led a rather sheltered life. Father took care of everything and gave her anything she wanted. My mother is like a spoiled child, Emma. She won't be a picnic to live with, I assure you. Are you sure you want to go along with this?"

Charles looked at Emma with a stern, unsmiling face.

"I'm sure, Charles. I've always gotten along with your mother and I see no reason why that should change just because we'll be living under the same roof. Besides, we have a whole year to get her used to the idea. So—what do you say, can we tell Mama now?"

"Alright, Emma. April 14, 1930 it is and let's tell your mother now. She will probably want to start cooking tomorrow."

Emma laughed as they linked arms and went out into the hall to call Julia.

Chapter 23

Julia agreed with the new plan and was secretly thrilled that she had regained control of her daughter's wedding. She called Jerry, now stationed at an Army base in Texas, to tell him the good news and remind him to arrange to get leave so he could be Charles's best man. She suggested to Emma that she ask her childhood friend, Anna, to be her maid of honor, but Emma wanted to wait a little longer as she still wanted to ask Ginger first.

Maude Carney recovered slowly but was still unable to accept the fact that she was now penniless. Charles arranged to hold onto their townhouse until the end of the year and then moved his mother and their few possessions into a small apartment. He and Emma didn't get to spend much time together as his mother occupied most of his time when he was not working. He had arranged for someone to come and stay with her on Saturdays, so he was assured of seeing Emma at least one day over the weekend.

By the winter of 1930, Charles had been able to dispose of many of their expensive household furnishings, including a grand piano and large ebony china cabinet filled with Waterford crystal. He closed on the sale of the townhouse by mid January, but he and Emma were unable to find a three bedroom apartment to accommodate them all after the wedding. Large apartments in Manhattan were still quite expensive and so they continued to forage the newspaper ads and call local realtors.

One day Charles's lawyer, Daniel Marks, suggested they consider buying a house outside of Manhattan in an area called Riverdale.

"Most houses are still owned by the banks, Charles. They were foreclosed on when well-to-do business men, like your father, lost them in the crash. The banks are more and more anxious to get rid of these homes," Mr. Marks advised. "After all, they are not in the real estate business, and don't want to be. You could probably pick up a three-bedroom house for a song. Let me recommend an agent in that area." Charles agreed and called Emma to tell her.

"Well, we have nothing to lose," said Charles. "Let's start looking this weekend. I never thought of looking at houses, but Mr. Marks may be right and we sure can't afford the price of an apartment in Manhattan. The commute wouldn't be bad from there and my mother might enjoy being out of the city for a change. What do you say?"

"I say yes, Charles. I never of thought of a house for us either, but it may be the answer to our prayers. Riverdale isn't too far from Hunts Point either so I could visit Mama whenever I want. Let's do it. Let's start looking."

After several weeks of looking, Charles and Emma were becoming discouraged. Suddenly, they got a call from a realtor who had found a house on Riverdale Avenue, not far from the prestigious Westchester County. They made an appointment immediately and two days later their bid was accepted by the owners.

"Our dream is about to be realized," said Charles. "The realtor says we can close by the end of March and that will give us a month to set up housekeeping before the wedding. We can have our honeymoon in our own home for a week before we move my mother in." he added with a grin.

"I am so excited, Charles. I can hardly wait to have our own home, and a whole week alone will be a wonderful way to start our married life together."

And so the plans for the fabled wedding proceeded under Julia's capable hands. Emma was able to reach Ginger to tell her the good news, but she was going off on location to shoot another movie.

"It's my first musical, Em, and I am so nervous. My co-star has already done two musicals and is a real pro they say. I sure hope I'll measure up."

"You haven't a thing to worry about, Ginger. You're the best dancer I've ever seen. Just wait till Hollywood sees how good you are. By the way, did Eddie ever make it to Hollywood?"

"Funny you should ask, Em. Eddie is here now and he got a job in the chorus line of this movie. He's still a dancing fool but I'm not interested in him as anything but an occasional dance partner. I'm just going to focus on my career right now and no man is going to distract me."

"You sound really dedicated, Ginger. I wish you all the luck in the world. I'm so sorry you can't be here for my wedding. I can't imagine getting married without my best friend, but I'll give you a full report after it's over. Please keep in touch when you can and let me know when the movie is coming out. I want to be the first one in line."

"I will, Emma. I promise. You know I'd be there if I could. Bye for now. I love you."

"Bye, Ginger. I love you too."

The next day Emma called her childhood friend, Anna, and asked her to be her maid of honor.

"Oh, Emma, I am thrilled. I accept, of course, and I couldn't be more pleased. My mother will be excited too. Thank you for asking me to part of your wedding."

"I am so relieved that you will be my maid of honor. After all, you were my best friend all through elementary school till we moved away from the old neighborhood. It's my fault we didn't keep in touch as much as we should. I was so busy modeling. Can you forgive me?

"Of course, and now that we've found each other again, let's promise to remain friends."

"That's a promise, Anna."

The two women embraced and Emma silently thanked God for her good fortune.

Chapter 24

"It's my wedding day," wrote Emma as she sprawled on her bed for what was to be her last journal entry for a long time to come.

I still can't believe it. In a few hours I will be Mrs. Charles Carney and we will be living in our new home in Riverdale. Charles and I just finished arranging the furniture last week. Mama and Papa gave us a beautiful new bedroom suite and all our friends from the old neighborhood gave us a kitchen set and all the gadgets we could ever need. Mama gave us beautiful every-day dishes and service for eight in silverware. The living room furniture came from the apartment Charles has been sharing with his mother. It is much fancier than I would have chosen but we're lucky to have it. It will make his mother feel more at home too.

Her bedroom suite is the same one she had in the townhouse when Charles's father was alive. It's really too big for her bedroom in the house, but she will have it no other way. We are trying to get her to leave the man's chifferobe behind, but she won't hear of it. Charles will try to convince her to let us put it in the hall for extra linen storage and that will give her more room to move around.

Charles and I will go to the house after the reception at St. Constantine's, and he has asked his aunt to stay with Mrs. Carney for a week in the old apartment before we physically move her and her furniture into the house. Charles says this will be our house honeymoon. He promises we will take a trip later on to make up for it.

There was a knock on the door. Emma put down her pen and closed her journal.

"Who is it?" she called out.

"It's the mother of the bride. I've come to tell you that it's time to get into your wedding dress. We must leave for the church in half an hour."

"Please come in, Mama. I'm anxious to get dressed and prepare to become Mrs. Charles Carney. Is Anna here yet?"

Julia opened the door and entered Emma's bedroom. Anna followed behind her.

"She's right here, Emma. We're both here to help you get dressed for your big day."

Emma hugged her mother and then embraced her friend.

"How do you like my new chemise, Anna? Isn't it just the prettiest thing you've ever seen? Mama made it specially to go under the wedding dress."

Before Anna could answer, Julia walked over with the wedding dress over her arm.

"Here is the piece de resistance—your wedding dress. Lean over just a bit so I can slip it over your head."

Emma did as she was told. The soft, white satin slid down her body like a sensuous second skin. Emma had been adamant about having a street-length dress that she could wear again and so she and Julia had designed this creation together. Anna gasped as Emma straightened up and struggled with the tiny covered buttons at the back.

"Let me help you with those," said Anna. "You look amazing, Emma—absolutely amazing. I have never seen a more beautiful bride."

"I'm glad you approve, Anna. Emma and I make a good design team. The only thing we could not agree on was the headpiece. I wanted a more traditional veil but Emma insisted on a tiny satin cap with a few white lilies. And so, as usual, she got her way."

Julia produced the head piece from a large hat box.

"What do you think of this, Anna?"

"Oh, I love it," Mrs. Pedesch. "Really I do. It's so delicate and chic and doesn't detract from the dress at all. I see now why Emma wanted to carry lilies in her bouquet. They carry out the theme from the hat. What a charming ensemble it makes. You two certainly are a good team."

"Well, to tell the truth, Anna, we have Annabelle to thank for that. She is a dear friend that works for me at American Chic and she designed the hat based on Emma's choice of flowers for the bouquet. A lovely idea, I thought. The main thing, of course, is whether the bride is pleased." Julia turned to her daughter.

"The bride is definitely pleased," answered Emma. "I only hope the groom will approve."

"How could he not?" said Anna. "You are a beautiful bride, Emma. Charles will be swept away when he sees you coming down the aisle at St. Constantine's."

"Speaking of St. Constantine," Julia broke in. "We had better get the bride to the church now. I know being late is fashionable, but I don't want to overdo it. Papa and Jerry are waiting downstairs and the car is already pulled up in front of the house. We'll get in back with the bride, Anna, and Papa will sit in front with Jerry. Are you all set, Emma?"

"Yes, Mama. I just have to put the pearl earrings in my ears and put on my shoes. Can you tell me if my seams are straight," she asked as she did a small pirouette in front of the mirror.

"Perfectly," said Julia, "but let's do a tradition check. Something old—your earrings, something new—the dress, something borrowed—my pearls at your throat, and something blue. Where is the something blue?"

"Relax, Mama, I am wearing the blue garter Ginger sent me just for this occasion. All traditions are present and accounted for, and the bride is ready to leave."

Julia started down the stairs, followed by Emma and then Anna. Jerry and George were waiting at the bottom of the stairs, pacing like expectant fathers.

"Here we are," said Julia, a vision in blue chiffon, reminiscent of her days in the employ of John Jacob Astor.

Anna's dress was soft rose-colored chiffon that came to mid calf and she was wearing a tiny ribbon of the same shade in her soft brown curls. A "wow" escaped Jerry's lips as he took in the scene.

"You ladies look gorgeous," he said with enthusiasm. "I can't believe my big sister is such a beauty and you and Mama look beautiful too, Anna," he added. "You were only a little kid when I saw you last, Anna. Boy, have you grown up."

Anna blushed and smiled up at the handsome young soldier. "Thank you, Jerry. You look pretty elegant yourself."

George meanwhile was speechless. Emma went to take her father's arm and realized that he was crying. "Papa, what's wrong? Why are you crying?"

"I am so happy, Emma. I am crying because I am so happy, and you are so beautiful."

George patted his face with a huge white handkerchief, took her hand, and led her out to the car.

When they arrived at the church, Charles was already there. Julia did a quick check of the church and could not believe her eyes when she spotted Maude Carney in the front row on the groom's side. Maude was decked out in a cream colored lace floor length gown. Her shoulders were laden down with stone marten skins.

"There must be a half dozen at least," noted Julia, "and this is the middle of April. She must be dying of the heat....and talk about over-dressed."

Julia scanned the interior of the church and saw that many of the pews in the huge cathedral were already filled with friends and neighbors of the Pedesch family from the old neighborhood. She spotted Louis on a side aisle and Pierre sitting next to him. Annabelle too was already seated and a few couples were moving into the pews behind Maude.

"The seating does look a bit lopsided," Julia said to George. "I guess Maude doesn't have a lot of friends. Most of the guests on the groom's side are Charles's age—friends from college and work I imagine."

George made no comment. "All I care about is getting my daughter down the aisle in one piece," George said. I am very nervous, *Juliashcam,* very nervous indeed."

"You will be fine, George," Julia assured him. "Just let Emma hold your arm and walk slowly. When you get her to the end where the priest and Charles are, then just go to the first row and sit down next to me. Fr. Dante will do the rest. There's nothing to it—really."

George sighed deeply and walked back out of the church to the narthex to await Emma's arrival. Julia followed behind him, and with a pat on his cheek she went off to the bride's room to check on Emma.

Emma entered the narthex and before she could find her way to her father, a limo pulled up outside the door, brakes screeching. Emma turned at the sound to see her friend, Ginger, alighting from the rear of the limo dressed in shimmering green silk and looking every bit the movie star that she was. She rushed up the steps to embrace the bride.

"I can't believe you're here," said Emma, fighting back the tears that were welling behind her carefully made up eyes. "Now that you're here to see me get married, everything is perfect. Your presence is the best gift I have received."

An usher rushed over to grab Ginger's arm and get her seated on the bride's side.

The other usher then led Julia down to the front pew. Jerry and Charles followed Fr. Dante out to the steps leading to the altar. A hush fell over the huge cathedral and the strains of the wedding march could be heard from the organ loft high up in the rear of the church.

The congregation stood as Anna began her walk down the aisle. Then George appeared in the middle of the beautiful marble arch with Emma on his arm. She was a head taller than her father, but today George seemed to equal her height. He carried himself with the inestimable pride of an army general about to sign an armistice. Emma was glowing as they made their way down the aisle, pacing them in time to the phrasing of the wedding march. When they reached the altar, George kissed her gently on the cheek and took his place in the front pew beside his wife.

The priest intoned, "Dearly beloved we are gathered together……." Emma and Charles gazed at each other as they held hands and made all the proper responses. In what seemed just a few minutes, the priest was saying, "I now pronounce you man and wife," and the service was concluded. Charles turned to Emma and they kissed passionately. He grabbed her hand and began to lead her back up the aisle where they would receive the congratulations of their guests. An usher rushed up the aisle to get Maude and bring her out of the church. Julia and George followed Anna and Jerry up the aisle behind the newlyweds.

Emma was overwhelmed by the sea of faces offering their congratulations and couldn't wait until they got downstairs to the reception. As the last guest kissed her cheek and shook Charles's hand, Julia signaled the couple to walk outside and take the side door into the basement of the church where the reception would take place. They were pelted with a shower of rice as they ran around to the side door. All the guests that were invited to the reception were now hot on the trail of the bride and groom. As Julia opened the door, the smells of good Hungarian cooking filled their nostrils and everyone rushed to find a table.

After everyone was seated, and with George at her side, Julia made a brief announcement and then George made a toast in Hungarian. Everyone raised their glass to the bride and groom and toasted them with the fruit of the vine. The festivities began.

Julia tried to make Maude feel at home and enjoy herself but it was difficult. She was afraid to try most of the food and was drinking more wine than anything else. Jerry even asked Maude to dance, but she refused. Charles did get her to dance once with him while Emma was dancing with her father but that was the extent of Maude Carney's participation in this extraordinary event.

"You have outdone yourself, Mama," said Emma. "The food is fabulous. I think you cooked every recipe you ever brought from Hungary. And the wine is extra special too, Papa," she added, bringing a huge smile to George's face. "This is certainly a party we'll not soon forget. Thank you both for making my wedding day so memorable."

Emma made it a point to spend some time with Ginger and so ordered the groom to dance with his mother and some of the other female guests. They had so much to catch up on.

"Thank you so much for coming, Ginger. I can't tell you what it meant to have you here. How long will you be staying?"

"I must return tonight, Emma. I have a shoot scheduled in three days and directors don't like to be kept waiting. You know how that is. I'm just so glad I made it. I wouldn't have missed it for the world."

The two girls hugged again and then Charles came to claim his bride for one more dance. The party finally came to an end. It was time for Emma to throw her bouquet and she tossed it high into the air, accompanied by the calls and cheers of all the female guests. As if fate would have it, the bouquet landed at Anna's feet. She snatched it up and held it aloft for all to see, smiling broadly. Jerry stood nearby watching and a grin creased his face.

Chapter 25

Emma and Charles spent their honeymoon in their new home on Riverdale Avenue. Their joy was complete as they discovered each other both physically and spiritually. Emma was so enamored with being Mrs. Charles Carney that she was not prepared for the letdown that occurred when her mother-in-law arrived.

Precisely one week after they set up housekeeping in their new home, Maude arrived and Charles ensconced her in the larger of the two small bedrooms on the second floor. She brought so many of her personal objects from the townhouse that the room was instantly cluttered. It reminded Emma of an intimate museum. Beaded lamps, small teakwood tables, a Victorian writing desk, huge tasseled pillows, a mahogany dressing table complete with cut glass jars, a rosewood hair receiver, silver-backed comb, brush and mirror all found a place of honor in Maude's domain.

"I will part with none of it," she announced. "These are the symbols of my life with Mr. Carney and no one—not even my son—is going to take them from me."

"I am not trying to deprive you of your personal belongings, Mother," responded Charles, a tone of desperation in his voice. "I just want you to have enough room to move around in. This room is so full of personal items that there is little room left for you. Please understand that I mean well and am only concerned for your comfort. I want you to be happy here with Emma and me; truly, I do."

"I will never be happy away from my own home, Charles, and there is nothing you can do to change that. All I have left of your father are my few meager possessions and now you want to remove them too."

"But I…………………."

"Silence, Charles. You have said enough. My room is, as you say, my room, and I will put in it whatever I wish. Now please leave me alone." With that Maude dismissed her son and closed the door behind him.

His was not a spontaneous courage that could appear in a fearsome moment, but a practiced courage that Charles attempted to use every day in dealing with his self-righteous customers. However, when it came to applying this courage to his mother, he was somewhat at a loss. He found that he had to constantly summon that courage from a deep well inside himself that he kept replenished through the pain and suffering she caused him on a daily basis. Maude refused to admit that their fortune had disappeared with the death of her husband. She was not only unaware of the debts Lawrence had left her son but she was also incapable of accepting the possibility of their existence. In her mind life would go on just as it had, and it was due to the stinginess of her son that she was relegated to this small room in this insubstantial house and was burdened with deprivations beyond measure.

Emma tried her utmost to placate Maude and alleviate her dark moods but it was always a thankless task. She had never felt close to her mother-in-law, even before her marriage to Charles, and the chasm between them was growing wider every day. It soon began to cause dissention between Charles and Emma. Emma found herself crying alone in their room more often than she wanted to admit. Charles could be found pouring himself another drink from the decanter on the sideboard.

The months passed in endless bouts of joy and pain intermingled with a constant stream of complaints from Maude. Charles was doing well at work and even managed a promotion but was still preoccupied with paying off his father's debts. He and Emma couldn't even think about having a family until these debts were a thing of the past.

Emma worked hard to get their new home in order and even began planting a garden in the small but compact back yard. One afternoon she was so consumed with nausea that she had to go inside and lie down. This condition reared its head more and more lately and finally Emma took herself to a doctor. The verdict stunned her. She was pregnant. She knew she had no right to be surprised as they had not been practicing birth control other than in the true Catholic tradition known as rhythm. *So much for that system*, Emma thought to herself as she digested the doctor's pronouncement. The timing couldn't be worse but, as Mama always said, God will provide. She vowed to tell Charles that evening after dinner when Maude retired to her room and they were alone.

She hurried home and was already forming the words in her mind. Would Charles be angry? Would he be happy? What would he say? She opened the door and was immediately confronted by Maude.

"Where have you been? How can you leave me alone all afternoon? Don't you have better things to do than go gallivanting all over the neighborhood? I haven't even had my tea this afternoon." She looked like a small deprived child, and rendered Emma speechless as usual.

"I'll get you your tea, Mother Carney," said Emma. "Go sit down in the living room and I will bring it to you in just a minute."

Emma headed for the kitchen and began to assemble the items for her mother-in-law's daily tea ritual. The silver tea service sat on the sideboard, a relic from the Fifth Avenue townhouse. Emma brought it into the kitchen and filled the urn with the requisite hot water. She got out the tea ball and filled it with the imported English tea Maude insisted upon. She sliced a lemon and put sugar cubes in a small silver container.

"Loose sugar is for common folks," Maude always insisted. "Those of us with breeding use cubes. Never forget that Emma, dear."

Emma buttered two pieces of bread and cut each slice into smaller pieces, careful to remove the crusts first. She gobbled up the crusts herself, enjoying what she had always considered to be the best part of the loaf. She puts two fresh flowers left from the garden in a tiny bud vase on a silver tray and added the necessary tea components. She poured the hot water into the samovar and put it on the tray as well. Balancing the tray carefully, she marched into the living room.

Her mother-in-law looked up. "Oh thank you, Emma, my dear. The tray looks lovely. You really are a good girl and I do appreciate your serving me my tea in the afternoon. It's my one link to the old life—before Lawrence...." Her voice drifted away as she took a linen hankie to her delicate nose and sniffled for effect.

Maude was always dressed for the occasion. Today she was wearing a simple mauve silk frock with delicate lace collar and cuffs. Her hair was combed in the Marcel tradition with only a few strands of grey visible. She had a ring on every finger and two silver bracelets jangled on her right wrist. She constantly asked Emma to dress for dinner but Emma continued to wear her cotton housedresses and save her few dressy clothes for church. Charles and Emma seldom went out socially and so far had made no friends in the neighborhood with whom to socialize. Emma hoped that would change as she was very lonely for female companionship.

She still helped her mother out at the Salon on Saturdays and that had become the bright spot of her week. Although Emma loved being married to Charles, she missed her modeling career very much. Stephen had called several times to try to convince her to come back to work but Charles was adamantly against it.

"No wife of mine is going to work. I'm the breadwinner in this family and that's that." He did allow Emma to help her mother but that was his only concession. Emma was further frustrated by the letters she received from Ginger who was now working on her second film in Hollywood opposite a new leading man, Dan Dailey. It all sounded so exciting and Emma couldn't help but feel a bit jealous. She and Ginger had such big plans for their futures. *Ginger is certainly living her dream, but what about me?* thought Emma to herself.

Emma finished pouring the tea and watched as Maude delicately wiped her mouth with a tiny tea napkin, another relic from her previous life. She was temporarily in another world, staring with expressionless eyes, lips moving silently, remembering another time and place. Emma removed herself from Maude's presence and returned to the kitchen, tears already beginning to slide down her cheeks.

Chapter 26

▼

Emma picked up her old worn journal and began to write.

It used to be such a secret joy to write in this journal, but now it is almost a chore, designed to save my sanity on days like today. Maude is so difficult and no matter what I do, it's never good enough. She is so unhappy living with us and is making Charles and me unhappy too. I want to write about my big news, but I am almost afraid to commit the words to paper. I don't know how Charles will react to the fact that I am pregnant. We didn't want to start a family just yet, but I guess the good Lord has made that decision for us. I'm going to tell Charles tonight as soon as I can get him alone without his mother around. I don't want her to know until I have told Charles. Please, God, please help me. Don't let him be unhappy about the baby. Maybe it will change our lives for the better. Maybe it will.......

Emma heard the door slam downstairs. She quickly put down her pen, closed the journal and returned it to its hiding place. She glanced in the mirror, pinched her cheeks to evoke a little color, smoothed her hair and rushed downstairs to greet her husband.

"Welcome home, Charles," she said, throwing her arms around his neck and planting a kiss on his mouth.

"Wow," said Charles. "What a greeting that was. What did I do to deserve it, Emma?"

"I'm just very glad to see you Charles. I'm so glad you're home. Please come upstairs with me so we can have a little time together before dinner."

"Can't I pour myself a drink first? It's been a rather long day," he said tiredly.

"Of course, but then bring it upstairs, will you? We can talk more privately in the bedroom.

"Alright," Charles agreed. "I'll be up in a minute. Did you want a drink too?"

"No thanks, Charles. I just had tea with your mother not too long ago. Just get your drink and join me upstairs."

A few minutes later Charles walked through the bedroom door and tossed his jacket on the antique mahogany valet near the bed. He put down the glass and proceeded to remove his shoes, tossing them casually one at a time toward the closet.

"Now, wife," he said with a grin, "what is all this secret talk about anyway?"

"Oh it's not a secret, Charles. I just want to talk to you in private. What I have to tell you is rather personal and I'm not ready to share it with anyone else just yet."

"By anyone else, you mean my mother, don't you, Emma? You don't want to share this with my mother."

"That's right, Charles. After all we're still really newlyweds, aren't we?"

"You're quite right, my dear, and if you put this off much longer, I'll be forced to show you just how newly wed I feel."

He laughed and lunged at her playfully, almost dropping the glass in his hand. Emma winced, realizing he had already had too much to drink and then turned to face him.

"There's no easy way to tell you, Charles. I'm pregnant. I saw the doctor today and he assured me that it's true. That's why I have been so nauseous and out of sorts lately. I know we didn't plan for this to happen, but it has and…….."

Emma stopped abruptly as she watched her husband's face contort. He was trying to speak but the words wouldn't come. He put down the glass and stood, swaying slightly, and walked toward her. Charles enveloped Emma in his arms and held her. She could smell the liquor on his breath. She snuggled close and waited for him to speak.

Charles held her away from him and looked deep into her eyes. "Pregnant? Are you absolutely certain?"

"Yes, Charles, absolutely. I hope you're not too upset."

"Upset? No, Emma. I'm not upset. I'm thrilled. I always wanted to be a father and now I will be. It will be a little difficult at first, but we'll manage. I'm expecting a promotion soon and meanwhile I'll work lots of overtime until it comes through so we'll have extra money for what we'll need for the baby. We even have a built-in baby sitter already," he grinned. "I can't wait to tell my mother. I'm sure she'll be thrilled for us."

"I'd like us to tell her together, Charles. We can do it at dinner tonight."

"I need another drink," said Charles. "This is reason to celebrate. How about joining me this time, Emma?"

"Alright but I'll wait till dinner if you don't mind. We can share a glass of wine then and you can make a toast. Speaking of dinner, I better get started. I know how you and your mother like to eat promptly at six o'clock. You chill the wine, and I'll start cooking."

Promptly at six Emma called Charles and his mother to the table. No sooner did they all sit down then Charles raised his glass in a toast. It's obvious to both women that Charles has already had a few drinks as his speech is a bit slurred and he appears rather flushed.

"Here's to us who are pregnant," he shouted. "May it be an easy pregnancy and a quick birth."

Emma looked over at her mother-in-law who had not lifted her glass or said a word. Her face seems to be frozen in time and was devoid of expression or color.

"Isn't that great news, mother?" Charles said turning to face his mother. "Emma and I are going to be parents. That means you are going to be a grandmother. Isn't that exciting news?"

Maude turned toward Emma. "I thought you were going to wait awhile. How are you going to have a baby in this little house? I hope you don't expect me to help you. You'll have to hire a nanny or someone to help you."

She seemed flustered and at a loss for more words. Maude rose from the table.

"I'll have my dinner in my room, please," she said and with that, she walked out into the hall and up the stairs to the second floor.

Emma and Charles looked at each other in amazement. Charles seemed to have sobered up almost at once, much to Emma's relief. Emma began to pass the plates of food to her husband and filled her own plate as well.

"I'd better eat. After all I'm eating for two now. I'll fix a plate for your mother and you can take it up to her," she added.

They ate in silence for a few minutes and then Charles spoke. "It's not important what my mother thinks, Emma. What we think is what matters. We both want children and even though this is a little sooner than we planned, we're both happy about it. We have another bedroom up there that we can turn into a nursery and I'm sure we'll be able to handle a baby without a nanny or anyone else to help us. Lots of couples do it every day. It's just that my mother never had to do it alone. She always had help and so she can't imagine us raising a baby by ourselves. I bet once it comes, she will love to help out. It's not that she doesn't like kids—she's just not too good with them. Please don't worry, Emma and let's just be happy."

Charles raised his wine glass and Emma joined him. "Here's to our new baby," they chimed in unison.

"Fix Mother a plate, Emma, and I'll take it up to her. We'll have coffee and dessert together when I come back down."

Charles brought dinner up to his mother who accepted it without a word. She seemed literally stunned into silence and Charles was grateful. He was not in the mood for a motherly lecture just then. He wanted to get back downstairs to his wife so they could enjoy the moment.

Emma was sitting at the table again cutting pieces from a warm apple pie. A cup of hot coffee was already at Charles's place. He sat down and picked up the steaming cup.

"I love you, Emma, and I'm really happy that you're pregnant."

"I love you too, Charles, and I'm happy that I'm pregnant, too. Do you care if it's a boy or a girl?"

"Not really. I just want it to be strong and healthy. My mother will come around, too. You'll see. She'll be happy for us too once she gets used to the idea. Now, how about a piece of that pie?"

Chapter 27

Emma and Charles began turning the tiny third bedroom into a nursery. Charles was pretty handy with tools and Emma found that she was quite talented with paint and brush. Before they knew it the room was transformed into a yellow and white haven for their first edition. They found a crib and a tiny dresser in the local furniture store. Both were unpainted and Emma set to work painting the pieces with white enamel and adding yellow decals for decoration—ducks and chicks so it would be good for either a boy or a girl.

One day Emma decided she wanted to wallpaper one wall of the nursery. Without checking with Charles first, she bought a roll of paper at the local hardware store and set to work. She dragged the small ladder up from the basement and set it against the wall. Before she got even one foot on the ladder, the phone rang. Emma went to answer it and was surprised and pleased to hear Stephen's voice on the other end.

"Hi Emma, it's me, Stephen. I just wanted to check in and see how you're doing. I'm still used to seeing you, at least occasionally, at the studio. I sure wish you hadn't given up modeling altogether. Don't you miss it, even a little?"

"Of course I do, Stephen, and I miss seeing you too, but you know how Charles feels about pregnant women modeling. Why don't you come and visit? You're still a dear friend, you know."

"I was hoping you would say that because I'm in the neighborhood right now and would love to stop, by if that's okay."

"You mean right now?" Emma exclaimed. "My mother-in-law is visiting a friend in Manhattan today so I'm here alone I'm just getting ready to wallpaper one wall of the nursery. I thought this would be a good chance to get this done."

"Well then, I can help. I'm done for the day and I can be there in fifteen minutes."

"Okay, come ahead. I'll leave the door open in case I'm up on the ladder."

Emma went to the front door and flipped the latch. She returned to the nursery and began mixing the glue and laying out the first sheet of paper. She set the pan on the platform of the ladder and started up. When she got to the top rung she suddenly became dizzy. The whole room started to spin and before she knew it, she was on the floor with wallpaper glue dripping from the front of her dress. Emma rolled over and then let out a low moan as she felt a searing pain in her belly. She crawled out into the hall toward the bathroom. Looking back, she saw a trail of blood behind her. Her heart sank and then everything went black.

"Emma, Emma dearest, are you alright? Speak to me."

Stephen was on his knees next to her on the floor. He leaned down and gently turned her over. His eyes lingered on the puddle of blood seeping from under her.

"Oh God, Emma, you're bleeding. Let me call the doctor. What is the number?"

"On the table, Stephen, next to the phone," she mumbled almost inaudibly.

"Don't move, Emma. I'll be right back."

Stephen stood up and ran to the phone. He dialed the number on the slip of paper lying there. The phone rang three times before a female voice came on.

"Dr. Kramer's office—who's calling please?"

"My name is Stephen Lang and I'm calling for Emma Pedesch. She's had an accident and I need to get her some help. She's bleeding and I'm afraid to move her."

"I'll get Dr. Kramer right away, Mr. Lang. Hold on."

The wait seemed interminable. Suddenly Dr. Kramer came on the line.

"Is Charles there, Mr. Lang? Where's her mother-in-law?"

"No sir, only me. I came to visit and found Emma on the floor with blood coming from under her. She told me she was going to put up wallpaper in the nursery. She must have fallen off the ladder. Please tell me what to do, doctor."

"Don't move her, Mr. Lang. I'll send an ambulance right away. Thank God you came to visit when you did. I told her not to do anything strenuous but she's as stubborn as her mother. I'll meet you at the hospital."

Stephen rushed back to Emma. "Hang on, Emma. The ambulance is on its way and the doctor will meet us at the hospital."

"Call Charles, Stephen. Please let him know," Emma murmured. "The number is on the wall by the phone."

Stephen found the number and dialed the phone once again.

"AT&T," came the voice on the other end.

"May I speak to Charles Carney, please? It's an emergency. His wife has had an accident."

"One moment please."

"Hello, this is Charles Carney."

"This is Stephen Lang, Charles. I'm at your house and Emma has had an accident. I've called the doctor and he is sending an ambulance right over. He will meet us at the hospital."

"An accident? What kind of an accident? Is she alright? And what are you doing there, Lang?"

"Slow down Charles. She was wallpapering and fell off the ladder. I called her earlier and had just stopped over for a visit. I found her on the floor and she was bleeding. Your mother isn't home so I took it upon myself to call the doctor. Emma wanted me to call and let you know."

"Tell her I'm on my way to the hospital and I'll be there when she arrives."

Stephen heard the slam of the receiver and returned to Emma. "Charles is leaving for the hospital now, Emma. He'll be there when the ambulance arrives."

"Thank you Stephen, but please don't leave me. I don't want to go in the ambulance alone."

Don't you worry, Emma. I won't leave you. I'll be with you all the way, I promise."

Just then the ambulance pulled into the driveway. Stephen rushed to the door to let the medics into the house. "She's in here," he said, indicating Emma on the floor in the hall.

A medical technician strode toward Emma and knelt down beside her. After checking her vital signs, he called for a stretcher. Another medic put it on the floor next to Emma and together they gently rolled her onto it. They picked her up on the stretcher and headed out the front door to the waiting ambulance. Stephen followed close behind and secured the door behind him. He climbed into the back of the ambulance with Emma.

"Are you the husband, sir?" asked the medic. "We need to get some information on the patient."

"No, just a friend of the family," Stephen answered. "I called and her husband will meet us at the hospital. He should be there when we arrive."

The siren screamed into the afternoon sunlight. Stephen held tight to Emma's hand and assured her that everything would be alright. She sighed and closed her eyes.

Chapter 28

Emma's miscarriage affected her greatly and Charles had trouble hiding his disappointment. Only Maude seemed to be taking the incident in stride.

"It was God's will," she admonished them.

"And God will let me get pregnant again," Emma reminded Charles in the privacy of their bedroom.

Eight months later Emma was indeed pregnant again. This time the doctor warned her to take it easy—no climbing ladders and no unnecessary exertion.

"Lots of bed rest is the order of the day," Dr. Kramer insisted, "and Charles will be my enforcer."

"You bet I will," agreed Charles. "I'll see to it that Emma behaves herself and gets lots of rest too. You can count on me."

Charles was as good as his word and Emma did nothing but the absolute essentials around the house. She fixed dinner most evenings and sometimes Charles brought it home with him. Maude was of no use in the kitchen at all—never having cooked a full meal in her entire life. She did however react to the situation and offered to "tidy up," as she called it. Charles was grateful for any help she offered.

The months passed uneventfully until May 29th when Emma announced that it was time to go to the hospital. She had her small overnight bag packed for a few weeks and it was positioned by the front door to accompany her to the hospital when the auspicious day arrived. Her water broke right after breakfast before Charles left for work.

"It's time, Charles," she announced at the breakfast table.

"Time for what?" Charles countered.

"To go to the hospital, silly. The baby is ready......."

Before she could finish her sentence, Charles leapt from his chair.

"I'll get the car, Emma. Just wait here and I'll be right back."

He rushed out into the hall and yelled up the stairs. "It's the baby, Mother. We're going to the hospital now."

Charles led Emma to the car. He put her gently on the front seat and tossed the overnight bag into the back.

"Are you alright, Emma? Are you in pain?"

"I'm okay, Charles. Just hurry please. The pains are coming pretty fast now."

Charles threw the car in gear and pulled out of the driveway and onto Riverdale Avenue. He was at the hospital in less than fifteen minutes and pulled up to the emergency entrance. An attendant came out with a wheel chair and helped her into it. He placed her bag on her lap and told Charles to follow him.

"Who is your doctor?" the attendant asked. "Have you called him yet?"

"Gosh no, I just didn't think," answered Charles. "All I could think of was getting my wife here as quickly as possible. Where is the phone so I can call him now?"

The attendant pointed to the phone on the counter at the end of the hall. Charles seized the phone and dialed the number.

"We're at the hospital, Dr. Kramer. Emma's water broke and I brought her right in."

Dr. Kramer assured Charles he would be there momentarily and not to worry. Charles hung up and followed the attendant toward the elevator.

"You'll have to wait out here," the attendant advised. "I'll take your wife upstairs. The nurse will be there in a minute to get her into bed and ready for the doctor. I'll call you as soon as I know anything. Meanwhile, just relax and wait for the doctor. These things can take awhile you know."

Before Charles could argue, the attendant had Emma in the elevator and out of sight. Charles found himself alone in the waiting area, and like many perspective fathers before him, he began to pace. Before long, Dr. Kramer appeared and greeted Charles reassuringly.

"I'm going right upstairs to Emma now. As soon as I finish examining her, I'll come back down and we'll talk. Relax, Charles. Everything will be fine. Trust me."

The doctor disappeared into the elevator and Charles continued pacing.

"Can I get you some coffee, Mr. Carney?" a nurse inquired. "It may be awhile before the doctor gets back downstairs."

Before Charles could answer, Dr. Kramer stepped out of the elevator and strode across the room. He looked very stern and Charles was immediately apprehensive.

"What's wrong?" he mumbled.

"Sit down Charles. Emma is fine but the baby is turned in the womb. I'm going to have to do take the baby surgically. It's called a Caesarian Section."

"Is it dangerous?" Charles interrupted.

"Not inherently, but the danger increases the longer we wait. I need your permission to operate, Charles."

"Does Emma want the operation, Dr. Kramer? Is it alright with her to do it this way?"

"She wants whatever is necessary for you to have a healthy baby. She understands that this is the only way to insure that."

"Okay then," said Charles. "You have my permission. I don't want her to suffer any more and I want our baby to be safe. Do whatever you have to do, doctor."

"Thank you Charles. I'll have Emma in the operating room within the hour. The next time you see me you will be a father."

Dr. Kramer was on his feet and heading for the elevator before Charles could say another word. "I'll be back as soon as it's over and Emma is in recovery," he said over his shoulder.

The elevator door closed and Charles was once again alone in the waiting room. For the first time in his life he experienced real personal fear. Even though the death of his father and the debts he left behind and the difficulties in moving his mother were debilitating experiences, they did not instill in Charles the fear he felt at this moment—the fear of losing his beloved Emma.

"Please, God, don't take her from me," he prayed. "I'll do anything you ask."

Just then the elevator door opened and Stephen Lang came walking toward him.

"Is Emma alright, Charles? Did she have the baby yet?"

"She's going to have surgery right now, Stephen, but how did you know we were here?"

"I called the house and your mother told me. I just had to come. I hope you don't mind."

"No, I don't mind. I was just surprised to see you. You always seem to be around when Emma's in trouble. I wonder why that is," Charles said thoughtfully.

Before he could answer, the elevator bell rang loudly and the doors began to open.

Chapter 29

Charles looked toward the elevator and was relieved to see Dr. Kramer walking toward him with a wide smile on his handsome face. He was removing his surgical mask as he walked, using it to wipe small beads of perspiration from his brow. He strode up to Charles and announced, "Congratulations. You are the father of a healthy baby girl. Wife and daughter are doing nicely."

"Thank you," Charles mumbled almost intelligibly, "I've been so worried. Thank God they're both alright and thank you, doctor, for making sure they were." He clasped the doctor's hand and shook it hard. "Can I see her now? Emma, I mean."

"Of course," answered Dr. Kramer. "And then you can go down the hall to the nursery and get a peak at your daughter. I'm sure you want to see her as well."

"I sure do," said Charles. "But first I want to see Emma. What room is she in?"

"Four twenty two, West Wing," was the reply. "Tell Emma I'll be back to see her a little later."

The doctor turned and strode from the room. Charles turned to Stephen.

"Please excuse me, Stephen, but I want to go see Emma now."

"Of course, Charles. Please tell Emma I will come visit tomorrow."

Without another word Charles hurried toward the elevator and pushed the button for the fourth floor. Emma's eyes were closed and she looked rather pale as Charles approached the bed. He leaned down to kiss her and her lids fluttered open.

"Oh, Charles, I'm so glad you're here. Have you seen her yet? Is she beautiful? I'm so happy. Are you happy too?"

"Whoa, Emma, slow down," gentled Charles. "I came here to see you first. I haven't seen the baby yet. I'll go see her after I leave you. But, of course, I'm happy. I'm just so relieved that you are alright. I was so worried about you—and the baby."

"You don't mind that it's a girl, do you, Charles?"

"Mind? Of course I don't mind. I just wanted a healthy baby. We have plenty of time to have a boy too, if we want. Just concentrate on getting some rest now, Emma. You had a tough time, Dr. Kramer said, and I want you to rest and get back to your old self again. By the way, Stephen was here too and will be back to see you tomorrow."

As Charles looked down on Emma, he could see that her eyes were barely open and sleep was fighting to overtake her. "I'm gonna leave you now, sweetheart, and go pay a visit to our daughter. I'll report back before I leave. Close your eyes now and take a little nap." He leaned down and kissed the tip of her nose and tucked the blanket around her frail shoulders.

Charles left the room and headed down the hall, following the sign directing him to the nursery. He came up to a long plate glass window. Two other men were glued to the glass talking in gibberish and pointing. He looked in through the glass and saw the row of bassinettes—some pink and some blue with tiny placards attached to each. He scanned the rows until his eyes lit on a card, "Baby Carney" it said in pink letters.

Charles drew in his breath. There in the pink bassinette marked Baby Carney was the most beautiful infant he had ever seen—not red and squalling like some of the others in the row, but pale pink with tiny wisps of blond hair and the most angelic expression on her countenance. He was speechless with joy. As he was drinking in the site, a nurse walked through the aisle between the rows and placed a tiny pink hat on the head of Baby Carney. She looked up and seeing Charles staring wide-eyed, she grinned. Charles grinned back.

Charles couldn't wait to get back to Emma. He rushed down the hall to her room and ran to her bedside. "Emma, she's not just beautiful; she's gorgeous. She's the most beautiful baby in the nursery. Wait till you see her." He paused to get his breath. "She's beautiful just like you are, Emma. I am so proud of you."

"I can't wait to hold her, Charles. The nurse said she would bring her in as soon as visiting hours are over. I'm going to try and nurse her if I can. I want our baby to have the best start possible. Did you call my mother yet and give her the good news?"

"Oh, my gosh, Emma, I didn't even think. I'll call her right now and my mother too. I was so worried about you and the baby I didn't think of anything else. Your mother will have my head." Charles grinned and left the room to call Julia and Maude and share the good news.

"Hello, Mrs. Pedesch," Charles spoke into the phone. "It's Charles. I'm at the hospital. Emma had a baby girl and she's just beautiful. Emma is fine and so is the baby." He paused, giving Julia a chance to respond.

"Thank you for calling me, Charles. I just called the house and spoke to Maude. She told me that you had gone to the hospital, and I have been so worried. Are you sure Emma is alright, and the baby too? I know they won't let me in tonight, but I'll be there first thing tomorrow. Tell Emma, will you? I can't wait to see her and my new granddaughter. Goodnight, Charles, and congratulations."

Charles dialed the phone again. This time his mother's voice came on the line. "How are you sweetheart? Has the baby come yet?"

"Yes, mother. We had a little girl and she and Emma are both fine. She's beautiful, mother—the baby I mean. I've never seen anything so beautiful. I'll bring you over tomorrow to see her. I'll be home soon. Emma needs her rest. I just wanted you to know you are a grandmother."

"Thank you, dear. That was very sweet of you. I'll go tidy up a bit so everything will be ready when Emma comes home. See you soon." The phone went dead. Charles shrugged and returned to Emma's room.

Emma was dozing when Charles entered. Seeing her beautiful pale face on the pillow tugged at his heart. He leaned down to place a kiss on her forehead. She stirred briefly but did not open her eyes. Charles tiptoed from the room. He decided to make one more brief stop at the nursery. As he approached the window, the nurse was pulling down the last shade, indicating that visiting hours were indeed over. He got one last peek at the bassinette marked Baby Carney and headed for the elevator.

As Charles walked toward the front door of the hospital he was consumed with thoughts. What would they call their daughter? Who would she look like? What would she want to be in her life?

He stepped outside. A strong spring breeze caressed his face and brought him momentarily back to reality. He reached up to smooth his rumpled hair and walked toward his car. I'm a father, he thought to himself—a father.

Chapter 30

▼

The sun shone brightly as the nurse wheeled Emma out the door of the hospital. Baby Joan was cuddled in her arms and Charles was following close behind. He had brought the car up to the front and went to open the door for her. He smiled watching Emma hug the nurse and make her way carefully toward the car, holding tightly to the tiny bundle that was their daughter. It had been a difficult delivery, Dr. Kramer had told him.

"Emma is very anemic and so has not bounced back as quickly as I expected," the doctor explained. "She will still need a lot of rest when she gets home; and remember, Charles, I don't want her getting pregnant again in the near future so you must be careful."

Charles nodded in assent, but inwardly thought about the son they would have one day. *Emma wants another child too he assured himself. Surely God will make her strong again, and then we can think about increasing our family.*

The toot of a car horn disturbed his reverie. Charles looked up to see Stephen Lang pulling up behind him. Stephen got out of the car, his arms full of flowers and a huge balloon. He rushed to the passenger side and knocked on the window.

"I didn't realize you were going home today, Emma. I would have come earlier if I had known. These are for you and the baby." He thrust the flowers toward the open window and then realized she had her hands full. He looked around flustered and then handed the flowers and the balloon to Charles. "Put them in the back seat, will you, Charles? I just wanted Emma to have fresh flowers when she returned home."

"Thank you, Stephen, I'll take care of them," Charles said coolly. "Now we really must be going. I have to get my family home."

Charles laid the flowers in the back seat and got behind the wheel. Emma waved at Stephen with her free hand and mouthed a thank you through the window. The car pulled out of the driveway and headed for the main road.

"Why does Lang have to be around all the time, Emma? After all, you don't work with him anymore."

"Stephen and I are friends, Charles. You know that. Whether we work together or not, we will always be friends. He is just concerned about me. Why must you refer to him as Lang? He's your friend too."

"No he isn't, Emma. He's your friend, and I don't like him hanging around my wife so much. How do you think I felt knowing he took you to the hospital instead of me?"

"Thank God he was there to take me, Charles. We owe him a debt of gratitude. Now please let's not talk about Stephen anymore. We have a new baby to bring home."

Charles reached over and patted Emma's hand as she held their tiny daughter. "You're right, Emma. Let's concentrate on us and the baby right now. I can't wait for my mother to see her."

"Why didn't Maude come to the hospital with you, Charles? I thought that was a little strange. After all, she is a grandmother."

"Hospitals make her too nervous, Emma, and it's even worse since my father died. She'll make up for it when you get home. You'll see."

They drove the rest of the way in silence. Emma concentrated on the tiny bundle in her arms. She studied the dainty pink and white features barely visible under the blanket.

Suddenly the car came to a stop and Emma knew that they were home. She looked out the window and felt a wave of joy.

"It's so good to be home," she said. "It seems like I've been away forever."

"I'm so glad you're home, too, Emma. It's been pretty lonesome here without you. Now we'll be a real family."

Charles came around and opened the passenger door and helped Emma get out with the baby in her arms. He put his arm around her and guided her up the few steps to the front door. Before he could ring the bell, Maude was standing in the open doorway.

"Welcome home, children, and now let me see my new granddaughter."

Emma stepped inside and went right to a chair in the living room. Charles helped her off with her jacket and she settled back and began to undo the wrapping surrounding the baby. Maude watched intently and then sat down on the adjacent chair.

"Do you want to hold her, Mother Carney?" Emma asked, as she removed the outer blanket that had been swaddling the baby.

"Oh no," said Maude. "I'll just look at her from here. I never even held Charles till he was six months old."

"But how did you feed him and bathe him, mother?"

"Well," said Maude hesitantly. "I didn't. The nursemaid did it all. I was just too nervous to handle a newborn." She lowered her head and sat back in the chair. "She is beautiful, Emma—so beautiful. Maybe you could just put her in my lap a minute but don't let go of her."

Emma looked at Charles. He shrugged and she knew he was embarrassed. Emma placed the tiny bundle in her mother-in-law's lap. Maude hesitated and then took one of the tiny hands in hers. Joan reached up and grabbed hold of Maude's finger and a tiny sliver of a grin crossed her baby face. Maude glowed. She looked down at the infant and then at Emma.

"I think she knows me," Maude said, and she was smiling from ear to ear. Emma had never seen her mother-in-law smile like that since the day they met.

"I believe these two are bonding," she said looking up at Charles.

"I believe you're right, Emma," said her husband. "This baby may give Mother's life new meaning."

And so Joan was officially introduced to Maude, and unknowingly re-charted the course of her grandmother's future. For the first time in her life Maude Carney felt a consuming concern for another human being. It was not that she did not love her son—she adored and admired him, but she never felt a responsibility for his happiness. She knew his father would take care of that and anything else he needed. This baby was different. She seemed so needy and had already engaged her grandmother in an emotional way totally unfamiliar to the dowager.

Emma rose from the chair and went to gather Emma into her arms. Maude resisted and held on to the infant like a child protecting her pet or favorite toy from an unsolicited playmate. Emma glanced at Charles questioningly. Sensing her discomfort, he intervened.

"I think Emma should take Joan upstairs now, Mother," Charles said with some authority. We want to get her settled in her new home."

Maude suddenly reacted. "Oh, of course, dear—here she is, Emma. All ready to go to the nursery." Maude moved to extract her finger from the infant's grasp but the baby held on. Maude looked up at Emma helplessly. Emma knelt down and gently scooped the tiny baby into her arms while relaxing the child's grip on Maude's finger and replacing it with her own. She stood up, adjusted the child in her arms and started for the stairs. Charles hurried to her side and followed her up to the second floor.

Emma and Charles settled Joan in her crib and returned downstairs. Maude was still sitting where they had left her. Maude looked up as they entered the living room.

"She's the most beautiful creature I have ever seen," said Maude, tears glistening at the corners of her eyes. "She is truly a gift from God. How Lawrence would have loved her. I am so happy to have a grandbaby. I will love her forever."

"We all will, Mother, but I'm happy you are so pleased with our new edition. She's lucky to have you, too, and I'm sure you two will become great friends."

Charles kissed her gently on the forehead and then followed Emma into the kitchen.

"I can't get over your mother's reaction, Charles. I've never seen her show this much emotion over anything before, much less a baby."

"I never have either, Emma. I think Joan is going to change my mother's life—give her something to live for—something special. I guess we won't have to worry about asking her to baby sit. She'll make herself available whenever we need her. A pretty good setup, huh?'

"I guess so, Charles, but I can't help but worry just a little. I hope she won't be obsessed with the baby and interfere with how I take care of her. I am the mother after all."

"You don't have to worry about that, Emma. My mother never took care of a baby in her life—not even me. The nursemaid did it all. I assure you she wouldn't know where to begin."

"I'm sure you're right, Charles, and I want her to do things with the baby, really I do. I just don't want her telling me how to take care of Joan. I want to make those decisions by myself—and with you. I am so excited about being a mother, and I can't wait to begin." She put her arms around her husband and held him close.

"I love you, Emma, and you will make a wonderful mother, better than mine ever was. Joan is a lucky baby to have you for a mother, and I will try to be the best father I can, I promise you."

As if to seal the bargain, a tiny cry could be heard coming from upstairs. Emma moved out of Charles's embrace and headed back up the stairs.

Chapter 31

The days passed in pure joy for Emma. Being a mother seemed to be the culmination of everything she had ever wanted. Julia came often to visit her new granddaughter and always brought food prepared with loving hands for Emma and Charles. Emma appreciated this as it afforded her more time with the baby and lessened her time in the kitchen.

Maude, on the other hand, was not thrilled with these culinary care packages or with their provider. She was the grandmother in residence after all and that should entitle her to special privileges when it came to Joan. She made it her business to be available for the baby whenever Emma had other duties to perform, but she often got upstaged by Julia when the 'other grandmother,' as she referred to her, came to call.

Joan reacted to Julia on sight whenever she came near her—gurgling and smiling as if she would burst with joy. She smiled often for Maude but never expressed such excitement at her presence. Maude resented this bitterly and put the blame squarely on Julia, not on baby Joan.

"You have bewitched her," she announced one afternoon. "You have cast some kind of spell on her, I know you have. She never reacts to me like that—only to you. It's unnatural, I tell you, unnatural indeed. I'm here for her every day. I don't just visit on a whim. She and I have a special bond. Can't you see that?"

Julia chose to ignore Maude's comments and placed the baby in her lap. "I have done nothing to this child but love her," Julia said. "She loves us both, just in different ways." She turned and left the room. Maude cuddled the baby firmly in her arms and relaxed again in pure joy.

"By the way, Maude, where is Charles? It's almost dinner time and he has not come home yet."

Before Maude could answer, the door slammed and Charles appeared in the hall.

"Emma, Emma, I'm home," he called out.

"She's taking a little nap before dinner, Charles," Julia informed him.

"Yes, she's been rather tired lately," added Maude. "I'm taking care of Joan though, while she's resting so there's nothing to worry about."

"I see we have both grandmothers in attendance," said Charles, slurring his words ever so slightly. He staggered somewhat as he entered the living room and Julia knew immediately that he had been drinking.

"Where have you been, Charles? You're a little late coming home this evening, aren't you?"

"Oh, just a little, Julia," he answered. "We had a late meeting at the office and then everyone went out for a drink to celebrate a big deal that was made." He stumbled as he made his way across the room to his mother.

"Good evening, Mother. Good evening, Joan," he mumbled. He reached for the baby in his mother's arms and she pulled back. "You're intoxicated," she said. "You will not touch this child until you are sober, do you hear me?"

Charles looked at his mother incredulous. "What do you mean—intoxicated? I am no such thing." He looked at Julia for support and found none forthcoming. For once the two grandmothers were in total accord.

"I've only had one or two drinks," he offered.

"I think you rather lost count, my dear," Maude said and looked at Julia who was nodding in agreement.

"Let me fix you some coffee, Charles," said Julia and she motioned for him to follow her into the kitchen.

"Okay, Mrs. P., coffee it shall be. I'll be back to see my daughter shortly, Mother." He followed Julia into the kitchen, weaving his way between the sofa and the coffee table.

Within a few minutes Julia had a steaming pot of coffee going on the stove and was getting out a cup to give Charles his first cup of the sobering brew. Emma appeared in the kitchen.

"What's going on, you two? I'm sorry I was napping when you came home, Charles. I am feeling a little more tired than usual today. Please forgive me."

"Emma, dearest," answered Charles. "There is nothing to forgive. I'm just enjoying a cup of coffee with your mother before going in to play with my daughter. Will you join us?"

Emma surveyed her husband and realized at once that he was under the influence of alcohol. She glanced at her mother before she spoke again. "I think you should go on upstairs after you've had your coffee, dear, and lie down for awhile. I'll call you when dinner is ready."

"Don't bother with dinner, Emma. I had something to eat after work. I'll just go up and rest for a few minutes and change into something comfortable. As always, it's a pleasure to see you, Julia. Thanks for the coffee." He lurched toward his wife to give her a hug. Emma could smell the liquor on his breath before he reached her. She turned her head as he put his arms around her and then gently pushed him away from her and toward the stairs. She could feel her mother's eyes on her, but she said nothing.

Julia stared into her coffee cup and then rose to take her leave. "I'd better get home and feed your father," she said matter-of-factly. "I left you a big bowl of stuffed cabbage in the refrigerator, Emma. You can enjoy it tomorrow. Can I fix you some soup or something before I go? You look a little pale."

"No, Mama, but thanks anyway. I'll be fine. I'm really not very hungry. I'll just feed Joan and then I'll fix myself something. Thanks for stopping by and for bringing the cabbage. That's one of Charles's favorites, you know." She opened the refrigerator and took out a bottle of milk and prepared to warm it on the stove. Julia watched as she set out the baby dish and spoon and opened a box of cereal that stood nearby.

"Joan really likes her cereal now, doesn't she? Shall I go and get her from Maude and bring her in to you?"

"No, Mama, I'd better do that. You know how Maude gets about sharing her granddaughter. I'm in no mood for any disagreements tonight. Please see yourself out and we'll talk tomorrow." She gave her mother a kiss and headed into the living room to retrieve her daughter.

Maude surrendered the baby to her mother and proceeded to go up to her room. The house was quiet now and Emma settled down to enjoy this quiet time with her daughter. The baby ate with a healthy appetite and finished all the cereal and the whole bottle of milk. Charles had not returned so Emma left her in the highchair while she cleaned up the kitchen. Then she decided to make herself a cup of tea and some toast before taking Joan up to bed.

As she reached the top of the stairs, she could hear Charles snoring in their bedroom. She tiptoed down the hall into the nursery and settled her daughter in her crib. After changing her diaper and putting on a clean nightgown, Emma kissed her gently on the forehead and left the room, closing the door softly behind her. She entered her bedroom as quietly as possible so as not to wake

Charles. She completed her evening ablutions and was about to climb into bed next to him, when Charles stirred.

He threw his arm across her, pinning her to the bed next to him. "Darling Emma," he mumbled as he rolled on top of her. Emma tried to move away but he was too quick for her. Even intoxicated and half asleep he was strong enough to maintain his position. Before she knew what was happening, Charles was penetrating her body. Every fiber of her being fought this invasion but it was to no avail. Fortunately for Emma, the onslaught was short-lived, and Charles rolled off her almost as quickly as he had begun. She clung to her side of the bed, breathless, waiting to be sure he had gone back to sleep before getting up and going to the bathroom. Tears filled her eyes as she stood before the mirror. She cleaned herself as best she could, changed into a clean nightgown and returned to the bedroom. She crawled back into bed but stayed as far away from her sleeping husband as the space between them would allow.

"Please God, don't let him wake up again and bless our baby and our family. Amen."

Chapter 32

She doubled up with the pain and slipped to the floor holding her stomach with both her hands. Emma knew before she reached the bathroom what was happening to her body. She had not told Charles about the suspected pregnancy because it would have made him angry. Dr. Kramer had warned him about getting Emma pregnant and here she was expecting again after only three months. He could never have accepted the blame for this loss.

He barely remembered the incident and since Emma had made no comment, she knew he assumed that he had gotten away with the drunken indiscretion. She must be more careful in future she knew but was not sure how. Charles came home in this condition more often of late and she had to be very inventive to avoid another mishap. Several times she slept on the couch, pretending to have fallen asleep there while reading.

By the time Charles came home, Emma had pulled herself together, although the ordeal was evidenced by dark circles under her eyes.

"You don't look well this evening, Emma," Charles said. "Are you sure you are alright"

"Of course, dear. I'm just a little tired. Joan was fussy today and kept me hopping more than usual. Your mother is visiting her friend downtown so I didn't have her to fall back on for a nap. I'll be fine after a good night's sleep."

They had a quiet dinner in the dining room and then Charles went upstairs to play with Joan while Emma cleaned up in the kitchen. She was grateful for the quiet and lack of interference from her mother-in-law as well as the fact that Charles was totally sober. Maybe she could actually get a good night's sleep. She folded the dish towel, turned off the light and went into the living room. Before she could get comfortable on the couch, the phone rang.

"Hello Emma," came the voice over the line. "How are you this evening?"

"Oh, Stephen, how good to hear your voice. I'm fine thanks. How are you?"

"Fine Emma but I sure do miss working with you. Milliken has started another ad campaign and he's having trouble finding another model as good as you. Don't suppose you'd consider going back to work?"

"Not a chance, Stephen. Charles would have a fit if he even heard you suggest it. I'm a new mother, you know. As much as I would love it, my place is at home with my baby. I'm sure you understand."

"Of course I do, Emma, but I just couldn't resist asking. It's just not the same here without you and besides, you were the best model Milliken ever had."

"Thanks, Stephen. I know you mean well. I admit I miss working sometimes, but Joan more than makes up for it. She's the light of my life. Speaking of Joan, we are going to have her baptized soon and I would love you to be the Godfather. What about it?"

"Me? Why, Emma, I would be honored, but what about Charles. I'm not sure he will agree with your choice, and what about Jerry?"

"Never mind, Charles. I'll handle him, Stephen. You're my dearest friend and after all, you were there for Joan's birth and that has to count for something, doesn't it? Jerry is stationed in Texas now and I know he can't get another leave right now. He'll understand and we'll ask him for the next one. I only wish Ginger were here so she could be Godmother. She's filming a movie and won't be able to come to New York for several more months. Mama keeps bugging me about not waiting too long so I have to get this Baptism taken care of. I'm planning on a week from Sunday if that's alright with you."

"A week from Sunday it is, Emma. There's no place I'd rather be. Since Ginger can't be here, who will you ask to be Godmother?"

"I'm going to ask Anna, Stephen. She was my maid of honor and now I'd like her to be Godmother. Next to Ginger she's the best girl friend I have. I'm going to ask her tomorrow. By the way, Stephen, you two would make a handsome couple, don't you think?"

"Stop matchmaking, Emma. You know you were the only girl for me. Tell that sweet baby that Uncle Stephen will be coming for a visit real soon, okay?"

"Make it soon, Stephen. Joan and I miss you. Goodnight now and God bless."

Charles came down the stairs as Emma was hanging up the phone. "Who was that Emma?"

"Stephen. He called to see how the baby is doing. I asked him to be Godfather for Joan," Emma blurted out before thinking.

"You what?" Charles asked, incredulous. "Why in hell would you ask him to be Godfather?'

"And why not?" answered Emma. "He's one of my dearest friends and he adores Joan."

"But you have a brother, Emma. What about him?"

"I already talked to Jerry about this, Charles, and he assured me that he cannot get another leave this year. Even he suggested Stephen and said to put him on the waiting list for the next edition."

Charles slumped into the big arm chair in the living room. "I don't understand you sometimes, Emma. Why does that man have to be such a big part of our lives? You know how I feel about him."

"Because he's my best friend, Charles. He's always been there for me even when Ginger and my own brother couldn't be. I want him to be part of our lives and I hope he always will be. You have no reason not to like him, so please don't be disagreeable about it. I asked him and he said yes and that's the end of it. I'm going to speak to Anna tomorrow about being Godmother. I think they'll make a great couple, don't you?"

Charles shrugged and stood up. "I guess we'll never agree on the subject of Stephen Lang," he muttered. "I don't want to fight with you Emma so let's call it a night. How about a game of cards before you get Joan ready for the night?"

As tired as she was, Emma agreed. "You want to lose at something else today?"

Charles shot her a look but then broke out in a smile. "Okay, smarty pants, we'll just see about who is the loser. Wait here and I'll go get the cards."

Chapter 33

▼

The sun was out in all its glory on the day set side for Joan's baptism. It penetrated the otherwise dark interior of St. Constantine's Church by streaming with unimaginable force through the beautiful stained glass windows. The nave was warmer and more inviting than Emma could ever remember. She had not been there since the day of her wedding to Charles, as they now attended a much smaller church a few blocks from where they lived in Riverdale. It was a pleasant church but did not possess the grandeur or childhood memories of St. Constantine's.

Emma knew her mother had her heart set on having the baptism in their old familiar family church and so she had gotten a dispensation from her parish priest to return there to baptize her baby. Charles did not seem to care where it was held as long as it was held soon. Maude was getting more nervous every week that passed without a date being set for this auspicious occasion. She was sure something terrible would happen to the infant if she did not receive this important sacrament in the immediate future. She was driving Charles crazy and he in turn was torturing Emma about setting a date.

And so it came to pass on August 3, 1932 in the Church of St. Constantine that Joan Helen Carney was rendered a member in good standing of the Roman Catholic Church. She was held tenderly by her Godmother, Anna, and lovingly comforted by her Godfather, Stephen. She smiled through the entire service, to the delight of her parents, the priest, and all in attendance.

Julia glowed with pleasure throughout the ceremony and George sat quietly beside her, beaming with pride in his first grandchild. Jerry and his wife, Rose, were unable to be there but had sent a card and a beautiful bouquet of flowers to mark the occasion.

After the service they all went to Julia's house in Hunts Point to celebrate. Emma would have liked to have the party at home in Riverdale, but Julia convinced her to take it easy for a while longer and she finally agreed. She still had not told her mother about the miscarriage but somehow Julia sensed that all was not right with her daughter. She knew better than to interrogate Emma but she knew that having the party in Riverdale would be too much for her right now. Charles did not seem to mind and Maude went along with whatever her son decided.

Because of the glorious weather, Julia decided to have the party outside next to the garden. George had built a small patio there under the grape arbor and it was a perfect place to celebrate this occasion. A table and chairs had been set up in the shade of the arbor and the aroma of flowers pervaded the area. Anna helped Julia bring out the pitchers of ice tea and lemonade and Stephen helped George carry the platters of meats and cheeses and salads.

"What a spread your mother has made," commented Charles, "and how delightful it is to have the party out here under the arbor. We could never have done this at home. I'm glad she convinced you to have it here, Emma; really I am."

"I'm glad too, Charles. Mama is always so good at parties."

Emma wheeled Joan into the shade and parked the carriage. It was an elegant coach-type conveyance—a gift from Julia and George to commemorate the occasion. The baby was reclining in a slightly upright position cooing and gurgling at anyone who would listen. Charles reached in to pat her pink cheek and Joan grabbed his finger immediately and wouldn't let go.

"May I pick her up, Emma?" he asked gently, leaning down into the carriage.

"Why of course you can, Charles. I think that's just what she was hoping for."

Charles grinned and swooped up his baby daughter and placed her ceremoniously on his lap. She quieted down at once and proceeded to stare at him with unabashed intent. Charles stared back, in awe of this wondrous creature that was the result of his love for her mother.

Then just as suddenly, Joan began to whimper. The whimpers became cries and Charles looked at Emma for help.

"She must be hungry, dear. I'll just take her inside now and give her a bottle. I'll bring her back shortly, not to worry."

Emma extracted the crying baby from her father's lap and headed for the kitchen door.

"Anything I can do to help?" asked Julia coming out of the door with plates of food in both hands.

"No, Mama. Joan needs to be fed now so I will do that in the house. Maybe she'll take a nap after that and I can sit down and eat with all of you."

"Alright, dear, but if she doesn't want to settle down inside, you can always put her down in the carriage and keep her outside with us. I'll go outside with our guests, but let me know if you need me."

Emma took the baby into the kitchen and juggled her in one arm while she prepared the bottle with the other. I'm getting pretty good at this, she thought to herself. Joan had stopped crying now, somehow aware that food was imminent. As Emma waited for the bottle to warm, Stephen entered the kitchen. Emma turned suddenly, not expecting anyone to be there.

"I'm sorry if I startled you, Emma," said Stephen. "I was just getting some more glasses at the behest of the hostess."

"That's alright, Stephen. I was concentrating on the stove and didn't hear you come in. Your Godchild is hungry so I am trying to warm a bottle for her before she starts crying again."

"Well, she is the guest of honor after all," quipped Stephen, "so I guess she has a right to want to be fed."

"And so she will be." Emma extracted the bottle of milk from the pot on the stove and attempted to test it on her wrist. "Will you hold her a minute, Stephen. I want to be sure the milk is not too hot." She handed him the baby and just as he settled her in his arms and planted a kiss on her forehead, Charles walked through the kitchen door.

"What the sam hill are you doing?" Charles admonished. "I thought you were feeding Joan, Emma." His face looked like a storm cloud.

"I'm just getting ready to, Charles. I was testing the milk and asked Stephen to hold Joan for a moment. What are you so angry about?"

Stephen handed her back the baby who was looking from one to the other and getting ready to howl at any moment. Emma grabbed the bottle and gently thrust it into the baby's mouth. Joan gurgled in gratitude and began sucking with gusto. Emma sat down on a kitchen chair and looked at her husband with disgust.

"The glasses you came in for are in that far cupboard, Stephen," she said, ignoring Charles's glowering looks.

"Thanks, Emma. I'll take them right out to Julia. See you both later."

Silence pervaded the kitchen as the door closed behind Stephen. Joan's steady sucking was the only sound in the room.

"I'm sorry, Emma.... I just thought......."

"You thought. You always think the worst when it comes to Stephen. He was just getting glasses for my mother. Why do you get so angry every time you see him with me or the baby? He's my friend, Charles. Remember that. And now he's Joan's Godfather so he has every right to hold his Godchild. I'm sick of the way you behave around him. Tears started to trickle down her cheeks and she juggled the bottle with one hand to have one free to wipe her face. Charles hung his head.

"I'm sorry, Emma, really I am. It's just that I see the way he looks at you and it makes my blood boil. I can't help it—I just can't."

"Well you'd better learn, because Stephen Lang is a part of our life, Charles, and a part of Joan's and that's the way it is. Now I suggest you go outside and join our guests while I feed the baby. I'll be out as soon as I'm done."

Charles stood up and walked quickly toward the door. "I love you Emma," he said as he pushed the door shut behind him.

Chapter 34

▼

The rest of the afternoon passed uneventfully. Everyone ate their fill of Julia's cooking, spent ample time with Joan, the star attraction, and generally enjoyed each other's company. Stephen and Anna seemed to get on well together Emma observed and this pleased her. Anna was a quiet girl, attractive in her own gentle way, and a good and loyal friend. Emma was very fond of Anna and secretly hoped that Stephen would come to appreciate her also.

As the last guest was leaving, Emma yawned and realized how tired she really was. She followed Julia into the kitchen and added some more dirty plates to the already mounting pile in the kitchen sink.

"Have you seen Charles, Mama?" queried Emma. "I haven't seen him for the last hour or so."

"I think he went down to the basement with your father," Julia answered. She looked at Emma and noticed that she was scowling. "Is that a problem, Emma?"

"Not really, Mama, unless he's joined Papa in too many glasses of wine. I think I'll go check."

She started down the cellar stairs and stopped midway when she heard voices. Her father's deep voice came to her first, followed by a peal of masculine laughter that could only belong to her husband. She continued down the stairs, stopping when she reached the bottom. The sight before her would have been laughable if it had not been so unnerving. There was Charles swaying comically with his arm around George's shoulder. Each man had a wine glass in his hand, and after further inspection, Emma could see that some of the wine had splattered onto Charles's shirt front. His necktie was totally askew and his hair was falling onto his forehead.

"Your father's teaching me the *Chadash*," mumbled Charles, waving the glass and sending more wine down his shirt front. "It's a very difficult dance you know."

Emma surveyed the situation as calmly as she could and addressed her husband.

"I think it's time for you to come upstairs and have some coffee, Charles."

"But I haven't finished my wine, Emma. I can't waste your father's wine."

"I'm sure Papa will forgive you, Charles. I need you upstairs now, please."

George looked at his daughter's stern face and suddenly the realization hit him. He was the cause of his son-in-law's drunken behavior. He had allowed Charles to drink too much of his homemade wine and thus he had disgraced himself in front of his wife.

"I'm sorry, Emma," said George humbly. "I gave Charles too much wine to drink and then we started dancing and things just got out of control. I forget he's not used to the strength of my homemade brew. Please forgive me."

Her father's contrite look melted her, and Emma turned to give George a hug. "It's alright Papa. Charles is a grown man. He's supposed to know better. I'll just steer him upstairs now if you'll help me."

George turned Charles around and guided him to the bottom step. "Up you go, son; you're needed on the upper floor." Emma took his arm and together they climbed the basement stairs that led into the kitchen.

"Sit down at the table, Charles, and I'll get you some hot coffee." Charles did not answer but did as he was bid. Emma put a steaming cup in front of him and then sat down opposite him. Julia had already made herself scarce so the couple was alone in the kitchen.

"I'm going to put Joan to bed now, Charles, and I will wait for you upstairs. Finish the coffee and then come up. It's been a long day and we could both use a good night's sleep."

Charles nodded his head and Emma went out in search of Joan. She found her in the arms of Anna on the back porch with Stephen sitting close by.

"Hello, you two. I'm going to steal my daughter away if I may. It's time for her to call it a day. She's had a pretty exciting time and I think she should be ready for some serious sleeping about now."

"I think you're just in time," said Anna. "Her eyes were beginning to close while I was holding her. It's time for me to be leaving too," she said, as she gently handed the baby girl over to Emma's waiting arms. She looked over at Stephen. He stood up.

"It's time for me to be on my way as well. Can I drop you off at home, Anna?"

"Thanks, Stephen, I'd appreciate that. Good night Emma and thank you for a lovely afternoon. I'll just go inside and thank your mother and father and then I'll be on my way."

"Goodnight, Anna, and thank you so much for being Joan's Godmother. One day she'll know how lucky she is."

"She's quite a lovely lady, isn't she Emma? said Stephen. This is really the first chance I've had to get to know her. Thank you for that."

"You're most welcome, Stephen, and thank you for taking Anna home and for being Joan's Godfather too. She is twice blessed and I'm so grateful to both of you."

"I'll just go and say goodnight to your parents too, Emma, and then we'll be on our way. I'll call you soon."

He went through the door into the main part of the house in search of his hosts. Emma headed up the stairs with her precious bundle. She peeked into the guest bedroom on the way to her mother's room and saw Charles sprawled across the bed still fully clothed. Another night on the couch for me thought Emma, as she changed Joan's diaper and dressed her in her night clothes for the trip home. She put Joan in the bassinette Julia kept there for her granddaughter to use when she visited, and turned her attention to an old trunk in the corner of the room. The trunk contained not only her wedding dress but many other mementos of her adolescence and childhood. It was not a large trunk, but it seemed to Emma, just then, that it was the most important thing she possessed.

Chapter 35

▼

Emma put Joan down for a nap and began cleaning out the old trunk she had brought home with her from Hunts Point. Her father had loaded it into the trunk of her car and she had gotten Charles to drag it into the house the next day before he left for work. He hadn't questioned her about the trunk, assuming it contained childhood keepsakes that Emma wanted to go through, perhaps to pass on to their daughter. He placed it in the small alcove off their bedroom as Emma directed.

Emma waded through several piles of embroidered napkins and pillow slips before she came to a group of old fashion magazines and a few treasured books. At the very bottom of the pile she spied a worn blue cover with a satin ribbon hanging loosely from one corner—her beloved journal. She pulled it free and settled on her haunches on the floor. She opened it gingerly and began to peruse the page open in front of her. She noted the date. It was the day Charles had called to tell her of his father's death and that their wedding would have to be postponed. She skimmed a few more pages and noticed Stephen's name on several of them. Stephen—she hadn't seen him since Joan's baptism.

I wonder how Stephen is doing these days, she mused. *I really miss him and the fun we used to have at modeling shoots. Next to Ginger, Stephen is my dearest friend. It's too bad he and Charles never got along. I would have liked him to be a part of our lives. After all, he is Joan's Godfather.* The phone rang, breaking into her reverie. She stood up and went to answer it.

"Hi Emma, it's me. I'll be a little late tonight. We have a dinner meeting after work tonight. Don't wait up. I love you."

"Alright, Charles. Thanks for letting me know. Maybe I'll go have dinner with Mama since you won't be here. See you in the morning, dear, and I love you, too."

She hung up the phone and realized that she still had the journal in her hand.

She went back inside and sat down on the floor again by the trunk. She picked up one of the fashion magazines. It was an old copy of Vogue. She thumbed through it slowly and stopped when she saw herself in a Milliken ad.

I can't believe I ever did this for a living. It seems like forever since I was a fashion model. It was hard work, but Stephen always made it seem like fun and he never let anyone take advantage of me, not even a client like Milliken. Stephen—she said the name out loud. *I wonder how you are and if you miss me too.*

Emma returned the journal to the lower reaches of the trunk and covered it over with several napkins. She stood up, walked to the phone and dialed Stephen's number. The receptionist answered, "Lang Studios—may I help you?"

"Is Mr. Lang there?" inquired Emma, beginning to wish she hadn't been quite so spontaneous. He was probably in the middle of a shoot, she thought to herself, and here I am interrupting his work.

"Just a moment," was the answer, "and who shall I say is calling?"

"Emma, Emma Carney."

Emma heard the phone drop onto the desk and then silence ensued. Suddenly a voice came on the line.

"Emma is that really you? I'm so glad to hear from you. How are you and why are you calling? Are you alright?"

"Of course I'm alright, Stephen. I just realized we haven't seen each other since Joan's Baptism and I thought maybe you would like to come over and have supper with me and your Goddaughter. Charles is working late tonight so I thought this might be the perfect opportunity." There was a pause on the other end and then Stephen spoke again.

"Are you sure he won't mind, Emma? You know how he feels about me."

"You are my friend, Stephen, and my daughter's Godfather. There's no reason in the world why I can't invite you over for supper. It's not like we're going to be here alone after all. Have you forgotten that my mother-in-law lives with us?"

"I guess I did forget that, Emma, but if you're sure it's okay, I'd love to come and see you and Joan and have supper. What time shall I be there?"

"Can you be here by five thirty, Stephen?" This way you will have time to visit with the baby before I feed her and whisk her off to bed. She can sit at the table now in her highchair if she's behaving herself and not over-tired. She's becoming a real young lady. I think you'll be pleasantly surprised."

"I can't wait, Emma. I'll be there on the nose. Is there anything I can bring?"

"No, just bring yourself, Stephen. I'll take care of everything else. I'm so pleased you can come. I can't wait to see you."

She hung up the phone and saw her reflection in the hall mirror. She was grinning from ear to ear. She looked around and saw Maude Carney staring at her.

"Who were you talking to, Emma? Is someone coming for dinner?"

"Yes, Mother Carney. I invited Joan's Godfather to supper tonight. He hasn't seen her since her baptism."

"Is that alright with Charles?" Maude inquired. "I got the feeling that he does not like that young man. And I wish you'd stop calling it supper, Emma. The evening meal is usually referred to as dinner, you know."

"Charles will not be home for sup....dinner, Mother Carney. He has to work late so it will just be the three of us and Joan, and it will be very informal. I'm just going to warm up some stuffed cabbage that Mama sent over the other day. That's one of Stephen's favorites and he doesn't get home cooked meals very often."

"I see," said Maude Carney, glowering down at Joan through her pince-nez glasses. "Am I expected to join you for this culinary occasion, or would you prefer me to take my evening meal in my room?"

"No, of course not, Mother Carney. I would like you to have dinner with us just as you normally do. You have always enjoyed Mama's cooking, even though it is a bit ethnic for your taste. I plan to make a cucumber salad to accompany it and I will even make tapioca pudding for dessert. I know that's a favorite of yours." Emma smiled at the older woman and waited patiently for her response.

"You're quite right, Emma. I do enjoy your mother's cooking, but I am feeling a bit peaked tonight so will eat my portion in my room if that is agreeable to you. Make my regrets to Mr. Lang and thank you for making the tapioca pudding. I will look forward to it." She returned her pince-nez to her skirt pocket and headed upstairs to her room.

Stephen arrived promptly at five thirty and surprised Emma with a beautiful bouquet of flowers—a mixture of lilies, snapdragons and Shasta daisies with sprigs of baby's breath scattered throughout.

"They're beautiful, Stephen. Thank you so much. I guess you know how much I miss my father's garden. I was used to picking flowers whenever I wanted and we got accustomed to always having them in the house."

"I'm sure Charles brings you flowers. He certainly knows how much you enjoy them."

Emma's only response was to take the flowers from Stephen and head for the kitchen. "I'll just put these in water right away so we can enjoy them while we have supper." She paused. "By the way, Stephen, what did your family call the evening meal—dinner or supper?"

"Gee, Emma, I never really thought about it. Supper, I think. Mom and Dad were pretty simple folk and the evening meal was always hardy but not particularly elegant. I guess I don't think of it as 'dinner' per se unless it's a big holiday meal or we are eating out a bit later in a restaurant. Why do you ask?"

"Well, Charles's mother always calls it dinner and she gets upset with me when I refer to it as supper, so I guess I was just looking for some moral support; and as usual, I found it." Stephen grinned.

"Glad to oblige, Emma. I always knew we thought alike on the important stuff."

Emma reached in the cabinet for a vase and set about arranging the flowers. She placed them in the center of the kitchen table and announced, "I think we'll eat in here tonight, if that's okay with you, Stephen. Maude sends her regrets so it will just be you and I and the baby. The kitchen is so cozy and we don't get a chance to eat supper—she paused for effect—in here very often. Why don't you pour us a glass of Papa's wine. The jug is over there under the counter. I'll go up and get your Godchild and we'll have supper going in no time."

Chapter 36

▼

Emma was pouring their last cup of coffee and refilling Stephen's dessert dish with the remnants of the tapioca pudding when Maude entered the kitchen. She was wearing a long silk wrap-around robe and looked like the typical Park Avenue lady of leisure.

"Good evening, Mr. Lang. I'm sorry I wasn't up to joining you and Emma for dinner, but I did want to at least take a moment to say hello."

"What a nice surprise, Mrs. Carney. We missed you at sup…., I mean dinner but I am glad you felt well enough to come down and say hello. It's always a pleasure to see you."

Maude smiled at the compliment, and walked toward the kitchen. "I'll just take my dishes into the kitchen, Emma, so you won't have to come and get them later. The cabbage was delicious, my dear, and the pudding was the highlight of my day. Thank you."

"You're very welcome Mother Carney. I would have come for the dishes, but I certainly appreciate your bring them down."

"Is Joan in the nursery, Emma?" inquired Maude. "I'd like to peak in on her before I call it a night."

"Yes," answered Emma. "I just put her down before Stephen and I had our dessert and coffee. She sat at the table with us in her highchair and was good as gold so I let her stay up a little later than usual. I'm sure she's sound asleep now."

"Well then, I'll just say goodnight and be on my way," said Maude. "Goodnight, Mr. Lang. It was a pleasure to see you again."

As Maude glided up the stairs, Stephen and Emma exchanged glances. As soon as she was out of sight, a giggle escaped from Emma and Stephen soon followed suit.

"She's really something, Emma. It must be quite a feat to live with her in the house all the time. Is she always so terribly proper?"

"She certainly is, Stephen, but I don't let it bother me anymore. It's just her way. She's really loves Joan and they seem to have a special bond, so that makes it all worthwhile."

Stephen nodded in understanding. "Well, enough about your mother-in-law, Emma. When are you coming back to work? Milliken has been asking for you again. You're still the best in the business, you know."

"Oh Stephen, you're just prejudiced. You know I'd come back if I could, but Charles would never allow it. As far as he's concerned my modeling days are over."

"That's really too bad, Emma. We could use you even for just a few hours a week. I would think the extra money would come in handy too. I know about the problems Charles inherited from his father."

"It would help a lot, Stephen, but Charles's pride won't let him admit that. As far as he's concerned, he is the sole breadwinner in this family. Besides, I don't think he'd trust his mother to take care of Joan, even for a few hours."

Stephen put down his coffee cup and studied his hostess across the table. "Well my dear, I think it is about time I made my exit. It's getting late and I'm sure your daughter dictates that you get up rather early in the morning; so I will take my leave. Thank you for a wonderful meal. It was so great to spend time with you and with my Godchild, of course."

"We loved having you, Stephen, and please don't be such a stranger. We'll do this again soon, I promise."

Emma walked with him to the front door and accepted his goodnight kiss on her cheek. She couldn't resist giving him a return hug. "You're always welcome in this house, Stephen, always."

"Thank you again, Emma, and with that I'll say goodnight."

Emma sighed as the door closed behind her good friend. How good it was to see him, she thought to herself. She set about collecting the dessert plates and the empty coffee cups and brought them into the kitchen. The clock in the hall was just striking eight o'clock as she was finishing up. She heard the door slam and headed for the dining room to put away some of the dishes they had used.

Charles stood facing her as she entered the room. He scared her so that she almost dropped the dishes she was carrying.

"I thought you were eating at your mother's," he growled with distinctively slurred speech. He took off his coat and tossed it onto a chair. "What are you doing here?"

"I didn't go to my mother's after all, Charles. Joan and I and your mother had dinner at home instead."

"What changed your plans? You told me you were going to your mother's. Since when do you use dining room dishes for you and my mother?"

Emma looked down at the dishes in her hands. She put them on the table and faced her obviously inebriated husband.

"We had company for supper. Stephen Lang came to visit Joan and he stayed and ate with us. You mother was here too. I warmed up Mama's cabbage and made Tapioca pudding." Emma realized she was babbling, but the more she looked at Charles the more afraid she became.

"That Lang guy again, huh? Can't seem to get rid of him, can I? Didn't I tell you I don't want him in this house? Why don't you listen to me?"

Charles was getting more and more agitated. Emma kept backing up to put some space between them, and this angered Charles even more. "Don't walk away from me when I'm talking to you, Emma."

He moved toward her and Emma automatically backed up again. Charles lost control.

He picked up a dining room chair over his head and brought it down on top of Emma. She crashed to the floor and lay there as still as death. Charles stared down at the inert body of his wife. What had he done? What in God's name had he done? He knelt down beside Emma's lifeless form and began to sob.

"Emma, Emma, wake up. Please wake up. I didn't mean it. I love you. I don't know what came over me. Please Emma, speak to me."

He heard footsteps enter the room and looking up, saw Maude Carney looking at him in abject horror.

"What have you done, Charles? What have you done to Emma?"

"It was an accident, Mother, believe me—an accident. I didn't mean to hurt her. I love her. You know that. I would never hurt her."

"But the chair, Charles—how did the chair get broken? Did Emma fall off the chair? What in God's name happened?"

"I lost control, Mother. I hit her with the chair. I don't know why I did it. She told me Stephen Lang had been here and I went crazy. I'd been drinking and I guess it just put me over the edge. The chair was right there and before I knew what I was doing, I picked it up and the next thing I knew Emma was on the floor with the broken chair on top of her. Oh God, oh God, what have I done? Help me Mother, please help me." He began sobbing uncontrollably.

Maude collected herself and took charge. Her son needed her and she was not going to let him down. She walked over to where Charles was slumped over Emma's body.

"Get up Charles," she demanded. "Get up right now, and get that chair off your wife while you're at it."

Charles responded like a zombie. He rose slowly, taking the broken chair with him, and moved to the other side of the room. Maude replaced him on the floor next to Emma. She put her fingers on Emma's throat and knew she felt a pulse. "Thank God," she said silently. There was no sign of blood but a lump was already rising on Emma's forehead. Maude rolled her over as gently as she could and tried to hold her in a sitting position against her.

"Get me a cold wash cloth, Charles," she ordered. She's unconscious but she's breathing. Then go up to my room and get the smelling salts, and hurry."

Charles did as he was told. Maude placed the cool cloth over Emma's forehead and eyes. When Charles brought the smelling salts, she got Emma into a semi-sitting position and put the open bottle under her nose. Emma moved slightly and then suddenly jolted almost upright in Maude's arms.

"Wh...where am I?" she groaned. "What happened?"

"It's alright, dear, not to worry. You're safe and sound. You had a bad accident, that's all," reassured Maude.

Charles blanched at the word, accident, but made not a sound. He watched the proceedings unfold like he was watching a play—a play in which he had no part.

"Just lie quiet for a few more minutes," said Maude, "and then Charles and I will help you over to the couch where you can be more comfortable."

Emma murmured her ascent and closed her eyes once again.

Maude looked over at her son and whispered, "Get ready to pick her up, Charles, so we can get her on the couch."

"I'm afraid, Mother. Suppose moving her makes it worse?"

"What choice do we have, Charles? Don't argue with me; just do what I tell you. Now pick her up—gently please—and lay her on the couch."

Charles did as his mother bid and lay Emma as gently as he could on the living room couch. Maude took the cotton throw that adorned the back of the sofa and covered her daughter-in-law.

"Make the wash cloth cold again, Charles. I want to try to keep the swelling down."

"How do you know what to do, mother?" asked Charles incredulous. He always thought of her as practically helpless.

"My sister Winnie was a nurse, Charles. She used to show us things while she was in training. I never thought they'd come in handy until today."

"Do you think she'll be alright, Mother? Shouldn't we call the doctor just in case?"

"I'll call Dr. Kramer in the morning, Charles. It's too late to call him now and there is nothing more to be done at the moment. I don't think she has a concussion, but he'll know better when he sees her in the morning. We'll let her rest now and you go on up to bed and sleep it off. We'll talk in the morning."

"Thank you, Mother. I'm so glad you were here. I don't know how I could have managed without you." He turned and headed for the stairs.

Maude returned to Emma. She took off her shoes and stockings and adjusted the blanket and then settled herself in the big leather easy chair. It would be a long night.

Chapter 37

Maude's eyelids fluttered open. Sunlight was pouring in the living room window. She bolted upright in the chair and looked at the clock on the wall. It was after nine o'clock.

"Oh my God," said Maude out loud. She looked over at the still-sleeping Emma and suddenly fear gripped her. "Maybe she does have a concussion," she murmured to the empty room. She sat up and went immediately to the telephone and dialed Dr. Kramer's number. The receptionist answered on the second ring.

"This is Maude Carney. I need to speak to the doctor right away. It's about my daughter-in-law, Emma."

"One moment please," was the reply.

"Maude, it's Sam. What's wrong with Emma?"

"She had an accident last night, Sam, and she's been sleeping ever since. I'm scared it might be a concussion. Can you come here and see her?"

"I'll be there in fifteen minutes, Maude. Meanwhile, wake her up if you can, and keep her sitting up till I get there. I'm on my way."

Maude put down the phone and went over to Emma. She looked so peaceful lying there. Maude tapped Emma gently on the cheek and when she got no reaction she tapped harder. Emma's eyelids fluttered and opened. She looked at her mother-in-law blankly.

"What's wrong, Mother Carney?"

"Oh, thank God you're awake, Emma. Nothing's wrong. You had an accident and Dr. Kramer is on his way. He wants you to sit up, Emma. Please sit up for me and we'll wait until he gets here."

Just then Charles came down the stairs, rubbing his eyes and trying to take in the scene before him. His gaze rested on Emma lying on the couch, and the realization of the events of the night before suddenly registered in his aching head. "Oh my God, mother, is she alright?" He rushed over to Emma and knelt by the couch. He took her hand.

"I don't know, Charles. I just called Dr. Kramer and he is on his way. When I woke up this morning she was still sleeping so I'm worried that she could have suffered a concussion. Sam said to get her to sit up. I managed to wake her but I haven't got her upright yet. Please help me do that."

Maude looked at her son pleadingly. Charles responded at once. He put his arm behind Emma's shoulders and slowly lifted her to an upright position. Maude grabbed two pillows and put them behind Emma as Charles adjusted her into a sitting position.

"It's like moving a rag doll," she said out loud to no one in particular.

Emma's eyes fluttered open again and she recognized her husband.

"Did I fall down, Charles? What happened to me?"

"No, Emma. It was me. I..... it was an accident." The tears that were pooling in Charles's eyes now came like a flood down his face. "I'm so sorry, Emma—so sorry! Can you ever forgive me?"

Emma looked at Charles questioningly. "Of course I forgive you, but I don't remember what happened. All I know is I am so very tired and I have a terrible headache."

Suddenly the doorbell rang. Maude went to the door and in moments Dr. Sam Kramer strode into the room. He put down his large black bag, threw his coat on a chair and went over to the couch. He surveyed the scene and immediately drew his own conclusions. He would find out the details later. First, he would attend to Emma.

"How do you feel, my dear?" he asked gently.

"I'm very tired," said Emma, "and I have an awful headache, but I don't remember what happened." She looked at Dr. Kramer, waiting for clarification. When none came, she turned her gaze on Charles.

"I lost control," he blubbered. "I didn't mean to hurt her. God knows I didn't. I love Emma. Everyone knows that. Please tell me she'll be alright, doctor."

"Be quiet, Charles," ordered the doctor. I need to concentrate on Emma. He was examining her eyes with a lighted instrument and then took out his stethoscope and listened to her heart. He examined the bump on her forehead which now was the size of a walnut. There was a small cut on the top of her head too, that indicated where the blow had struck her. Dr. Kramer finished his examination and stood up.

"Put another cold compress on her forehead, Maude. I want to talk to Charles in private for a minute." Dr. Kramer grabbed Charles's arm and steered him through the doorway and into the kitchen.

"What the hell happened, Charles? What did you hit her with and why?"

Charles began to sob again but he managed to tell the doctor what had occurred the previous evening. "I don't know what came over me. I've never done anything like that before, and I hardly ever lose my temper with Emma." He looked up at the bewildered doctor.

"It seems to me, Charles, that the blame is on the alcohol, or rather, your over-consumption of it. You must have been drinking a great deal for it to have this effect on your personality. Did you realize what you were doing? Emma is only five feet one and a hundred and ten pounds. My God, man, you could have killed her."

Charles began sobbing again. "I know, I know," he sobbed. "I wasn't thinking. I don't even recall picking up the chair. It's like it was someone else who did this and I was a bystander. God help me, I never meant to hurt her. I wasn't myself. I…….." His voice trailed off, lost in the flow of tears.

"It's lucky for you, Charles, that Emma doesn't remember what happened. If she did I doubt if she'd ever be able to forgive you. We're going back in there now and tell her she fell. That will placate her this time, but if anything like this ever happens again, I will report it to the police. Do you understand me? And I recommend that you stop drinking from this day on. It has a terrible effect on you as this situation illustrates. If you love your wife, you'll give up the alcohol. That's all I have to say on the subject. Now, pull yourself together. Your wife needs you."

Sam Kramer turned from the weeping Charles and went back in to the living room to attend to Emma. Maude had placed a cool cloth on her forehead and was holding her hand and trying to be of comfort.

Dr. Kramer looked at Emma. "You have a mild concussion, my dear, but no permanent injuries I am happy to state. I suggest you sit up as much as possible for the remainder of the day and make every effort to stay awake. We can move you up to the bedroom if you would be more comfortable or Maude can help you freshen up and you can remain down here if you prefer."

"I prefer to stay here, Dr. Kramer, but I still want to know what happened to me. Did I faint? Why did I fall?"

Dr. Kramer cast a sidelong glance at Maude. She stood up.

"You tripped, Emma. You tripped over the little embroidered foot stool in your haste to greet Charles when he came in last night." She looked over at Charles standing across the room. "Isn't that so, Charles?"

"Why yes, Mother, that is what happened," Charles mumbled.

"I can't believe I was so clumsy," said Emma. "I am becoming a real klutz, as Ginger used to say. I'm so sorry I caused you all so much alarm. I promise to be more careful in the future."

Maude looked away and Charles came over to the couch.

"You're not a klutz, Emma. It was just too dark in the room to see properly. Now let's not talk about it anymore. Let Mother help you get comfortable, and I will be your slave for the remainder of the day. I will fetch and carry whatever your heart desires. I love you, Emma, and I'm so relieved that you will be alright."

"Try not to nap for at least eight hours," reminded Dr. Kramer. "That's the only way to fight a concussion you know. I'll stop by tonight after we close the office to check on you."

"Thank you, Dr. Kramer. I promise to be a good patient."

"I'll show you out, Sam," said Maude. He gathered his instruments and put them in the bag, picked up his coat and followed Maude to the front door.

"Keep an eye on her, Maude, and don't let that son of yours anywhere near the liquor cabinet again. He may need help if he can't control his drinking. I had a talk with him in the kitchen but I'm not sure he realizes how dangerous his drinking can be. Lawrence could handle his liquor well but his son does not take after him. Good day, Maude. I'll see you all later."

Maude Carney watched the doctor go down the front steps to his car. "Oh Lawrence, I wish you were here," she whispered to the photo on the hall table. "Sam is right. Charles can't hold his liquor like you did—he can't seem to hold it at all. I'm worried about him. I'm worried about them both."

Chapter 38

The next few weeks passed without incident. Charles avoided liquor like the plague and never came home late from the office. He attended to Emma's every need and eventually was making her crazy with all his abject attention.

One night, about two months after the unfortunate incident, Charles came home with a bottle of wine and suggested they all have a glass together at dinner. Maude looked a little doubtful but went along with the idea, as it seemed to please Emma, and added a festive spirit to an otherwise ordinary meal.

Charles proposed a toast. "To my darling wife and the mother of my beautiful daughter."

Emma smiled and raised her glass. Charles clinked his glass with hers and downed the amber liquid in one gulp. He began to fill his glass again. Maude looked nervously at her son but kept silent. She didn't want anything to spoil this festive mood.

Emma sipped her wine slowly as did Maude, so Charles drank the bulk of the wine during the meal. When they were savoring their second cup of coffee, Maude excused herself and went to her room. Emma and Charles made small talk, and then Charles helped Emma clear away the dirty dishes. He was a bit unsteady on his feet but Emma didn't seem to notice.

"I'll bring the dishes in and you can start washing them," said Charles. "I think we should make an early night of it, Emma. What do you think?"

Emma noted the gleam in his eye and began to suspect what Charles had in mind.

"It has been a rather long day, dear. Why don't you go up now and I'll follow as soon as I finish in the kitchen."

She turned back to the sink. Charles came up behind her and kissed her on the neck.

"Don't be too long, Emma. I'll be waiting for you."

When Emma entered the bedroom, she thought Charles was already asleep. She undressed quietly and finished her bathroom ablutions and crawled beneath the covers next to her husband. She knew immediately that she had misread the situation. As soon as she pulled the covers up to her chin and turned on her side, Charles's arm flew across her body pinning her to the mattress. He groaned as he made contact with her warm body, and before Emma could move a muscle he was on top of her.

Emma attempted to dissuade Charles as she suspected that protection had not been on his mind when he got into bed to wait for her. She whispered softly in his ear.

"It's not the best time of the month, Charles. Maybe we should wait another week. I haven't taken my temperature today but I'm sure it's that time of the month." She waited for some reply but got none. Charles was already embarked on his appointed course. There was little she could do to prevent this marital assault. She remembered the words of her mother. "When sex is inevitable, just relax and enjoy it."

"I guess I have no choice, Mama," she thought to herself as she rolled over to accept Charles's clumsy caresses.

It took awhile for Charles to complete his mission, doped up as he was with the large quantity of wine. When he finally rolled off her, Emma almost cried out with relief. She went into the bathroom to clean herself up and returned to the bed, clinging to her side as far from the sweaty body of her husband-lover as possible. She fell asleep praying that God would make Charles's seed infertile. She wanted another baby, of course, but not just now.

Emma's prayers were not answered. When they were celebrating Joan's nine-month birthday, she knew she was pregnant again. She hadn't called Dr. Kramer because she knew he would be furious, especially after his stern warning to Charles. She hadn't told Charles either because she couldn't bear the look of guilt that would take over his countenance. And so she had just persevered, telling herself that God would take care of the problem. God did just that.

At four o'clock in the afternoon, just after getting Joan up from her nap, Emma felt terrible contractions. She called to Maude to come downstairs and look after Joan who she had put in her highchair with a small cup of cold cereal morsels. Maude came at once, drawn by the anxiety apparent in Emma's voice.

"I'm not feeling well, Mother Carey." I need to get to the bathroom and I may be in there for a little while. Please do not worry. Just keep the baby occupied till I return." Emma rushed off in the direction of the bathroom.

It seemed to Maude that an hour had passed and Emma had not reappeared. She checked Joan's harness in the chair and went to knock on the bathroom door. "Emma are you alright?"

There was no answer. Maude called again and when no answer came, she turned the doorknob and opened the door. Maude gasped. Emma was lying on the floor in a pool of blood, seemingly unconscious. "Oh my God," said Maude out loud. "She's miscarried again."

She went to check on Joan and then called Dr. Kramer. "Sam, its Maude," she said when his voice came on the line. "It's Emma again, Sam. I think she's had a miscarriage. Can you come?"

Without hesitation, Sam Kramer responded. "Don't move her, Maude. I'm on my way."

When Sam Kramer looked at the fallen Emma he wanted to cry. "I told Charles how serious it was not to get her pregnant again. Why in God's name doesn't he listen?"

He put smelling salts under Emma's nose and waited for her to come around before he spoke again. "Emma, I'm going to pick you up and carry you upstairs. Just put your arm around my neck and hang on." He turned to Maude. "Go ahead of us and put an old blanket down on the bed so we won't get blood all over the spread. Emma will kill me if I ruin the bedspread Julia made for her. Hurry Maude, I'll be right behind you."

Sam got Emma upstairs without further incident. He laid her gently on the bed where Maude had placed the blanket.

"Help me get her skirt off, Maude, so I can examine her"

"No, Sam, I can't...the blood....I can't stand the sight of blood. You know how squeamish I get." She turned her face away as Sam, disgusted, began ripping off Emma's skirt and stockings and then her underwear.

"Well at least get me a basin of warm water, Maude, and some towels. I've got to clean her up and I don't want to move her again. Hurry, Maude, she's lost a lot of blood."

Maude gathered her wits about her and did as Sam Kramer ordered. She returned in a few minutes with a large basin of water and several towels.

"Shall I call Charles, Sam?"

"Absolutely not, Maude. He's no good to us now. He's already done his damage. Move the basin closer and hand me a towel."

Maude obeyed like a robot but still could not look at Emma or the bloody garments Sam Kramer was removing.

"Get something to put these in," said Sam, pointing at the pile of bloody clothing. "I'm going to check her internally now." Maude couldn't wait to leave the room. She was beginning to feel sick herself and felt the bile rising in her throat. When she returned, Dr. Kramer had finished his examination and had cleaned up Emma's lower extremities

"Can you get me a nightgown to put on her, Maude? I don't want to put her to bed like this."

Maude went to the dresser across the room and found the drawer containing Emma's nightgowns. She selected one and brought it over to the bed. "I can get her into the nightgown, Sam," she said apologetically. "It's the blood I can't handle. I'll have her in bed in a jiffy."

Sam Kramer smiled. "It's alright, Maude. Lots of people can't stand the sight of blood. Don't be too hard on yourself. I'll go wash up in the bathroom while you get Emma settled. I'll be back in a few minutes. When he re-entered the room, Maude had Emma tucked under the covers wearing a clean nightgown. Her upper clothing had been removed and hung over a chair. Her hair had been combed and rested on her shoulders. The bloody clothes were covered by a large canvas laundry bag. Sam stuffed the soiled clothes into the bag and carried it downstairs to the laundry tub in the basement. He returned to Emma, who was lying in the bed staring up at him.

"I've lost another baby, haven't I, Dr. Kramer?" she said in a whisper.

"I'm afraid so, Emma, but thank God you are alright. You lost a lot of blood this time though and it will take a while to get your strength back. You'll have to stay in bed for a day or two at least, and that's doctor's orders, young lady."

"I'll do whatever you say, Dr. Kramer, and thank you again for coming to my rescue."

"You can thank your mother-in-law for that, Emma, but your husband is another matter. I told him how important it was that you not get pregnant again so soon after Joan. Doesn't he listen?"

"It's because he loves me, Dr. Kramer. Sometimes he can't help himself. I try to remind him but if he's been drin......" She stopped in mid sentence, not willing to continue further.

"I think I understand, Emma, but I will have to have a serious talk with him. I know he loves you and I'm sure you love him, but your health must take precedence now. You may have another child some day but not if you continue to abuse your body this way. Please, Emma, I am only saying this for your own good. Have Charles call me so we can arrange to get together very soon. Meanwhile, stay off your feet and let Maude and your husband wait on you."

"But I have a baby to care for," she interrupted, alarm evident in her voice.

"Stay in bed today, Emma, and tomorrow you can care for Joan. Just nap when she does and don't stay on your feet if you don't have to. Give your mother a call. Knowing her, she'll be here in a flash to pitch in and help. Meanwhile, Maude or Charles can pick her up to go in the highchair or into the crib. I don't want you lifting anything for a few days, understand?" He turned from the bed and addressed himself to her mother in law. "Maude, will you see that she follows my orders?"

"Of course, Sam. I will be like an army sergeant, and if she disobeys, I'll report her to the general—that's you." She laughed at her little joke and reached down to pat Emma's hand.

"Well then, Emma, I think I can be safely on my way. You are in good hands. I'll call you tomorrow to see how you're feeling. Be sure to have Charles call me as soon as possible. Goodbye now."

The door shut quietly behind the doctor and silence pervaded the room. Maude looked down at her charge. Large pools of water were forming in her eyes and beginning to run down her alabaster cheeks. Emma turned her head on the pillow and looked at her mother-in-law.

"That's the second one, Mother Carney—the second baby I've lost. God must be so angry with me…he's punishing me. I know he is."

Chapter 39

Julia arrived early the next morning in response to Maude's call.

"I'll be staying a few days, Maude, just until Emma is back on her feet. You could use a break too I'm sure. Why don't you get away for a few days yourself. Go and visit your friend, Esther, in the Bronx. I'll be here to look after Emma and Joan. You deserve a change of scene after what you've just been through. Thank God you were here, Maude. I will be forever in your debt for taking care of Emma through this." Julia reached out and hugged Maude. They seemed to have a bond now that they had never had before.

"I think I will go visit Esther, Julia. Thank you for being here and allowing me to take a little break. I'll be back in a few days, but I'll have a talk with Charles when I return—about the drinking I mean. He has to get that under control. I can see that now."

Julia nodded in agreement and went upstairs to attend to Emma and little Joan.

When Charles came home that night he was surprised to find his mother-in-law in residence and his own mother conspicuously missing. Great smells were emanating from the kitchen and he knew immediately their home had been invaded by his mother-in-law. He loved her cooking but was not anxious to engage her in conflict. He knew she must be furious at him over the recent events. He would have to tread very easy so as not to engage her wrath.

He decided to go upstairs to greet his wife and meet his mother-in-law head on. Better to get this over with now rather than prolong the agony. Julia was just coming out of the nursery with Joan in her arms as he stepped on to the upper landing.

"Well, good evening, Charles," said Julia. "I'll be staying for a few days to take care of Emma and Joan while your mother takes a break. She's gone to visit Esther in the Bronx so I'll be staying in her room for a day or two. I hope you will find that satisfactory." She looked up at him with one eyebrow arched.

"Of course, Julia. I am delighted to see you and I'm sure mother could use a change of scene after all that has been going on here. Thank you so much for coming to our rescue. I'm sure Emma is thrilled to have you here."

He turned to continue up the stairs to go see Emma. "Just a minute, Charles. I would like to talk with you," said Julia, as she steered him into Maude's room.

"This has got to stop, Charles. Dr. Kramer has explained this to you so I know you understand. Emma cannot get pregnant again. She's not strong enough right now. I suspect it's the liquor that creates this problem although she won't tell me. Your wife is completely loyal to you. I hope you know that. I don't live here so I can't accuse you. All I know is Emma has more sense than to let herself get pregnant again right now but she would never say no to you in the bedroom. I know my daughter. So you have to be the responsible one. You have to, Charles, or you will kill her. Do you understand what I'm saying to you? Do you?"

Julia stood back with arms folded across her chest and stared at her son-in-law. She was a fearsome adversary, especially when she was protecting Emma. Charles knew better than to argue with her. He nodded his head in agreement.

"I understand, Julia. I assure you Emma will not get pregnant again until she is strong enough and Dr. Kramer says it's alright. He looked at his mother-in-law and added, "I promise you."

Julia nodded and said," You've given me your word, Charles. I want to believe you, but you and I both know that liquor is a problem for you. Only you can control your demons where that is concerned. God help you if you don't."

She turned on her heel and went in to the nursery to settle Joan in for the night.

"May I see my daughter and say goodnight, Julia?" Charles asked sheepishly.

"Of course, Charles, take a few minutes with Joan and I'll go attend to Emma. Then come and see your wife. She's been asking for you."

Charles went into the nursery and peered down into the crib at his beautiful baby daughter. She began to make baby sounds as soon as she saw him and he leaned down to pick her up. She smelled so sweet; it brought tears to his eyes.

"I love you so much, precious Joan, but I've been a bad daddy I'm afraid. I made Mommy get sick again and I must never do that again. So be patient with me, little one. You will have a brother one day, I promise you that, but we have to give Mommy time to get stronger. I love you both so much."

He planted a kiss on the tiny forehead and laid her gently back down in the crib. Charles put the blanket over the tiny body and walked out of the room. He went down the hall to the master bedroom and entered quietly. Emma looked up as soon as he entered.

"Oh, Charles, I'm so glad to see you. I'm so sorry about this. I didn't mean to get sick again. I'll be strong again in no time."

"Emma, Emma, please forgive me," he said. It's not your fault; it's mine. I love you so much and I am so sorry you had to go through this again. I will never touch another drop of liquor. I promise you—never."

"I know how much you want a son, Charles, and we will have one. I just need to get my strength back. It won't take long. I know it won't. Mama will have me strong and healthy again in no time, you'll see."

She smiled up at him and Charles thought his heart would break. How he loved this woman—with every fiber of his being. He knew as he looked at the beautiful pale face that he could never take another drink—not when it did such terrible things to his beloved Emma. He leaned down and kissed her tenderly on the mouth.

"I love you Charles. You mustn't blame yourself. It was God's will, but things will be fine now. I just know they will. I'm gonna be strong again in no time. You'll see."

Julia came back into the room and Charles went into the bathroom to wash up for supper. "I want to go downstairs for supper, Mama. Charles can carry me down and bring me back up when it's time for bed."

"Alright *Emmushcam*, I guess that would be alright. I'll go downstairs now and put the finishing touches on our meal. Charles can bring you when he's ready."

Emma slid back against the pillows and let her mind wander. Hers was not a spontaneous courage that appeared in a fearsome moment, but a practiced courage that she used every day in her role as Charles Carney's wife. She had chosen a life that required her to constantly summon that courage from a deep well inside of her that she kept replenished through faith and suffering. With God's help she knew she would be alright and eventually she would fulfill her husband's dream of having a son to carry on his name. She sighed deeply and smiled up at Charles as he came out of the bathroom and approached the bed.

"Can you carry me downstairs, Charles? I want so much to have supper in the dining room tonight. Mama has made us a wonderful meal and I want to do it justice."

Charles smiled and picked Emma up like she was a feather and carried her downstairs.

Chapter 40

The months and years passed without further incident. Emma gained strength every day and Charles managed to keep the demon liquor under control. He never really gave it up, but he never again came home drunk until early in September of 1936.

Charles received another promotion at work. He was made assistant to the chief engineer of the Borough of the Bronx. His friends at the office threw him an impromptu party to celebrate. They took him across the street to their favorite watering hole and proceeded to buy him boilermakers. By the time Charles climbed into the car and began the drive home to Riverdale, he was thoroughly ossified.

When he arrived at home, the house was dark. The only light Charles could see was the one over the front door. Emma always left this one on till he got home. He managed to navigate the driveway and bring the vehicle to a halt. He stumbled out of the car and found his way to the front door. He was fumbling in his pocket for his keys when Emma opened the door.

"I'm so glad you're home, Charles. I was getting worried and you didn't call me."

"I know, Emma. I'm sorry, he slurred. "The party was a *s'prise*..... *I din't know*....I just.... He leaned against the door jamb for support. "I got promoted, Emma," he mumbled. "I'm *assssssssssssistant* to the chief—we celebrated."

"I can see that," said Emma. "Shall I make you some coffee? Come out to the kitchen and sit down. We don't want to wake your mother or Joan."

"I don't want coffee—I just want my wife." He lurched toward Emma and pushed her against the wall before she could step out of the way. "You're *soooooooooooo beau'ful,* Emma. *Don'* pull away. *Lemme* hold you." He reached for her and when she moved aside, he slid to the ground.

"Please Charles, let me make some coffee. You're in no shape to go upstairs like this."

"I said no coffee, Em. All I want is you. Sit down here with me and we'll talk this over." A stupid grin covered his face and Emma felt the first hint of fear tremble through her. He reached up and pulled her down next to him on the floor. Before she knew what was happening, Charles had her in a death grip and was dragging himself on top of her. She heard the tearing sound as he removed her nightgown. Emma willed herself not to scream. The smell of Charles's breath on her face was making her feel sick to her stomach. She tried to reason with him.

"I love you too, Charles," she gasped under his weight, but her next words were smothered by his mouth on hers.

Charles Carney was not susceptible to reason or cajoling at this moment. He had one thing, and one thing only on his mind. Emma knew she could not fight him off and so stopped trying. His assault lasted only a few minutes, but to Emma it seemed interminable. When she felt his body slump next to her, she slid away from him and tiptoed over to the sink.

She attempted to clean herself up and put on the torn nightgown; then she surveyed the scene in front of her. How was she going to get Charles upstairs? She knew immediately that this was out of the question. Charles's six foot one inch frame was sprawled across the kitchen floor and his trousers were in total disarray. She decided to try to pull up his pants, tuck in his shirt and buckle his belt, giving him some semblance of order and then just leave him there. She had no other choice. He would have to concoct some explanation to satisfy his mother in the morning, and Emma would make up some silly story to satisfy Joan's four year old curiosity.

Emma rose from the kitchen floor, suddenly aware of the pain in her back from being pushed down hard against the linoleum. "If only you could control the liquor," she said to the comatose body on the floor. She turned away from her silent husband and walked wearily up the stairs.

Emma awoke the next morning to the voice of her daughter at the edge of the bed.

"Mommy, mommy, wake up and play with me. Nana gave me breakfast in my room and now I want to go downstairs. Please get up, please."

"You had breakfast in your room?" asked Emma, puzzled. "Where is Nana, Joan? Please ask her to come to my room. I need to talk to her."

"Okay, Mommy, I'll go find her."

Joan skipped out of the room and a few moments later Maude Carney entered the room.

"Good morning, Emma. I hope you're feeling alright. Joan is in her room just now."

Emma looked incredulous. "Where is Charles, Maude? Did you see him downstairs?"

"I certainly did, Emma, and I was not about to let Joan see him too, so I woke him up and made him go out to the car and go get himself some coffee. I told him to clean himself up too. He looked a disgrace, and I for one am disgusted with him—even if he is my only son," she added grimly.

"God bless you," said Emma with a grateful sigh. "I didn't know what I was going to tell Joan to explain why her daddy was on the kitchen floor."

Maude interrupted. "More importantly, Emma, are you alright? I don't know what happened down there last night but I have my suspicions. Charles has been good for quite a while now but something must have pushed him off the wagon. Do you know what it was?"

Emma told Maude what Charles had said—something about a promotion. "I'm sure he'll explain it all to you when he comes home today," she added. "Thank you so much for keeping Joan upstairs, Mother Carney. I'll get up now and we can both take her downstairs."

"I'll take Joan down, Emma. You take your time and come down when you're ready. We'll be just fine for now. Joan and I will fix you some breakfast for a change."

"C'mon Joan, we're going to make mommy some breakfast," Maude called. Joan appeared around the corner grinning broadly.

"We're gonna cook, Mommy. Nana's gonna show me how. Come down soon."

Emma smiled. *Nana cooking—we've come a long way*, she thought to herself.

Chapter 41

Emma suspected she was pregnant almost at once. Her breasts began to hurt and her body was sending her the telltale signals. She had been through this three times before so was quite sure she was right. She said nothing about her suspicions to Maude or to Charles. She wanted to be absolutely sure. She would call Dr. Kramer and have him check her out before she said a word.

Sam Kramer looked at Emma with disbelief and shook his head.

"I had hoped we would never see this day," he said. "I know Charles still wants a son, but I thought I had made it abundantly clear how dangerous another pregnancy would be for you, Emma. Was it the liquor again? He's been sober for a few years now so I guess I thought it would be forever. Apparently, I was dead wrong, and here you are again."

Emma explained briefly what had transpired a few months before. She told Dr. Kramer how contrite Charles was over the incident and that he promised it would never happen again. Sam Kramer shrugged.

"It's too late for promises now, Emma. You are very pregnant and the only thing we have to concentrate on now is keeping you healthy and giving that baby every chance to survive. Will you follow my instructions, Emma? If you don't, I cannot guarantee that you or the baby will survive. Do you understand me?"

Emma stared at the doctor. "Is it really that serious? It's been three years since the last miscarriage and I've been as healthy as a horse since then. Why are you so concerned this time?"

"Emma, you must understand that your body took a terrible beating with the last two miscarriages because you never really regained your strength after Joan's birth. You are still very anemic and your weight is still below what it should be.

You may look healthy on the outside, but your insides are in a very weakened condition. I'm not sure that your womb will be able to hold another infant to full term, if at all. The tissues are very weak and your tendency to bleed is an ever present concern. You will have to stay in bed for the duration of your pregnancy if you entertain any hope of having this baby and surviving yourself. Do I make myself clear?"

Emma looked up at Dr. Kramer and answered in a strong, sure voice. "I understand perfectly and I will follow your instructions to the letter. It will be alright, Dr. Kramer. I know it will. God will take care of me and the baby. I am convinced of that. I'll ask my mother to come and help take care of us until the baby is born. I'm sure she won't mind. Annabel can run the salon for her and Mama can go in once a week or so to check things out. I'll make arrangements as soon as I get home. And remember, Mother Carney will be there too and she has become more of a help than she knows—especially with Joan. Those two really get on well together. You'll see, six months from now I'll have a healthy baby boy."

"Oh a boy is it?" said Dr. Kramer. "You're sure about that, are you?"

"Very sure," answered Emma. "This is my last chance, and I know it. God will give me a son this time—a Charles, Jr. to carry on the Carney name."

"I won't argue with you Emma," said the doctor. "I'll feel better about everything once I know that your mother will be staying with you to help out. Please call me at the office tomorrow and let me know when you've made the arrangements. I'd like to talk to Julia, and Maude too, if you don't mind. I want to be certain they understand the seriousness of your condition. Meanwhile, take it easy, young lady, and be sure to take the vitamins I recommended. My nurse will give you some samples until you can get the prescriptions filled at the drug store. Goodbye, Emma, and I'll talk to you tomorrow."

Emma patted his hand and turned to leave the office.

As soon as she arrived home, she called Julia and explained the situation, downplaying the more dangerous aspects. She knew Sam Kramer would make those abundantly clear when he talked to her. "Will this be terribly inconvenient for you Mama?" she asked. "Will Annabel be able to take over for you for a few months? I'm so sorry to be such a nuisance, but I promised Dr. Kramer I would follow all his instructions to the letter. I want this baby, Mama. I want it desperately, and I know it will be a boy."

"Of course I will come, *Emmushcam*. Where else would I be when my daughter needs me? I'll stay over during the week and go home on weekends to take care of Pappa and check in on American Chic. Maude will be there when I'm not and I'll have all the food cooked ahead for the weekend before I leave. I'm sure we'll manage nicely, as long as you will cooperate and stay in bed and not try to do too much. Will you promise?"

"Yes, Mama, I promise. I will be good as gold for you and for Mother Carney. It will give me a chance to have some real quality time with my daughter too, and I intend to make good use of that time."

"Then it's settled," said Julia. "I will call Annabel now and make all the arrangements. Papa will want to come and see you before I come to stay over. He won't be able to once I have moved in except occasionally on the weekend if I have time to drive him over. He misses you so much already, Emma. This will really upset him unless he can visit now."

"I would love to see him, Mama. Can we all have dinner together here tomorrow?"

"That's a fine idea, Emma. Papa will be thrilled. I'll make some homemade noodles and pot cheese and bring it with me when we come. Maude will just have to learn to eat peasant food as that's all I can put together in such short notice. I know it's your favorite, so that will be my excuse. You can show her how to make the pear salad to go with it, eh?"

"That's a deal, Mama. It will make Maude feel like she's helping and, besides, I think she is beginning to like being in the kitchen—just a little anyway. I'll see you tomorrow."

Emma hung up the phone and turned to see her mother-in-law standing in the hallway.

"Was that your mother you were talking to, Emma?" she asked.

"Yes, Mother Carney. She will be coming to stay with us during the week for awhile. I'm pregnant, you see, and Dr. Kramer has insisted that I stay in bed until the baby is born. She will be here to help take care of me as I don't want the burden of this family to fall on you. I hope you understand. I want this baby very much, Mother Carney, but Dr. Kramer says if I do not take to my bed and follow his instructions I may not be able to carry the baby to term. He insisted I ask my mother to come and help out. She'll be here tomorrow with Papa for dinner and a visit and then she'll be staying over until the weekend. I told her that you and I could manage the weekends ourselves. Charles will be home then too to help out so it should work out just fine, don't you think?"

Maude Carney shook her head. "I'm so sorry, Emma. I know this is Charles's fault. He drank too much that night after his office party. I'll do everything I can to help you through this. I love spending time with Joan and will be able to amuse her and read to her while you are resting and your mother is cooking. I know she will be doing a lot of cooking." She looked at Emma and grinned sheepishly.

"Speaking of cooking, Mother Carney, Mama is making noodles and pot cheese for sup…dinner tomorrow night and wants us to make the pear salad to accompany it. How about if I sit in the chair and tell you where everything is and we put the salad together that way?"

"Please feel free to call it supper, Emma. I'm getting used to the Hungarian ways. You know I'm not much in the kitchen, but I'd like to be better. Little Joan gets such a kick out of it, too. Can I call her in to help with this salad project?"

Emma smiled at the reference to supper. "What a wonderful idea," she exclaimed. "This will be a fun project for all three of us." She walked into the kitchen and sat down.

"I'll get Joan," said Maude and she turned to go up the stairs to the second floor.

Joan had been napping in her room but sat up when her Nana entered.

"Is Mommy home yet, Nana? Can I see her?"

"Yes she is, Joan and of course you can see her. I was just coming to get you. Mommy is going to teach us how to make pear salad. Grandma Julia is coming tomorrow with Grandpa to have dinner here and we're in charge of the salad. Isn't that exciting?"

"I love it when we cook, Nana. Let's go down right away." Joan hopped out of bed and ran to the stairs.

"Hi, Mommy. I'm ready to cook." She stopped abruptly, noticing that her mother was sitting in the chair with her feet up on a box, rather than standing at the sink or the stove as she usually did.

"What's wrong, Mommy? Are you sick?" asked the little girl with concern evident on her small round face.

"No, Joan, I'm not sick. I am going to have a baby soon and Dr. Kramer just wants me to take it very easy so I won't get too tired. That's why you and Nana are going to make the pear salad."

"A baby? A real live baby? You mean I'm gonna have a baby brother like Daddy promised I would?"

Maude looked at Emma and shrugged. "Yes, darling, that's what I mean. If I do everything Dr. Kramer says, in a few months you'll have a baby brother. Are you pleased about that?"

"Oh yes, Mommy. I've wanted a brother for so long. I'll be in school soon so I'll be able to teach him all kinds of things, won't I?"

"Of course you will, Joan, but right now I think we'll concentrate on the pear salad."

Chapter 42

Emma was so excited about the prospect of giving Charles a son that she could hardly contain herself. Now that she would have so much time on her hands, lying in bed like a prima donna she determined to take up her journal writing again. She left her childhood one in the trunk and asked Julia to pick up a new one for her at the stationers. Emma wrote in the journal every day, chronicling the progress of her pregnancy.

December 2, 1936:
Charles was so thrilled when I told him about the baby. I thought he would burst with joy. Of course, he says it will be a boy and I am agreeing with him. It can't be any other way—it must be a boy—it must!

He wasn't too thrilled about Mama moving in with us during the week, but after he spoke with Dr. Kramer, he raised no more objections. I think he realizes how serious this is because I am not as strong as I should be. He will try to get along with Mama for my sake. I'm sure of it, and besides, they're really only together at meal times. Mama makes every effort to leave us alone in the evenings so we have quality time together.

We had lots of togetherness at Thanksgiving and Mama made us a wonderful meal to celebrate the holiday. Maude was a real help in the kitchen too. I can't believe how much she has changed recently. Joan is enjoying it too.

December 14, 1936
He moved today—not a lot, just a little—but enough to let me know he is there. I talk to him, like I did to Joan; to be sure he knows I am aware of his presence inside

me. *It's very cold outside and the stores are already beginning to decorate for Christmas, Mama says. I wish I could see them. I dearly love this time of year and I do miss the fun of Christmas shopping and the holiday visits with friends and neighbors. I wish Ginger were here. I miss her so much. She doesn't write nearly as often as she used to. She's so busy making movies these days. I can't believe my best friend is now a big-time movie star.*

Christmas came and went in the Carney household. Joan was thrilled with all the attention she was getting from her mother and two grandmothers. Even Charles was especially attentive these days. He and Julia even took her ice skating on the local pond. Christmas brought so many presents, including new ice skates she could attach to her shoes. She was overwhelmed. Her favorite though was her Sonja Henie doll, complete with her own tiny ice skates—not like Joan's, but real shoe skates—white with tiny laces.

Sonja had started skating as a young girl too, her mother had told her. She had won her first competition in Norway when she was not quite fifteen and her first Olympic Medal in 1928 at Saint Moritz, Switzerland. Sonja turned professional in the U. S. in 1936 and became a citizen in 1941. She was little Joan's idol.

February 17, 1937
The baby is moving more and more each day. I think he is getting stronger than I am. I feel so tired and listless from lying in this silly bed. I cannot believe this is doing me any good, but I dare not defy the doctor. Both Mama and Mother Carney keep a close watch on me and even Charles checks up on me more and more as time goes on.

Papa came to visit again this weekend and I was so happy to see him. He brought me beautiful flowers from his garden and a lovely pair of rosary beads that Mama must have purchased for him to give to me. He is so sweet and dear. Even though he was never a real force in my life, I miss seeing him more often. Just knowing he was around somehow was a comfort to me.

April 10, 1937
The baby was moving so much yesterday, but today it seems to be sleeping all the time. I feel very unsettled and am having some mild cramping, but don't want to alarm Charles or my mother. My appetite seems to be decreasing too. I know I have to eat for two, but it is getting harder every day. Even Mama's cooking, just doesn't appeal to me. All I want to do is sleep and that's not like me. Maybe I'm just having a bad day.

April 11, 1937
The cramps are getting worse. I think Mama will have to call Dr. Kramer. I feel really awful today—don't even feel like writing.

"In here, Sam. She's on the chaise. There was a lot of blood in the bed so I had to put her there in order to change the bed clothes. What's happening? Is she losing the baby?"

"I don't know, Julia, but I'm not going to take any chances. I'm calling an ambulance. We've got to get Emma to the hospital as quickly as we can. She's having mild contractions and I want her to hold off if she can."

"But it's barely seven months, Sam. How could a baby survive after only seven months?"

"It's a dangerous time, Julia, but if we hurry, we might be able to save Emma and the baby. Help me get her ready for the ambulance. We'll talk about this later."

Julia moved like a robot, following the doctor's instructions without a word. Emma was semi-conscious so was as pliable as a doll. When the ambulance came, Charles came rushing back into the bedroom.

"Can I ride with her to the hospital, Dr. Kramer?"

"Of course, Charles, but just talk to her and try to keep her calm. I don't know how much she is aware of right now but having you there should be a calming influence. Julia will stay here with Maude and Joan. The poor child is frightened to death that her mommy is going to die. She doesn't understand what is happening. They'll try and reassure her. Now let's get to the hospital."

Charles Lawrence Carney, Jr. came into the world very quietly on April 12, 1937. Dr. Kramer took him by Caesarian Section at three o'clock in the morning. No squalling infant this three pound, one ounce babe, unable to breathe on his own.

"He has all the requisite fingers and toes, Charles," Dr. Kramer assured him, "but his lungs are not fully developed; and his little heart is not strong enough to pump the blood through his tiny veins the way it should. It's going to be touch and go for awhile I'm afraid. We'll have to keep him in the incubator until we feel he can breathe on his own. That may take a few weeks so you must have faith and be patient."

"Does Emma know? Has she seen him yet?"

"No to both questions, Charles. I am going in to talk to her now. You may want to come with me to be of comfort to her. I have to be honest, Charles. I'm not sure the infant will survive and I am also worried about Emma. She lost a lot of blood and her pressure keeps dropping. I think some prayers are in order."

Charles looked aghast at the doctor. "Do you mean I might lose them both—Emma too?"

"Yes, Charles. That is a distinct possibility, but you can't let Emma know that. You have to be strong for her. Do you think you can do that?"

He looked at Charles and frowned. Perspiration was running down Charles's face and he looked a wreck.

"I can't lose her, I can't. She's my whole life, Dr. Kramer, my whole life. Please don't let her die, please." He began to sob. Sam Kramer put his hands on Charles's shoulders.

"Pull yourself together, Charles. Emma needs you now and she needs you strong and firm in your belief that they will both make it. There is no time now for tears. God willing, there will be no need for tears now or later. Come with me to see Emma."

Charles straightened and wiped the perspiration from his brow with his handkerchief. He ran his fingers through his hair nervously and followed Dr. Kramer down the hall to the maternity wing.

Chapter 43

▼

The room was dark. All the blinds had been drawn. Emma looked like a child in the huge hospital bed with tubes coming out of her and an IV running at the side of the bed. Charles rushed to her side and pulled a chair up as close to the bed as he could get. He picked up her hand and held it to his lips.

"Oh, Emma darling, I love you so much. Please fight hard to get well so we can be a family again. I promise I'll never let you get pregnant again—never."

Dr. Kramer interrupted. "Let me take a look at her Charles. I need to check her vitals."

He moved to the other side of the bed and put his stethoscope gently on Emma's chest. After a few moments of silent listening, he took Emma's wrist in his and checked her pulse. A nurse entered and Dr. Kramer asked her to take Emma's temperature and blood pressure while he was there. She did so immediately. Emma stirred when she put the thermometer in her mouth, and then she spoke.

"Charles, is that you? Where is our son? I want to see our son"

Dr. Kramer signaled for Charles to answer. He picked up Emma's hand again and spoke ever so softly.

"I'm here, Emma, and our son is in the nursery. You can't see him just yet because he is in an incubator and is still very weak. He came a bit early, you know, so he will have to get his strength back before we can take him home. You have to get your strength back too, Emma. You've been through a terrible ordeal."

"But I want to see him, Charles. Please let me see him."

Dr. Kramer interrupted. "Emma, the baby must stay in the nursery, but when you are strong enough, we will take you down there in the wheel chair and let you visit him. I promise you."

Emma turned to look at the doctor. "When will that be?"

"The minute you are strong enough. When you can sit up and take some solid food and can get into the wheel chair, we'll take you. And speaking of food, how about trying some soup and Jell-O for me, for starters?"

Emma nodded. "Is little Charles alright?" she asked. "Does he have all his fingers and toes?"

"Yes, Emma, he has all his appendages. He's just very tiny and cannot yet breathe on his own. A machine is breathing for him now but he is taking a little milk from the bottle and we even heard him cry a little this morning."

"Cry? You sound like that's a good thing," said Emma.

"It is," said the doctor. "That means his tiny lungs are developing. It's when babies don't cry that we worry." He smiled at Emma reassuringly. "Now, how about that soup, young lady?"

He motioned to the nurse standing in the back of the room by the door and she exited immediately. She returned almost at once with a small bowl of soup and a few saltine crackers on a tray. She plumped the pillows behind Emma's back and rolled a tray across her lap where she proceeded to place the small repast.

Emma pushed herself to an almost sitting position and studied the soup. "I think I'd better have a towel under my chin, Charles, or I may have more soup in the bed than in my mouth," she quipped, trying to sound light hearted. Charles obliged her by putting a small hand towel under her chin.

"If I need to get strong to see my son, then I'd better start now." She lowered the spoon into the bowl and lifted it to her mouth. A trickle of soup slid down her chin. Charles smiled and wiped her chin with the napkin. "How does it taste, darling?" he asked.

"Not bad, Charles, but it is rather hot so I will have to eat it slowly."

"I don't care how long you take, Emma, just so you get it down. Eat one of the crackers too." He sat back in the chair and surveyed her. She was trying hard to be cheerful and eat as she was directed. Dr. Kramer watched, a smile curling his mouth.

"Well, if you keep that up, Emma, we'll have you in the wheel chair in no time. I must be going now but I will check in on you later this evening before I head home."

"Good bye, Dr. Kramer, and God bless you. Thank you for everything, but mostly for saving my baby. I will work hard to get better, I promise. I want to see my son more than anything in the world. By the way, how is Joan? Is Mama staying with her? I hope I didn't scare her too much. Wait till she hears she has a baby brother. Won't she be thrilled?"

"Your mother is with Joan and she has told her she has a baby brother. Julia explained that he is too little to bring home yet but, hopefully, it will not be too long. You can talk to Joan on the phone tomorrow. I'll arrange it. Goodbye for now."

The doctor strode from the room and Charles leaned in close to his wife. "Don't worry about Joan, dear. She's in good hands with two grandmothers to take care of her. She'll probably be spoiled rotten by the time you get home."

Emma smiled, thinking of her little girl now five years old and anxious for the arrival of a sibling. "I hope we won't be here too long—little Charles and I," she said wistfully. "I want to be home and be a family again."

"Finish that soup now dear and then you should rest. I'm going to take a walk down to the Nursery and check on our son and then I'll report back."

Emma nodded and turned her attention back to the soup bowl. Charles kissed her on the forehead and left the room. He followed the signs in the hall that led to the Nursery. He walked up to the long glass window and peered inside. There was a row of cribs with a tiny sign at the head of each one announcing the last name of the infant resident. There was no sign saying Carney there. Charles looked further into the room and toward the back wall he spied what he assumed must be an incubator. A nurse was sitting close by writing things on a chart attached to the side. She looked up. Charles tapped on the window and she got up and came over to the glass.

"Carney?" he said with a question in his voice. "May I see my son?"

"Oh, you are the baby's father," she said. "Come over to the door and I will let you in for a minute. You can't stay long," she said. "This is a controlled environment. You must put on a hat and a gown before you can come in."

Charles donned the designated garments and followed the nurse to the incubator. He stopped short when he looked in and a gasp escaped from his lips. He had never seen anything so tiny before in all his life. He could barely tell that this was a baby—there were so many wires attached to the tiny body. He was speechless.

The nurse explained about the tubes that were helping the tiny infant breathe. "Ordinarily, we could let you touch the baby, but not in this case. We must preserve the germ-free environment within the incubator and maintain its high temperature at all cost. I'm sure you understand. But at least you have seen him and now you can tell your wife."

She smiled at Charles who looked back at her blankly. He was totally in awe of the sight in front of him. Tears filled his eyes and began to trickle down his cheeks. A sob escaped. He mumbled his thanks to the nurse and made his way to the door. Outside he saw a sign that said Chapel and an arrow pointing down the hall. He followed the arrow and when he came to the Chapel, he entered and knelt down in a front pew. He put his head in his hands and let the tears flow.

"Dear God," he whispered in a trembling voice. "Please save my son. I haven't asked you for much but I'm asking now. Please don't let Charles, Jr. die and please help my dear Emma to get her strength back so we can all go home together and be a family again. I promise you, God, I will never get her pregnant again—never. This was all my fault. My drinking did this to Emma and the baby. I take full responsibility, but I will make it up to them, Lord. I will. Just let them both live. Please, Lord, I beg you."

The tears stopped and Charles wiped his face with his handkerchief. He blessed himself and stood up. He needed to get back to Emma and assure her that their baby son would be alright. He could taste his helplessness. Charles prayed that everything would work out. He blessed himself again as he crossed the threshold and headed down the hall toward the maternity wing.

Chapter 44

Three weeks passed before Emma was able to leave the hospital. Charles, Jr. had to remain behind as he was still in an incubator. Dr. Kramer looked worried when he arrived to check Emma out and she was very much aware of his anomalous expression.

"Charles is getting better, isn't he, Dr. Kramer? He'll come home soon, won't he?"

"He's holding his own, Emma, but quite frankly, I had hoped for more progress. I want to get him out of that incubator and we cannot do that until he can eat and breathe totally on his own."

"Charles and I will come visit him every day," said Emma, the tears welling again. "I'm trying to be strong, but I want so much to bring my baby home. Poor little Joan doesn't understand why she can't see her new baby brother either. I don't know what to tell her any more."

"Think positive, Emma," said the doctor. "You have made amazing progress these past few weeks and now you're going home. This will give you a chance to get re-acclimated before you have to care for an infant again. It's been five years remember. The baby is getting excellent care here and you can rest up and prepare for his homecoming."

Emma sighed and nodded her head. She knew the doctor was right but she felt so guilty leaving her son behind. Just then, Charles arrived.

"I have the car out front, Emma. Are you all ready to go?"

"Yes, I'm ready, Charles, but would you wheel me down to the Nursery first before we go? I want to see little Charles one more time."

Charles nodded and helped Emma into the wheel chair. He pushed her down the hall to the Nursery. When they arrived, the curtain had been pulled across the glass window. Charles knocked on the door. A nurse answered and informed them that the baby had developed a problem and had been moved to a special heat room at the rear of the nursery. They would not be allowed in until he was moved back to the main Nursery.

"But I'm leaving today," Emma sobbed in an effort to abrogate the decision. "I have to say goodbye to my son; I have to."

"I'm really sorry," said the nurse, "but that is impossible. Please speak to Dr. Kramer. He'll explain the situation to you." She closed the door and left Emma and Charles staring after her.

Charles wheeled Emma back to her room and spotted Dr. Kramer filling out the last of Emma's discharge papers.

"They wouldn't let us see him, Dr. Kramer."

"I know," was the reply. "I got a call from the Nursery right after you left. It's a temporary setback. We're having trouble stabilizing his body temperature."

Emma was a pitiable sight, slumped in the wheel chair and Charles felt totally at a loss to cheer her up. "Let's go home and see our daughter, Emma. She needs us too. Dr. Kramer will keep us informed of the situation here, won't you doctor?"

"Of course I will, Charles. I think it's important to get Emma home now. Julia tells me that Joan is beside herself waiting to see her mother after all these weeks. Get going you two. I'll go down to the Nursery now and I'll call you later in the day. I may even stop by on my way home tonight."

A nurse picked up Emma's small suitcase and the last vase of flowers and followed Charles and Emma to the elevator. Charles wheeled her over to the car and helped her in. Then he put the suitcase and the flowers in the back seat before he got behind the wheel.

Emma was still wiping her eyes when they pulled into the driveway. She didn't want Joan to think she'd been crying. She took a deep breath and waited for Charles to open the car door. Before she could get her feet on the ground, two chubby arms engulfed her.

"Mommy, Mommy you're home! You're really home! I missed you so much," the little girl exclaimed. She covered her mother's face with wet kisses.

Emma hugged her daughter to her, swept up in this surge of emotion from the tiny five year old. "I missed you too, my darling. I can't tell you how much." Emma kissed the little girl and then held her away from her. Joan frowned, not understanding.

"I think you've grown an inch since I saw you last." Emma said. "You're growing up right before our eyes." The child grinned now and stood straight and tall as is if to punctuate her mother's observation.

"I have grown, Mommy, but I'm still only five. How old is Charles?"

"He's almost two months old already, Joan, and we hope to have him home real soon. He wants to meet his big sister."

"Did he say that, Mommy? Did he?"

Emma laughed. "Not in so many words, dear—he's only a tiny baby, but I could tell by his eyes when I told him about you."

Charles interrupted. "How about us getting Mommy into the house now, Joan? She's pretty tired from the trip home and will have to rest a bit I think. You can talk to her more later after I get her upstairs."

"Oh no, Charles," said Emma. "Don't make me go upstairs just yet. I don't want to see a bed for awhile I can tell you. Let me rest on the couch in the living room. This way Joan and I can talk and I can read to her too."

Charles shrugged. "I guess that will be okay. Joan, go tell Grandma to get the couch ready for Mommy because we're going in now." He grabbed Emma under the arm and guided her up the path to the front door. Maude was waiting just inside the door and greeted Emma with a big smile and some tears she could not hold back. Julia was in the living room plumping pillows on the couch and holding an extravagant lap robe.

"Hello Mother Carney. It's so good to see you." She turned then and saw her mother. Before she knew it, the tears were streaming down her face. "Oh, Mama, I missed you so much. Thank you for being here for Joan and taking care of the house and everything. I could never have gotten through this ordeal without you."

"I had lots of help, Emma. Maude and Joan have worked just as hard as I have, believe me. We missed you, too, and we are so glad to have you home. I will bring Papa by tomorrow to see you. If I don't, he won't give me a minute's peace. Come now; let's get you settled here on the couch."

Emma smiled and did as her mother instructed. Joan did not leave her side for an instant. "Grandma made noodles and pot cheese for lunch, Mommy. It's your favorite, right?"

"It sure is, Joan, and I can't wait to taste it. They don't cook Hungarian in the hospital you know."

Joan clapped her hands gleefully. Maude, who had been staying in the background, came over to the couch and sat down on the ottoman. "Emma, I am so glad you are alright and that you are home with us again. I have been praying every night and I know the baby will be getting stronger—maybe not in our time, but in God's own time. Please don't worry and just get your strength back so when he does come home you will be ready for him."

"Thank you for that, Mother Carney. I have been praying, too, and I believe that the baby will be home soon and will be strong and healthy in no time. Thank you so much for all your help through this. Thank God we have you with us." She hugged her mother-in-law and Maude hugged her back.

"I'm going to put lunch on, Emma, Julia yelled from the kitchen. I hope you are all hungry."

"As a matter of fact, I am," said Emma licking her lips. "I haven't really been hungry in quite a while. All it takes is Mama's cooking I guess."

Charles took her arm and led her into the dining room. "I'll stay for lunch but then I have to go into the office for an hour or two, dear. I hope you don't mind. I've been out so much lately and there are a few pressing matters I must attend to."

"Of course I don't mind, Charles. I understand totally. You do what you have to do and I'll see you this evening for dinner. But right now, let's enjoy this wonderful lunch Mama has prepared. Maybe we'll hear some good news from Dr. Kramer before you return tonight. He said he'd call or stop by."

"I'm sure he'll be in touch as soon as he has some news, Emma. Let's pray that the news will be good news."

Julia made a toast with apple cider to Emma's homecoming and they all sat down to enjoy the meal.

"Thank you God for bringing my mommy home," said Joan raising her glass. "And don't forget my baby brother. Bring him home soon, too, please, and thanks for lunch."

Everyone answered, "Amen."

Chapter 45

A month had passed before Dr. Kramer called to say that they could consider bringing the baby home.

"Ordinarily I would keep him in the hospital several more weeks but he is not improving as fast as I would like. I feel that the baby needs his family around him. I know that sounds a bit radical, but I think we could take better care of him at home where he can begin to bond with his mother. It will be very difficult, Charles. I will need your full cooperation."

The doctor looked up at Emma and Charles with deep concern etched on his face and then continued. "We will have to keep the nursery at ninety three degrees around the clock."

Emma interrupted. "But we planned to keep him in our room for the first few months. Are you saying we can't do that?"

"That is precisely what I am saying," Sam Kramer answered. "This baby is still in an extremely delicate condition, but I honestly feel we can take better care of him at home than they can at the hospital. We can only do this if you and Charles cooperate and do everything I tell you. Can you do that?"

"Of course we can," they both answered at once. "Just tell us what you want us to do."

"First of all, you and Charles can be the only ones allowed in the room until I tell you otherwise. This means both grandmothers and Joan are barred from the room until I give permission. We cannot afford any outside contamination until he reaches at least six pounds. You will both have to wear hospital gowns and hats and wash your hands thoroughly before doing anything for the baby. It isn't going to be easy, Emma. Do you think you can do this? Please be honest with me. Your child's life depends on it."

Emma looked up at Charles questioningly. He nodded and put his arm around her shoulder. "We'll do whatever it takes. We'll give our son the best care we can and we'll follow all your directions to the letter. I promise."

Sam Kramer smiled. "Somehow I know you will. I just wanted to be sure you understood the sacrifices this will entail. I will try to explain a little to Joan but you and Charles will have to convince her that her absence in that room is essential right now. That goes for the grandmothers too. Hopefully, in a few weeks the ban can be lifted and your son can begin to bond with his whole family."

The ban remained in place a bit longer than Sam Kramer or the parents expected. It was mid September before Joan, Julia and Maude got to meet Charles Carney, Jr. Joan had already begun attending Kindergarten before she was permitted to meet her baby brother for the very first time.

On October 1st Emma led her daughter by the hand into the nursery. Joan was beside herself but kept very quiet as her mother had instructed. Shaking with anticipation, she tiptoed over to the crib and looked in. Charles was sleeping and Joan put her chubby hand through the bars of the crib and touched his tiny infant hand with one finger. The baby's eyes did not open but immediately one tiny fist opened and wrapped itself around her finger. "Oh" erupted from Joan's mouth and she looked up at her mother.

"It's okay, Joan," Emma said. "Sit here in the rocker and I will let you hold him."

Emma extracted Joan's hand from her brother's grasp and bent down to pick up her son. She carried him over to the chair where Joan was seated and waiting expectantly.

"Here's your new brother, Joan. Hold him gently but firmly and just talk to him softly."

Joan did as she was told and within a few minutes the baby's eyes fluttered open. His gaze rested on his sister's face and slowly a shy grin spread across his tiny countenance. Anyone watching could tell it was love at first sight and a sibling bond was forged that day that would never be broken. Joan smiled back and held her brother to her tiny bosom, rocking him back and forth with childlike reverence.

"Oh, Mommy, I love him so much," said Joan. "May I take him to school for show and tell? I want to show him to all my friends in school."

Emma laughed. "No, my darling, but you can bring your friends over to meet him when he gets a bit bigger and stronger. God has done a wonderful job of taking care of him and now we can all be a normal family again."

As the days continued, Charles got stronger and stronger and before they knew it he was a healthy one-year old. He was a bit smaller than most babies his age but he was strong and inquisitive and getting into everything. To the delight of his sister, his first word was "Doan," but by the time he was two, he could yell Joan with a vengeance.

Charles was proud of his son but tended to be quite strict when reprimanding him. Charles, Sr. worked many long hours so the two males in the household spent little quality time together. Charles, Jr. was smothered with affection by his "harem" as his father called it—Joan, Emma and the two doting grandmothers.

In 1939 a terrible event occurred which changed the course of the family's life forever. Their next-door neighbors were their dearest friends. They were so close in fact that 7-year old Joan called them aunt and uncle. Uncle Karl often watched out for Joan playing in the front yard while Emma had to do an errand. One afternoon Emma had to take young Charles to the doctor and Maude was away visiting a friend so Joan was playing with her dolls on the front lawn while Uncle Karl was mowing the lawn. Joan asked if she could go inside his house to use the bathroom. He said she could but added in a stern voice, "do not touch the pictures on the kitchen table."

Joan entered the house and headed for the bathroom. As she passed the kitchen she peeked in and saw that there were indeed a lot of pictures laid face down on the kitchen table. With a natural child's curiosity, she turned over one or two of the pictures. She saw that they were of naked men and women and she didn't like what they were doing to each other. She was studying one of them intently when Uncle Karl came in. He grabbed her by the arm and shouted, "I told you not to touch those pictures. You are a bad, bad girl."

Joan began to cry and before she knew what was happening Karl had dragged her into the bedroom. He threw her onto the bed and was coming toward her brandishing a hairbrush. Joan didn't know what was happening and began to scream. This made Karl very angry and he tried to hush her up with his hand. As he pushed her down on the bed she was so terrified that she screamed again. Before Karl could cover her mouth again, a knock sounded at the front door.

"Mommy, Mommy," screamed Joan. Emma's voice came from behind the door.

"Let me in Karl. Please let me in. I can hear Joan screaming. What's happening?"

Karl didn't answer but he let go of Joan and ran into the bathroom. Joan raced to the front door and opened it. She threw herself into her mother's arms sobbing. Emma scooped her up and ran next door to their house.

When they got inside Emma tried desperately to calm Joan down. Little Charles was in the carriage where he had been while on the outing with his mother. Emma managed to soothe Joan and finally got her to tell her what happened. Joan explained through her tears the situation as she remembered it.

"He got so mad 'cause I looked at his pictures, Mommy. I thought he would hurt me. He kept telling me to shut up and I didn't know what to do. Uncle Karl never yelled at me before—never. What's wrong with him? Why did he get so mad at me?"

"I don't know, Joan. He must not have wanted anyone to see those pictures. You shouldn't have touched them. That's what made him so mad. We'll call Daddy and ask him to come home. He'll know what to do. I'm sure he will."

Charles was furious when Emma told him the story, but instead of taking the side of his daughter, he placed the blame on her. "She must have done something more to aggravate Karl," he said. "He never loses his temper, Emma. You know that. Karl and Esther have been our dearest friends since we moved here. Don't do anything until I get home—nothing, do you hear?"

"Yes Charles," agreed Emma and she hung up the phone. Joan was still sobbing in the next room and Emma went to comfort her daughter.

When Charles came home, he called for Joan immediately. "What happened, Joan? Tell me everything."

Joan repeated what she had told her mother and the tears begin to course down her cheeks once more.

"What kind of pictures were they?" asked her father. Joan described what she had seen, "people with no clothes on doing funny things to each other. I didn't like them, Daddy, and I put them back, but Uncle Karl got mad anyway." She looked up at her father waiting for him to take her in his arms and tell her he understood.

Instead Charles Carney rushed out the door and headed across the yard toward his neighbor's house. Esther answered the door and Charles asked to speak to Karl. "He can't talk to you right now, Charles. He's sick."

"What do you mean sick? I have to speak to him and right now. Where is he?"

Esther had just come in and hadn't even had time to take her coat off. She had found her husband in the bedroom sobbing with his head in his hands. Photographs were strewn all over the breakfast nook as if blown by an angry wind. She hadn't even had a chance to pick them up and look at them. She was too intent on calming her husband down and finding out what was wrong.

"You can't see him now, Charles. I told you he's sick," she insisted.

Charles walked past Esther into the kitchen and saw the pictures scattered over the table and the floor. He reached down and picked up two of them. As soon as he looked at them he knew Joan had been telling him the truth. He gasped in utter disbelief and rushed past Esther and out the door. When he arrived back at home he went to find Emma and Joan. They were upstairs in the bedroom and Charles raced up the stairs two at a time. He walked into the room and seeing the state his daughter was in, knelt down on the carpet in front of her and pulled her toward him.

"I'm so sorry, Joan. Please forgive me. Daddy knows you were telling the truth. I'm not mad at you, only at Uncle Karl. He is very sick, Joan, and that's why he lost his temper. You won't be able to go over there ever again."

After Emma got Joan calmed down and settled in her room she returned to their bedroom to talk to Charles.

"I've called the Police, Emma. I reported an attempted molestation and named Karl as the guilty party. The Police are on their way. I had to do it, Emma. His mind must have snapped for him to do such a thing—and to our daughter too. I still can't believe it."

The next few months were a nightmare. Every time Emma or Joan went out of the house Esther would call obscene names out the window at them. The Police had taken Karl away that day and were holding him for trial. They informed Emma and Charles that his defense would be criminal insanity. They also advised that little Joan would have to appear in court. Charles fought this tooth and nail but to no avail. Joan, now 7-1/2 was subpoenaed to appear at the trial scheduled for thee months hence.

Meanwhile Emma demanded that they move. She convinced Charles that they must get Joan away from here and the sooner the better. She had been sharing the nursery with Charles and was now at the age when she should have her own room anyway. Charles agreed and they began house hunting the next weekend. They found a three-bedroom house in Yonkers, NY with room for expansion of a fourth bedroom on the third floor. It was near enough for Joan to walk to the elementary school and it was also a short walk to the local high school. Joan could share a room with her Nana for awhile until Charles could finish the fourth bedroom for Joan.

Two weeks after the trial the moving van was at their front door. The trial was a nightmare for little Joan who had to take the witness stand and answer questions put to her by the Judge. Several times she broke down in tears and had to be taken out and walked around by the kindly Bailiff. Karl had been seated in stony silence in the front of the court room with his lawyer, and his unwavering stare, directed at the little girl had unnerved her completely. She was terrified just to be in the same room with him. Emma was not permitted to comfort the child and had to rely on the compassion of the court as manifested by the Bailiff.

Karl was found guilty by reason of insanity and committed to the local mental hospital for an indeterminate period. The two weeks before they moved were agonizing for Emma. Esther became more abusive every day and little Joan was afraid to go outside the house. Emma no longer took her to the bus stop to go to school but drove her there everyday until they moved to Yonkers.

Early in May the move was accomplished and Joan had her eighth birthday in the new house in Westchester County.

Chapter 46

Emma loved the new house. It was an English Tudor with a green lawn down to the sidewalk that ended in a rock garden on either side. A huge old oak tree shaded the right side of the house and the backyard seemed to go on forever. The grass actually ended several hundred yards from the back of the house and was marked by forsythia hedges, but there were what seemed like miles of empty fields behind that. Everyone in the neighborhood infringed on that vacant land and the Carneys would be no exception.

Charles put in a huge vegetable garden with trellises for tomatoes and lots of green leafy vegetables. Emma loved the garden but spent most of her time cultivating the flowers that surrounded it. Charles even put in a 9-hole putting course for himself and Charles, Jr. eventually, so they could practice their golf game.

Joan was a bit withdrawn at first but once she got to know her neighbors and was convinced that they would not hurt her, she began to relax and became a bit more outgoing. Emma took her into the tiny village nearest their house to go shopping and showed her where her school was located. There was even a movie theater in the village and now that she was eight years old, she would be allowed to go to the movies more often Emma told her. Joan loved the films but had never seen anything but Shirley Temple, which Emma took her to on the trolley car when they lived in the Bronx.

Maude was the only one not happy about the move. "I am stuck out here in the country without any of my friends and no way to get to see them," she complained. "I've lived in the city all my life. How can you expect me to survive in this God forsaken place?"

Emma and Charles tried their best to placate her but it was no use. All she did was complain, and poor Joan got the worst of it because they shared a bedroom. Charles had not yet had time to fix up the bedroom on the third floor for Joan so she and Maude had twin beds in the second bedroom which was quite large. Unfortunately, Maude insisted on having a lot of her things from the City house with her in the room. This left little room for Joan and her dolls and other toys. The one concession Maude made was letting Charles put a small roll-top desk in the room so Joan could do her homework.

Charles did clean up the cellar and, although they could not afford an actual playroom down there, he painted the walls, put down an old piece of carpeting and built a toy box for Joan and Charles to keep their toys in. He put up some book shelves too, and this is where the children spent most of their free time when they weren't outside playing.

Life was good for the Carneys. Charles got promoted again and this time to Chief Engineer of Westchester County. Emma was very proud of him. They had spent the last few years paying off the remaining debts from Charles's father and then buying this new house so additional income would be very welcome. The only reason they could buy a house like this, Charles reminded her, was that during the war the banks foreclosed on a lot of them and now had to sell them off at low prices to get their money back. Maude still didn't understand about the debts and when Charles denied her anything she got furious. She figured if they could afford this house, they could afford anything she wanted. She was getting older and seemed to suffer from various ailments and so made Charles's life increasingly difficult.

As he progressed up the business ladder, Charles began to drink more and more frequently and, as a result, had frequent fits of temper. Young Charles was often the recipient of his father's rage, but Emma seemed to get the brunt of it.

One evening Joan was doing her homework upstairs when she heard a commotion in the living room. She went downstairs and saw her father, in a rage, pick up a lamp and bring it down on her mother's back, knocking her to the floor. Joan was terrified. Her huge intake of breath caught Charles's attention and he turned toward her as if to strike again. Instead of running away, Joan ran to where her mother was lying still. This was not the first time this had happened, she remembered vaguely.

"Mommy, Mommy," she cried. "Speak to me. Please speak to me."

Joan looked up at her father in fear and disgust.

"You've killed her. You've killed my Mommy."

This outburst from Joan had an immediate sobering effect on Charles. He dropped to his knees, cradling his wife in his arms and rocking her back and forth. He wept out load and his keening lamented his actions. As he rocked her, Emma stirred.

"It's alright Charles. Don't cry. You didn't mean it. I know you didn't. Let me rest a minute and then help me upstairs."

Joan was aghast. How could her mother forgive such behavior? She hated her father at that moment and wished he would just die and leave them alone. She knew this would not happen. She also knew that, despite the violence brought on by liquor, Charles Carney worshiped the ground his wife walked on. He loved her beyond all understanding, but this love did not prevent these bursts of cruelty. It was as though he knew he would be forgiven unconditionally, and knowing this, he used Emma as a means to vent his crippling anger. Joan vowed she would never forgive him for his actions. Maude was no help. When Charles became violent, Maude disappeared into her room. She refused to get involved in 'family disputes' as she called them.

Charles Carney's insecurities aggravated by liquor, manifested themselves in pure unthinking rage. These insecurities had their foundation in his upbringing. Maude had trained him to be afraid. As a young child she would drag him into the basement of the townhouse whenever there was a thunder storm and they would huddle there together till the storm passed. She insisted on double locks on all the doors and even had his milk shipped from the City when they went on vacation to the mountain resorts her husband favored, because she was sure the country milk would poison him. Maude was also a hypochondriac and Charles followed in her footsteps.

His treatment of Charles, Jr. was excessively strict and the introverted young boy never had the courage to defend himself against his father's bullying. Joan, on the other hand, would stand up to him and fight back. Although it roused her father's anger on many occasions, Charles Carney did have a deep respect for his daughter because she would not allow him to browbeat her. Joan became her brother's protector and intervened whenever she could to save him from a punishment, especially one he didn't deserve.

One day, when Emma was out shopping, Charles accused his son of stealing coins from his dresser. Joan was convinced of her brother's innocence but failed to deter her father from beating him. He kept on hitting and pushing him out the front door and down the steps to the sidewalk. The child lay bruised and battered on the sidewalk when Joan rushed to his aid.

"I'll kill you if you hit him again," she shouted.

Charles raised his fist but lowered it slowly and walked back into the house. He found the missing coins the next day. They had slid off the dresser onto the floor and were underneath his chifferobe. Emma spotted them when she was running the carpet sweeper. He said nothing to her, nor did he offer an apology to his son. He put the coins in his pocket and forgot them and the incident forever.

Chapter 47

Emma recovered fully from the incident with the lamp but when she went to Dr. Kramer for a checkup he spotted the bruises on her back. When he questioned her, Emma came up with some rather lame explanations.

"They're from Charles, aren't they, Emma?" Sam Kramer asked.

Emma was silent but her silence only punctuated the obvious. "You can't sustain this sort of treatment, Emma. If he doesn't get help for his drinking, one day he'll kill you. You know that, don't you?"

Emma shrugged. "I know you're right, Dr. Kramer, but I don't know what to do about it. Charles loves me. He would never deliberately hurt me. Even you know that. But when he drinks, he becomes another person—an unthinking animal. He loses all control." The tears began to flow and before long, Emma was sobbing. The kindly doctor took her in his arms to soothe her.

"I've known you since you were a little girl, Emma. I can't just sit by and watch this happen. Ask Charles to come and see me. Perhaps I can convince him to get help."

"I'll do what I can," Emma murmured, wiping the tears from her cheeks. "Please don't mention this to Mama," she pleaded. "She'd kill him if she knew."

"Don't fret, Emma. This will be our little secret, but if you can't convince him to come in, I'll have to resort to other measures."

Emma nodded and left the office.

When Charles came home that night, she could tell he had been drinking. He wasn't drunk but the smell of alcohol was clearly on his breath. He looked at her through dazed eyes and went upstairs to change his clothes. Maude passed him on the stairway.

"He looks very tired, Emma. Don't you think so? He's definitely not himself." She sat down on a kitchen chair and waited for Emma to answer. When none came forth, she spoke again.

"Is Charles ill, Emma? Is there anything wrong with my son?"

Emma turned to face her mother-in-law. "He drinks too much, Mother Carney. That's what's wrong with your son. He just doesn't know when to stop and sometimes it makes him sick."

Maude gasped but didn't answer. She knew Emma was right but she had chosen to ignore it for quite some time. Before she could say another word, a crash sounded from upstairs. Emma reacted immediately and dashed up the stairs.

The door to the master bedroom was closed. She tried the door, and though it wasn't locked, she had trouble opening it. It was as though something or someone was preventing her from opening the door. She pushed harder but the door only opened a crack. She peered in and realized that it was Charles that was holding the door shut. His prone body was visible through the crack. He was apparently lying on the floor immediately in front of the door, thus preventing Emma from opening it.

"Mother Carney, please come up here. I need your help," she called.

Maude heard Emma's cry for help and went up the stairs to see what was wrong. She saw Emma pushing hard against the bedroom door and surmised what the problem might be.

"Charles is lying across the door, Mother Carney. I'm not strong enough to push the door open with his body in the way. Do you think you could help me?"

"I'll try, Emma. I'm stronger than I look you know. She put her shoulder to the door next to Emma and they both pushed as hard as they could. After several tries, the door began to move inward. It finally opened enough for Emma to slide through the opening and get into the room.

"Wait here, Mother. I'll try to slide Charles's body away from the door so we can get it open. In a few minutes the door was open wide enough to allow Maude Carney entrance into the room. She looked down at her son sprawled across the carpet and began to weep.

"Get hold of yourself, Mother Carney. We have to get help. I'll call Dr. Kramer and you stay here with Charles in case he wakes up. Thank God Joan and Charles are still at my mother's in Hunts Point. They're not due to come home till after dinner. Maybe the doctor can get here before then."

Emma ran down the stairs to call Dr. Kramer. As soon as he heard the agitation in her voice, he knew something had happened.

"I'll be right there, Emma. Don't move him. Just leave him be until I get there."

She heard the phone click and ran back upstairs to talk to Maude.

"He's coming; Dr. Kramer is coming right away. He said not to move him. Did he wake up at all? Has he said anything?"

"No, Emma. He appears to be unconscious," said Maude, wiping the tears that were still trickling down her cheeks. "I can't imagine what happened."

Both women walked over and sat down on the bed. Emma felt as though her legs were made of lead. She sighed deeply and then put her arms around her mother-in-law. "He'll be fine, Mother Carney. Please don't worry. Dr. Kramer will be here soon and then everything will be alright."

Moments later the doorbell rang and Emma let Sam Kramer into the house. He followed her up the stairs and took in the scene with a practiced glance. Charles was indeed unconscious but did not seem to have any injuries. The smell of alcohol struck him as the doctor knelt next to the body and listened to Charles's heart with the stethoscope.

"Drinking again, I wager." He looked at Emma with a raised eyebrow. "I'm going to call an ambulance and get him to the hospital, Emma. That's one place we can get him to dry out, although I think there is more going on here than just too much alcohol. I'll go downstairs and call. Get a small bag packed for him—his toiletries and some pajamas and a robe—just the necessities.

Emma moved like a robot and did as Dr. Kramer commanded. As she filled a small canvas bag with Charles's belongings she prayed. "Please God, watch over Charles and if it is your will, take away his need for alcohol and make him well again."

The ambulance was there in twenty minutes. They carried Charles out on a stretcher and Emma went with him to the hospital. Maude agreed to stay home and wait for Julia to return with Emma and Charles, Jr.

Emma waited in the lounge outside Charles's room. It seemed like hours since they had brought Charles in and gotten him a room. A nurse came over to her with a cup of coffee and a sandwich.

"Dr. Kramer insists that you eat something, Mrs. Carney."

She thrust the food at Emma and walked briskly away down the hall. Emma was not hungry but she knew she had better keep up her strength so she took a bite of the sandwich and followed it with a large swallow of the hot coffee. It actually tasted good, and she realized it had been about eight hours since she had eaten anything. She had called Julia after she got there so her mother would be prepared to explain their father's absence to the children. Julia said she would stay at the house until Emma came home.

Emma had just finished the sandwich when Dr. Kramer came around the corner. She stood up and waited for the doctor to speak.

"He's going to be fine, Emma. He's had a nervous breakdown. It may have been alcohol induced but there are other factors going on here also. Charles's nerves are shot and he's going to need a lot of rest. I venture to say he'll not be able to go back to work for several months. I'll call his office and give them the necessary medical explanation. I'm sure they can arrange for a medical leave for him. He needs complete bed rest and, of course, no alcohol at all. It won't be easy for you having him home all the time, but at least you do have Maude there as well. She's going to have to pitch in and do her share. After all, he is her son."

"May I go in and see him, Dr. Kramer?"

'Yes, but just to say goodnight, Emma. I've sedated him and he won't be able to stay awake much longer, I assure you. After that, I'll take you home. It's been a long day for both of us."

Emma nodded and went down the hall to Charles's room. He was almost asleep when she entered the room.

"Forgive me, Emma," he rasped. "You know I love you and….." His voice trailed away, and the hum of regular breathing was the only sound in the room.

She kissed his forehead and whispered, "I'll be back in the morning, dear. Have a good night."

Chapter 48

▼

Charles came home from the hospital two weeks later—a remnant of his former self. He had lost nearly fifteen pounds and his demeanor was sullen and withdrawn. Emma tried to ignore his attitude and did everything possible to keep him calm and entertained. He was taking rather strong medication for the depression, and Dr. Kramer recommended some various methods of therapy to keep his mind and hands busy.

He suggested that Charles crochet rugs from scraps of cloth that Julia could provide in abundance from the cutting room of her salon. Emma was afraid to even mention this suggestion to her husband, afraid he would take offense at the demeaning activity. To her surprise, however, he took to it immediately.

Julia brought several boxes of scraps to the house and several large wooden crochet needles. She started the first rug for Charles and taught him the same way she had learned from the priest's housekeeper in Budapest so many years ago. He seemed anxious to learn and was fascinated at how the rug grew longer. He became angry the first time Emma stopped him, until she explained that it was long enough now to make a rug out of it.

"You've made a beautiful new rug for the foyer, Charles. I'm so proud of you. Mama and I will sew it together and then you will be able to enjoy your handiwork."

Charles smiled, not entirely understanding. "I want to make more," he said. "May I make another rug, Emma?"

"Of course you can, dear, but perhaps you'd like to try something else for a change."

"No, Emma, no. I want to make another rug. I don't want to try anything else. Bring me the crochet needle and some scraps."

Emma could see that Charles was getting agitated. She brought the needle and the material and laid them in his lap. *Was this all he was ever going to do with his life?* she thought.

One day followed the next and soon Charles put back some of the weight he had lost and color began to return to his pale cheeks. He was on his third rug when he admitted to being a bit bored. Emma took this as a good sign and suggested he try something new.

The latest rage in the stores then was painting by numbers. Famous works of art were copied onto canvases and marked off into many sections. Each section was assigned a number and each number referred to a specific color paint. Emma had purchased a set of three canvases—all religious masterpieces taken from the Vatican collection. Charles was enthralled but apprehensive too.

"I've never painted anything in my life, Emma. I have no artistic talent at all. All I know about art is the drafting we learned in engineering classes at Columbia."

"You don't need artistic talent to paint these pictures, Charles. You just need patience and a controlled hand. I think you will do very well."

Charles agreed to give it a try and before long all three canvases were completed. By the time Christmas rolled around, there were few spaces left on the walls of the house where Emma could hang Charles's artwork.

Emma devoted all her time to Charles's recovery but had to find a way to make some extra money to cover the deficit in pay while Charles was out on disability. She began to sell brushes from their home, using the ping pong table in the basement as her staging area for merchandise going out. She got her friends and neighbors to give brush parties where she could sell her merchandise.

His pride forced Charles to explain his wife's working as a "side business," of his own design. He determined at the outset that the money she earned would only be used to purchase AT&T stock, something they could no longer due on his reduced income.

Emma did very well and was earning more and more each month. Many deliveries were made late in the evening after the dinner dishes were cleared away. Sometimes, after an unpleasant exchange of words with her bored and ailing husband, Emma would bundle Joan and little Charles into the car and head out to make deliveries, vowing never to return. They always did come home, of course, and Joan and Charles, Jr. began to accept these midnight jaunts as a normal way of life at home. These trips were Emma's only way of blowing off steam and standing up to the emotional cruelties often heaped on her by an unstable husband.

One night Emma awoke to hear Joan crying in her room. She got out of bed and padded down the hall to the room still shared by Maude and Joan.

"Mommy, she won't wake up and she's making awful noises," cried Joan.

It took Emma only a moment to realize that her mother-in-law was dying. What her daughter was hearing was not the old woman's usual snoring, but the rattle of breathing that precedes an imminent death. She gathered her daughter into her arms to soothe her.

"Wait here, Joan. I'll go wake Daddy," Emma instructed. She returned to her bedroom and awakened Charles.

"It's your mother. I think she's dying. Please come at once, Charles. Joan is very upset. She doesn't understand what's happening."

Charles rose at once, threw on his robe and followed Emma down the hall. By the time they reached Maude's bedside she had passed. Joan was huddled under her covers sobbing.

"I'll call Kramer, "he said. "He'll have to fill out a death certificate." His face was impassive. "I'll go get dressed and then you can bring Joan into our room."

Maude Carney passed to her reward with little fanfare. She did not attend church and had very few friends left that he knew of, so Charles did not waste time or money on a wake. He arranged for a small funeral service at their local Catholic church and buried her in a nearby cemetery. Emma felt the loss of her mother-in-law more than she thought she would.

Eventually, Charles recovered sufficiently to return to work on a reduced schedule. Emma insisted on keeping the business going and despite his recriminations, she did just that. She cut back on her brush parties and relied mostly on her re-order business which was sizeable. Charles did not complain too bitterly as Emma's earnings allowed them to purchase more stock than they would have otherwise.

With Charles back at work and permanently sober, the children thrived. Even young Charles was doing well in school now that his father was calmer and less judgmental where he was concerned. Joan was in high school now and had just been elected to join a sorority.

Emma had to fight with Charles to get him to allow Joan to date. "She's fourteen years old, Charles, and all her friends are dating. The dances she wants to go to are all supervised and attended by chaperones. You can't keep her at home forever."

"I want to meet any young man she goes out with, Emma, and I expect her to adhere to my curfew no matter what. Is that clear?"

Emma tried to intervene on Joan's behalf whenever she could. She trusted her daughter completely but getting her father to ease up on his stringent rules was an impossibility. Mother and daughter had an amazingly strong bond and Joan appeased her father as much as possible for the sake of her mother. The memories of her father's prior violence toward her mother would always be with her.

Joan was preparing for graduation from high school in 1950 and had been accepted into New Paltz State Teacher's College. Emma was so proud of her daughter and Charles was eminently pleased. He had wanted more for her academically but did not want to pay the tuition that a non-State school would require. Emma was aware of his miserly nature but was thrilled that Joan would be fairly close to home while getting her education.

The world came to an end one evening at dinner when Joan announced that she had changed her mind and was not going to go away to college. Emma listened silently, but Charles threw his plate across the room in a rage and thundered his displeasure.

Unbeknownst to her parents, Joan's current boy friend, Alan, had given her an ultimatum. "If you go away to school, that will be the end of us."

Being newly eighteen and convinced she was in love with this tall, handsome young man five years her senior, Joan had agreed.

"I want to go to Katharine Gibbs in New York City," she said authoritatively.

"And where did that idea come from?" bellowed her father. "You always said you wanted to be a teacher and that's what you're going to be."

"I said that because I knew that's what you wanted me to be," said Joan. "I want to work in an office. I'm going to learn how to be a secretary and then I can work in New York City and earn money right away."

Charles was furious and swore he would give her no financial help to achieve this ridiculous scheme. Joan stood firm and, as always, Emma became the peacemaker. She pleaded with him not to abandon his daughter, and eventually she wore him down. Even in anger, Charles found it hard to refuse his wife when she had made up her mind. He agreed to pay for one year at Gibbs.

Joan entered Katharine Gibbs in the fall of 1951 and, ironically, Alan was drafted in November of the same year. Joan was devastated but the die was cast and she had to live with her decision. Emma was relieved that Alan was vacating Joan's life, but she never let on.

And so, two years passed. Joan graduated and started working at ABC-TV in Manhattan. Charles had been restored to his old position by now and was up for another promotion. He soon became General Manager of Westchester County and looked forward to the day when his son would join him in the business.

Things were more or less peaceful in the Carney household until Alan returned from Korea in 1953. He returned with an engagement ring and a determination to get Joan to marry him forthwith. Emma begged Joan to stall, knowing Charles would be livid. Alan was not rich, not Catholic and had no college education. To Charles he had no redeeming features whatever as a perspective bridegroom. He was not worthy of his only daughter—not by a long shot. Charles put his foot down—Joan was not to see Alan Greene ever again.

That was all the incentive Joan needed. She not only saw him but she agreed to wear his engagement ring. Joan told Emma her secret, but both women kept Charles Carney in the dark. The subterfuge continued until March 1954 when Joan confided to her mother that she and Alan planned to marry in May—with or without Charles's permission. Emma gave Joan her blessing but kept silent. When Joan told her father at the end of March that she planned to marry Alan Greene on May 22nd, he went wild. He ranted and raved, threatened and cajoled. Nothing worked. Emma continued to keep silent until the tirade ran its course. She talked softly to Charles and finally soothed him into accepting the inevitable marriage.

Charles fought the idea with every fiber of his being. At first he refused to pay for the wedding but then his pride got the best of him. Joan had been paying board since the day she graduated from Gibbs, so that money would be used to pay for the wedding he decided.

"You must stay within the allotted amount, as I will give you no more," he announced. "Do you understand me?"

Joan and Emma agreed that they could do this. If they had the reception at the local women's club and served only champagne and hors d'oeuvres they could pull it off.

"Thanks for being on my side, Mommy," Joan said as they left the Women's Club with the signed contract. "Now if we can just keep Daddy from killing Alan before the wedding, we'll be fine."

Emma grinned at her daughter, knowing that there was more truth than fiction in that statement than she knew. "Don't worry, honey. You'll make it down that aisle; I promise."

Chapter 49

Before preparations for the wedding even began, Emma received a phone call that temporarily took Joan out of the limelight where Charles was concerned. The modeling agency, where she had worked more then twenty years ago, wanted a mature hosiery model. Emma was forty eight by then and so was very flattered to be considered as a potential model. She made an appointment and went by train into New York City to the agency. Edward Milliken, older and wiser now, was still head of the agency. He drew Emma to him and hugged her like a long lost niece.

"Walk across the room for me, Emma, and do a slow turn," he requested.

Emma followed his instructions.

"Wow," were the only words Milliken uttered. "You've still got the best pair of gams in New York City, Emma. When can you start work?"

Emma was both shocked and pleased.

"Well, I don't know Mr. Milliken," she finally managed to say. "I'll have to check with Charles and get back to you. I'm sure he'll be as excited by your offer as I am. He always was proud of my modeling. I'll call you tomorrow if that's okay."

"Okay," said Milliken, "but don't keep me waiting too long. I need someone now for our new client. Hanes has a whole campaign going—magazines, newspapers and catalogs too. Call me tomorrow, Emma, please."

"I will," she agreed and hurried out of the studio, anxious to get home and tell Charles the exciting news. *I won't have to sell brushes anymore*, she thought. *I sure won't miss that.*

- 209 -

When she stepped inside the front door she realized that Charles was already at home. The television was on in the living room and he was seated in front of it.

"You're home early, dear," she said.

"Yes, I am. I had a meeting off site and it ended earlier than expected so I came home instead of going back to the office. Are you glad to see me?"

"Of course I am, Charles, and I have some exciting news to tell you." Emma sat down on the sofa opposite her husband.

"I was just in the City myself and I can't wait to tell you my news."

"Well hurry up and tell me," said Charles a little impatiently.

"I had a call from Mr. Milliken a few days ago. You remember him, don't you? He was the head of the hosiery company I modeled for. Well, he called and asked me to come down to see him and so I did."

"Get to the point, Emma. You drag everything out so."

"He asked me to come to work for him, Charles."

"He what?" Charles snorted. "You're fifty years old, Emma."

"Forty eight, Charles," corrected Emma. "Milliken's looking for a mature model and he said I still have the best gams in New York. Imagine that?" she concluded with satisfaction.

Charles gaped at his wife. "I can't believe what I'm hearing, Emma. You aren't really considering his offer, are you? You're too old to be a model anymore. What a ridiculous idea. Just call him back and tell him you aren't interested, and if you don't, I will."

"What is so ridiculous about it? I still have my figure and my legs haven't changed since I was a bride. I'd love to get back into modeling. It sure beats selling brushes."

Charles bristled at this comment. "I never told you to go and sell brushes, Emma. You did that all on your own."

"Yes I did, Charles, and you didn't mind the money coming in to buy your precious stock either, did you? I thought you'd be flattered that your wife could still be a model. I know I am and I'm not going to turn this offer down."

Charles Carney turned on his wife, eyes blazing. "I can support my family with no help from you, Emma, so put this modeling idea right out of your head—now! The answer is no and that's all I'm going to say about it."

He cleared his throat and stormed out of the room. Emma just sat there, unable to believe her husband's unreasonable outburst. Joan passed her father in the hall and went to her mother to see what had happened. Emma explained the situation through a trickle of tears and Joan put her arms around her to comfort her.

"Maybe he'll change his mind, Mommy, when he cools off and thinks about it a little. I think it's neat! Imagine my mom a model again after all these years. I'm so proud of you."

"Thanks for the vote of confidence, Joan; but I don't think Daddy will change his mind. He seemed really upset at the idea of me going back to work, especially as a model. I'll have to call Mr. Milliken tomorrow and tell him it is out of the question."

"I'm so sorry, Mommy. I know how much you'd like to do this. Why does Dad have to be so stubborn? He can't stop you if you really want to do it, can he?"

"Not really, Joan, but he sure could make it unpleasant around here. He's still the boss in this family and if he says no, I won't fight with him over it. It's just not worth it, honey. Dad thinks I am too old to consider modeling, especially stockings. It's undignified, he says."

"Well, I think he's wrong, Mom. You're still a beautiful woman and would make a great model. I'm very proud of you and how you look and all my girl friends say so too. They all wish their moms looked as good as you. I bet Grandma Julia would be thrilled for you also.

"Thank you, honey; I really appreciate you saying that. Your grandma would be on my side too, I know, but Daddy has the final word. It was nice just to be asked and I'll always have that to remember. Let's not talk about it anymore, Joan. It just wasn't meant to be. Now I've got more important things to think about like what I'm going to feed this family for dinner." Joan smiled and followed her mother into the kitchen.

Chapter 50

Joan's wedding day dawned bright and sunny.

Charles was still reminding his daughter, "You don't have to go through with it, you know. We can still call it off."

"Stop talking like that, Daddy. I am marrying Alan today and that is that. Now please go and bring the car around."

Emma said nothing. She led her daughter down the stairs to the hall. She held the train reverently behind her as they approached the front door. Charles had pulled the car in front of the steps and was coming up the walk. Joan took a deep breath and stepped through the front door. Just as her feet touched the bottom step to the front path, the first raindrops fell. Joan could not believe it. She could feel the curls in her hair falling along with the drops. Then just as suddenly as it began, the rain stopped. Was this an omen, Joan wondered?

Mother and daughter continued the parade down the path to the sidewalk. Emma held the train as Joan got into the car. Charles went around and climbed in on the driver's side and turned the key. Nothing happened. He tried again. Nothing happened. He looked at Emma in the back seat and growled. "The car is dead. The battery must have died. Call Wally next door, Emma. Ask if we can borrow his car."

"But he has a coop, Charles. How will we get Emma into a coop with all this train behind her?"

"Do as I say, Emma. It appears we have no choice and the wedding is scheduled to go off in fifteen minutes. Hurry up. We'll wait here."

Emma jumped from the car and ran across the street to the neighbors. Wally and his wife were just getting ready to go to the church.

"Can we borrow your car, Wally? Ours is dead in front of the house," Emma cried. "We were just taking Joan to the church when it gave up the ghost. We're desperate."

"Not to worry, Em," said Wally with a shrug. "Take my car and I'll get yours charged and drive it on down to the church. I'll pull it out and Joan and Charles can jump right in and get to the church. Good thing Helen and I are always late, eh?"

"Bless you Wally. You are the best neighbor we could ask for. I'll go tell Charles the plan."

Emma raced out to the car and as she was explaining the plan to Charles, Wally pulled up next to them. Emma helped Joan out of the Buick and into the front seat of Wally's roadster. The long white train was bunched up in her lap as she overflowed the narrow front seat of the sports car. Wally and Charles traded places and Emma jumped into the back before she got left behind in the exchange.

"Thank God the church is only a few blocks away," said Emma.

"I'm sure this is a bad omen," grumbled Charles. "I told you this wedding was a bad idea."

Emma bit her lip and said nothing. Joan was also suspecting the motives of her higher power at this point but kept quiet. "Just get me to the church, dear Lord," she prayed silently.

They were only ten minutes late and, Emma noted, Alan Greene was early for the first time in her memory. He had a perfect record of being notoriously late picking Emma up, but today he had broken his record. God certainly does have a sense of humor decided Emma.

The ceremony went off without a hitch and the reception at the Women's Club was adequate and satisfying. Many cases of champagne were consumed and the endless array of hors d'oeuvres were creative and delicious. Charles got in a fight with the photographer who made the mistake of calling him Pops, but other than that, all went well. The couple stayed the requisite amount of time and then left on their honeymoon amid a fanfare of rice and well wishers.

Charles couldn't wait to get home and put this magnificent folly behind him. He had had a few glasses of champagne so was in a rather ominous mood. Emma was aware of his state of mind so stayed her distance. Charles, Jr., though only seventeen, had partaken of a glass or two of the bubbly as well and was feeling a bit frisky. Emma did not want any confrontation between her husband and her son this evening. They had all had quite enough excitement for one day. Besides, she was feeling a bit under the weather herself—probably a result of all the excitement that day she thought.

"I'll put some coffee on, dear," said Emma. "Do you want anything more to eat before I go up and change my clothes?"

"Not now, Emma. I ate enough of those canapés to last me awhile. Coffee is all I want right now. Where's our son?"

"He's gone up to his room to change I think. He was anxious to get out of that tuxedo I can tell you. Seventeen year old boys are really not into dressing up you know."

Charles didn't answer so Emma proceeded up the stairs to the bedroom. She suddenly felt very tired and decided to take a hot shower to relax her weary body. She shed her mother-of-the-bride gown quickly and arranged it on a hangar and hooked it on the door to air before putting it away in the clothing bag in the far reaches of her closet. *I wonder if I'll ever wear it again,* she thought.

Emma stepped into the steamy water and began to lather up. As she moved the wash cloth slowly across her chest she paused. Was that a lump she felt? She retraced her movements and then stopped. "My God," she murmured. *It is a lump—under my left breast. It wasn't there yesterday. I'm quite sure of that. I guess I'd better call Dr. Kramer tomorrow and make an appointment to see him. I'm sure it's nothing but I shouldn't ignore it.*

She finished her shower, wrapped her hair in a towel and put on her robe. *What an anticlimax to Joan's wedding day,* she thought. She sat at her dressing table and studied her face in the mirror. *Could it be? Could I have cancer?* She continued brushing out her long hair and drying it with the towel. Emma's long hair was still her pride and joy although she wore it in a chignon or a French twist most of the time. Charles had forbidden her to ever cut it and she had honored his wishes. She finished her ablutions and moved her body onto the bed.

The next thing she knew she felt Charles climbing in beside her in the double bed. *I must have fallen asleep,* she thought to herself. She turned and moved closer to her side of the bed. Charles tended to sprawl and she wanted to be sure he had enough room. She made no indication that she was awake. She was in no mood for a discussion right now. Her head was full of her own thoughts and so she began to pray silently.

Dear Lord, I don't want to have cancer, but if it is your will, I will accept it. I think you must have a sense of humor because removing a breast from me is almost funny—I am so flat-chested. The poor surgeon will have to really dig to remove something that almost isn't there. And to think that's what made me such a successful model all those years. All my friends had to bind themselves to be in fashion, but not me. I was always built like a boy—flat as a pancake. And now I may lose the pancakes as well. One has to see the humor in that. Please don't let this upset my husband or my children. Charles is just recovering from his dreadful nervous breakdown and I wouldn't want to be the cause of a relapse. He couldn't handle that just now, dear Lord. My daughter will be upset of course, but after we talk, she will be my support system. We have that kind of a relationship. We are good, good friends as well as being mother and daughter. Young Charles will take it hard but teenagers have a way of putting things aside that really do not affect their lives specifically. He'll get used to the idea and deal with it with the help of his sister. He looks up to her and they are very close. That will help him get through this. I guess I am making the assumption that it is cancer, Lord. Why is that? Forgive me for upstaging you. I will put this out of mind now and wait until I see the doctor. Whatever the outcome, your will be done.

Emma turned over on her side and felt her body relax.

Chapter 51

▼

"Faith is the realization of what is hoped for and the evidence of things not seen," said Fr. Nevins. "And your faith is very strong, Emma. You will survive this crisis and your faith will be the reason. God bless you and keep you, Emma. I'm so glad you came and shared this with me. Remember, you are not alone in this journey. If you need me to talk to Charles, you have only to ask."

The priest held Emma close and kissed her cheek. He had been a close confident since the Carneys had moved to Yonkers. He knew better than anyone what Emma went through living with the unpredictable and irreverent Charles Carney.

"Goodbye, Emma. You are in my prayers."

"Thank you Father. Talking with you has helped relieve the burden more than you know, but now I must go home and tell my family."

Emma left the rectory and headed to her car for the short drive home. Dr. Kramer had examined her a few days ago, ordered x-rays and a biopsy and determined that she did indeed have third stage breast cancer. The left breast would have to be removed and he had already set up a date for surgery. Emma would have to check into the hospital two days hence and the surgery would be performed that day. Dr. Kramer had already introduced her to the surgeon who would operate on her and she liked him immediately. Dr. Healy appeared competent but also very kind and compassionate. He had gone over all the details of what she could expect and told her to ask him any questions that might be bothering her. Now she must tell Charles and the children.

Emma arrived home just a few minutes before Charles. She barely had her coat off when he walked in the door.

"Are you coming or going, Emma?" he inquired. "I guess I have time to shower before dinner," he went on without waiting for her to answer.

"You're right, Charles. I just got home from seeing Dr. Kramer, so I haven't started dinner yet. Go and take your shower and I'll call you when it's ready."

She turned and walked toward the kitchen. Charles followed her.

"What were you doing at the doctor's? Is anything wrong?"

"No, nothing's wrong really. I have to go in for surgery in a few days, that's all."

"Surgery? What do you mean—surgery? What's wrong, Emma. Tell me at once."

Charles was becoming agitated so Emma turned back and addressed him quietly.

"Let's go into the living room for a moment before you take your shower, Charles, and I'll explain."

She led him to the sofa and he sat upright and stiff just staring at her.

"Well?"

"I found a lump. Charles. It's in my left breast and it turned out to be cancer. Dr. Kramer says it has to come off right away."

"Come off? What has to come off? Charles interjected.

"My left breast," Emma answered. "The cancer is too far gone to remove just the lump so they have to take off the entire breast. In my case, it won't really make much difference, will it?" she quipped, attempting to ease the situation with humor.

"That's not funny, Emma. You know I love you just the way you are. But how did this happen? When did you find the lump? This is all so sudden."

He put his head in his hands. Emma moved toward him to comfort him.

'Please don't worry, dear. I've met the surgeon already and I will be fine. He's pretty sure he can get it all and I can have a prosthesis made to wear in my bra so I'll look just the same as I do now. So you see, there's nothing for you to worry about. Mother will help out while I'm in the hospital and I'm sure Joan will too. It will all be over before you know it."

Charles raised his head from his hands, his eyes searching his wife's face. He moved closer and took her in his arms.

"Don't leave me, Emma. Please, don't ever leave me. I couldn't live without you. You know that, don't you?"

"I'm not leaving you, Charles. I will only be in the hospital a week to ten days, Sam says. There is nothing to worry about. I'll be good as gold in a month or two. Now, go and get your shower so I can start fixing us some dinner."

"When will you tell Joan and Charles, Jr.?

"Tomorrow. That is plenty of time for him to know. I can't tell Joan until she returns from her honeymoon in Florida, and by that time it will all be over. Now scat; I have work to do."

Emma pushed her husband toward the stairs and headed for the kitchen.

Emma took Charles, Jr. aside in the morning and briefly informed him that she would be having surgery in the coming week. She did not go into a myriad of details. He took it in his stride and assured her that he knew she would be just fine. They hugged, and that was that. Telling Joan would be quite a different matter. Emma wished she could tell her before the surgery but was just as determined not to disrupt her daughter's honeymoon. After all, there was nothing Joan could do right now. She knew her daughter would be upset that she had gone ahead with the surgery without telling her, but Joan would forgive her once she understood.

Emma's next task was to call Julia. She had told her mother about the lump but had not passed on the results of the biopsy as yet. They made arrangements to meet for lunch at a little café they both liked near American Chic and Emma was looking forward to the trip downtown. Julia took the pronouncement in stride, but Emma could read the lines of fear etched into the still beautiful face.

"You are a strong woman, Emma—like your mother." She smiled and continued.

"I would trust Sam Kramer with my life—and with yours as well. He is a fine doctor as well as our dear friend, and I'm certain his choice of surgeon is an excellent one. God will be with you Emma, just as he has always been with me. He will not abandon you in this test of your faith. Please, believe me."

"I do believe you, Mama. I have already been to talk to Fr. Nevins and I know God is with me. I am not afraid, Mama, really I'm not. My concern is for Charles and the children. I don't want them to be worried, especially Charles. You know how dependent he is on me lately. I assured him that you would help out while I am in the hospital. I hope that wasn't too presumptuous of me."

"Emma, my dear, how can you say such a thing? Of course, I will help out while you are in the hospital—and for as long as you need me afterward." She put her arms around her daughter and held her close. "You are my life, Emma, you and Joan and Charles, Jr. There is nothing I wouldn't do for you. You must know that."

Emma, more palpable than usual, hugged her mother and the two women clung together momentarily. Emma broke first.

"Let's enjoy our lunch now, Mamma. "It's been awhile since we've had an outing together and I want to remember this one. There is one more favor that I would ask though."

"Anything," answered Julia with concern clear in her voice.

"Please help Joan to handle this and to forgive me for not telling her before the surgery. I just can't break into her honeymoon. I just can't."

"I promise you, Emma. I will make Joan understand. She and I have a special understanding. You know that. She will be fine. I'm not sure I can say the same about Papa though. He will be distraught when I tell him you are going into the hospital. He will want me to bring him there as soon as you are allowed visitors. Are you alright with that?"

"Oh yes, Mama. I love Papa and seeing me is the only thing that will ease his mind. You bring him as soon as I am awake. I don't want him to worry. He is such a dear, sweet man and I......"

Julia interrupted. "Pish posh—You never say those things about me. What is so special about that old man anyway? I could never see it."

Emma laughed. "Don't be so hard on him, Mama. You know you love him—in your own way, of course."

Before Julia could answer, the waiter brought the check. "Let this be my treat today, Mama. You can treat next time we do this—when I'm out of the hospital and back to normal."

"That's a date, my darling," said Julia. "We will have that to look forward to."

The two women parted outside the café with hugs and kisses. Emma assured her mother she would call her before going to the hospital. Charles had insisted on taking her there himself and Emma agreed that they would do this together. Charles needed to feel somewhat in charge and Emma wanted to appease him at all cost. God would be in the back seat—this she knew.

Chapter 52

▼

The surgery went well. Dr. Healy was very optimistic and the prognosis was good. He assured Charles that they got all the cancer that was visible, including in the lymph nodes and that Emma was expected to make a full recovery. Charles was jubilant. Emma took a bit longer to get her strength back than Dr. Kramer had predicted, but they all agreed that another week in the hospital would do her a world of good.

Julia had the situation in Yonkers well in hand and even George had been placated, once he was permitted to see his darling daughter. Joan, on the other hand, was still a bit miffed that no one had called her in Florida to let her know about her mother's surgery. Charles assured her that he was only following her mother's wishes, and for once Julia chimed in agreement. Emma's wishes were followed to the letter by those who loved her. Joan finally gave in and accepted the explanation. Since returning from her honeymoon, she spent her lunch hour every day at her mother's side. Joan adored her mother and, next to Alan, she was the most important thing in her world. Life without her was not a plausible consideration.

Emma got her strength back and was finally released from the hospital at the end of June. Summer's heat had not yet invaded the Westchester County area, so Charles was able to keep her quite comfortable with a few large fans placed strategically throughout the house. Julia stayed on for the first few days with Joan coming in at dinner time to help with the workload and give her grandmother some much needed moral support.

Julia and Charles constantly rubbed each other the wrong way and it was an effort on Julia's part to keep a budding revolution from erupting. Joan could see the danger signs and tried to play peacemaker at every turn. It was easier to keep her father distracted and away from Julia than visa versa so that's what she did as much as possible. By week's end, Julia had reached her limit and announced she was returning home to take care of "poor George." Charles was delighted to bid her farewell and Joan was relieved now that the tension would be lessened.

Emma rose to the challenge of taking care of her home, husband and son in short order. Once Julia had left, Emma picked up where her mother had left off and resumed being mistress of her household, much to Charles's utter joy. Charles made every effort to be home on time for dinner and to do some of the household tasks like taking out the garbage, although he preferred to leave these chores to his son. Young Charles spent as little time as possible in the company of his parents. He and his father were constantly at cross purposes and the young man knew that this upset his mother no end. He decided the best way to handle this uncomfortable situation was to absent himself as much as possible. Emma tried to talk to him on several occasions but he continued to spend more time away from home. He loved his mother very much but was never sure how to show that love without angering his father. Sometimes it seemed to the younger man, that he and his father were in competition for his mother's affections.

Time passed and Emma's health improved daily. Even Dr. Kramer was pleased.

Joan visited her mother as often as she could, but working in the local insurance office kept her pretty busy during the week. Things progressed normally until the following March when Joan announced she was pregnant. Emma was thrilled, but Charles was not overjoyed at the prospect of being a grandfather and perhaps having to spend more time in the company of his son-in-law who he still disliked intensely.

As far as Charles was concerned nothing had changed about Alan Greene. He was still not rich, not Catholic, not college educated, and, in Charles's opinion, not up to his social standards. What Joan saw in this tall, lanky young man was more than he could figure out. He had hoped it wouldn't last, but now that Joan was expecting a child, his hopes had crashed and burned. He put on an act for Emma's sake, but Joan knew his real feelings. She always could read her father better than anyone, but sometimes he made her wonder. He had always made a show of telling his daughter that if they ever needed financial help, they had only to ask. Joan kept this information close to her heart, hoping she would never have to ask. Emma remembered too.

Maybe the time will be coming soon, thought Emma, *although it would take a lot for Joan to ask her father for help. But now that a baby was on the way, they would have to move out of their tiny one-bedroom apartment. If they wanted to buy a house, they would certainly have to get some help from Charles as they had nothing saved and Alan's mother was just getting by as a dressmaker. His father had been dead for years. His mother supplemented her income by taking in borders in the big house on First Street.*

Emma kept all these thoughts to herself and just reveled in the idea of becoming a grandmother. She was thrilled at the prospect and shared her joy with her daughter. Joan worked until the last week she was due which was the week before Christmas.

"Most first babies are late," informed Emma, and this was no exception. They got through the holidays without incident. They all celebrated Christmas at the Carneys and Emma watched anxiously as her daughter helped clear the table and pick up the piles of wrapping paper strewn in the living room.

Two days later Elyse came into the world weighing 6 pounds 2 ounces and perfect. Alan had hoped for a boy and made that known to everyone in the family, but he seemed pleased that his wife had produced a healthy, normal baby. Emma watched her son-in-law as he gazed down at the tiny bundle.

There will be a bond between these two, she thought to herself. *Despite what he said about wanting a son, I can see the delight in his eyes. She will be special to him—very special.*

Alan named the baby without even discussing it with Joan which upset her slightly. She had wanted to name her daughter Alison, but Alan had filled out the papers already and Joan didn't want to make a fuss and upset him. She asked him where he got the name from but he was never able to provide a satisfactory answer. Joan was afraid the priest would not baptize her with that name but when she checked with Fr. Nevins, she found it was a derivative of Elisabeth, so was totally acceptable to the church.

Emma fell in love with the child immediately and vowed to be the best grandmother she could be. Her only request was that she be called Nana as Charles's mother had been. Joan had no problem with that and before Elyse turned 13 months old, she could say Nana loud and clear. Joan spent as much time as she could with Emma. Alan refused to let her go back to work so she brought Elyse over to her mother's house several times a week. The three generations of women flourished together for the next few years.

After two years had passed Joan was disappointed that she had not become pregnant again. She complained to Dr. Kramer, who was now retired, and he sent her to one of his young students who was just starting out.

"You may never have another baby, Joan," he informed her. "After all it took you a year to conceive Elyse. I cannot find anything physically wrong with you. Do you think we should have your husband tested?"

"Oh no," answered Joan. "That would make him furious. We've been trying for the past three years but without success. Maybe it's God's will. If I just relax and stop trying so hard maybe it will happen."

Joan proved the doctor wrong, and three months later she was pregnant. Now the time had come to think about moving. They needed more room to accommodate another child. Joan and Alan began house hunting in the surrounding area. They even looked further up the county where several of her father's young engineers had purchased starter homes. Charles had raved about their choices, so Joan, remembering her father's offer, decided to take the bull by the horns. She and Alan went to see him one evening and asked the fateful question. The answer had been a resounding "no" with no explanation other than, "those houses aren't worth it." Joan was hurt beyond words and Allan was furious. He made no bones about that and told Charles where he could stick his damn money. Joan let it go and did not bring up the subject again. Before she knew what was happening, Alan announced that they were buying his mother's big old house on Front Street and she was going to live with them. Joan begged and pleaded to wait until they could find something they could afford, but Alan was adamant. This was the answer to their financial problems and Emma's father be damned.

"I'm the head of this house," Alan shouted, "and I'll make the decisions. We don't need your father and his damn money anyway. Our baby will be born in the new house and my mother will be there to help, and that's final."

Joan threw in the towel and stopped fighting him. She had more important things on her mind right now. Emma was back in the hospital preparing to lose her other breast.

Dear God, let me live to see my second grandchild, Emma wrote in her journal. *I haven't asked you for much lately but if it isn't your will, I understand. Could you make it a boy this time? Alan wants so much to have a son. And please, Lord, help Joan to get along with her mother-in-law and find happiness in her new home.*

The Lord answered half her prayers. Emma did indeed survive another breast surgery and tolerated some ugly treatments with mustard gas, the best antidote available at the time. Joan had another girl and this one, also 6 pounds, 2 ounces but 19-1/2 inches long, she named Alison. The nurses laughed when they heard because the doctor who delivered the infant was named Allison—two ll's instead of one but never-the-less the sound was the same. The doctor was pleased too even though Joan explained that he was not really the baby's namesake. Joan cried again when she came out of the anesthetic when she heard it was a girl, thinking Alan would be furious. Disappointed was a better word. He was so happy that they proved the doctor wrong and produced another offspring that he didn't mind that it was a girl.

"We can always try again," he assured Joan.

Chapter 53

It took Emma several months to recover from the second surgery and the mustard gas treatments took their toll. Julia helped out again and Joan did her best too, but with a four year old and a new baby in the house, her time was very limited. On top of that, when they bought the house, Alan decided it needed to be completely renovated. Construction was definitely his forte but when they started Joan had been very pregnant with Alison and could not do a lot to help her husband with the painting and wallpaper removal. It was a long arduous project and, they soon realized, would take several years to complete.

Alan's mother had given them the master bedroom which had an alcove off of it to contain the new baby. This worked out fine until three months later when Joan discovered she was pregnant once again.

"This can't be happening," she said to Emma. "First the doctor says I'll have no more and now I can't seem to stop. These babies will only be a year apart, Mom, and it will be born in December again just like the other two. The month of March seems to be my nemesis."

"Don't worry, Joan," cajoled Emma. "At least they're not twins and Elyse will be able to help you even more by then. She can already give Alison a bottle, and she's only four years old herself. What an amazing child she is."

The year went by before either woman realized it, and suddenly on Friday, December 13th there was another addition to the growing family—another girl. Joan was mildly hysterical this time as she heard the nurse's voice through the haze of the anesthetic pronouncing that it was a girl.

"Alan will never forgive me," was all she could think. She began to cry as soon as her husband walked in the door. The crying stopped abruptly though when he informed her that he had once again named a baby without consulting her. He had named the new infant Betty Lou—the name of a former girl friend and a name that Joan detested. Even in the haze of anesthesia, Joan found rage. "How could you do that?" she screamed. Alan only grinned and left the room. Joan called the nurse at once and demanded that the birth certificate be held up and not sent to the registrar.

"I want the name changed," she insisted, "and I will not take no for an answer." The nurse knew instinctively that she meant business and went to the head nurse with Joan's demand. The forms were supplied and Joan filled them out without hesitation.

"I want at least one daughter to be named for my mother," she stated vehemently. "This child will be called Elizabeth—my mother's middle name. I wanted to call her Emma but my mother dislikes the name so I will settle for Elizabeth, and we can call her Beth for short."

"Shall we have your husband co-sign the request?" asked the nurse.

"Absolutely not," said Joan. "I am making this decision on my own and I don't need him to approve it."

The nurse shrugged and took the forms from Joan's outstretched hand. "I will take care of this at once, Mrs. Greene. Have no fear; your daughter will be officially named Elizabeth."

Joan settled back on the pillow and breathed a sigh of relief. She would have a few choice words to say to her husband when he returned for visiting hours.

Alan shrugged off his wife's tirade and insisted she had lost her sense of humor. Emma usually didn't take sides, but this time she agreed with her daughter that his actions were not humorous. She was pleased to have her granddaughter named for her and thanked Joan for selecting Elizabeth rather than Emma which she disliked. Charles came to visit one evening with Emma but it was obvious to Joan that he thought another daughter was a terrible mistake.

Joan recovered quickly and was back home with the new baby in three days. Alan had worked hard to finish one more bedroom so they could move Alison in there and keep the new baby in the alcove with them. Emma, as always, agreed to come over during the day and give Joan a hand with the new baby. Having Alison and Beth a year apart was a lot of work and Emma knew her daughter could use all the help and moral support she could provide. Charles objected, stating Emma's tenuous health as a reason to decline, but she ignored his warnings.

There was little joy in her life anymore, Emma reflected, except for her daughter and her grandchildren. Charles's disposition had gotten worse with each passing year and many of their so-called friends no longer invited them into their homes. Everyone adored Emma, but few could tolerate Charles and his cantankerous attitude. Emma understood and forgave them, but she did miss the social interaction she was used to. Many of her women friends would invite her for lunch or some other social outing, but she and Charles were seldom included as a couple on their neighbors' guest lists.

Charles, on the other hand, didn't seem to mind their exclusion. He was becoming more and more antisocial and preferred to have Emma at home all to himself. Emma still kept in touch with Stephen now and then but was never able to mention that to Charles without invoking his ire. Stephen had never married and this fact, coupled with the fact that he still called Emma from time to time, was fuel for Charles's anger. He was convinced that a man and woman could not be just friends. Emma knew that Stephen still had deeper feelings for her but she trusted and cared for him more than anyone else in her past.

Ginger had totally disappeared from Emma's life years ago—shortly after Joan was born. She had sent congratulations when the baby was born but made no mention of coming east in the near future. She was totally absorbed in her career in Hollywood and Emma was no longer a part of her world. Emma felt no ill will toward her childhood friend but couldn't help missing her just the same. They had shared so many memories from their high school and modeling days.

She missed her friend, Anna, too. Anna had finally married and moved to a city in the Midwest and was now busy raising a family herself. They kept in touch for awhile but as often happens, life got in the way and the two women stopped writing and finally lost touch with one another, except for an occasional Christmas card. Joan was Emma's main link to happiness now and the two women became closer and closer as the years went on.

In 1960 the ides of March foretold again that Joan would have another baby. Emma tried to ease her daughter's angst but Joan was not to be consoled.

"There will barely be two years between Beth and this baby," Joan wailed. "I can't believe I am pregnant again."

Emma knew that her daughter's marriage was a bit rocky at the moment. Alan had been drinking more than Joan would have liked and Emma suspected that this pregnancy was a result of a recent drinking binge. In anger Joan had alluded to being raped by her husband and Emma had been shocked but just listened.

"What can I do when my mother-in-law is sleeping in the next room?" Joan cried. "He's awful when he's been drinking, Mom, just awful, and I don't know what to do about it. We didn't want another baby and now here I am pregnant again. That's how Beth was born too. I wouldn't trade my kids in for anything, Mom. You know that, but a little family planning would have been nice."

Emma held her daughter close and tried to console her. "I'll be here to help you again, honey. Don't worry; we'll get through this just like we did before."

Joan rested her head on her mother's shoulder and let the tears come. "I don't know what I'd do without you, Mom. You're what's holding me together. I love you so much."

Emma came over almost every day to give Joan a hand. As long as she was back home when Charles walked through the door, all was well. She had been feeling more tired than usual lately and decided to go to Dr. Healy for her checkup a bit earlier than usual. He ordered some x-rays and a blood test and she went back to his office a week later to get the results.

"Emma, the results are not good. The cancer is back but this time it is in your intestines. It must have been seeded there like grass seed even when your first breast was removed, and now it has sprouted and is a full blown threat to your life."

Emma sat silently for a few moments. "Poor Charles," she said. "How will he ever manage without me?"

"Emma," responded Dr. Healy, "it's not Charles I am worried about; it's you. Do you understand what I am telling you?"

"Yes, of course I do doctor. You're telling me I'm going to die and I can't help but worry about my husband. He needs someone to care for him and he won't understand. How long do I have?"

"It's hard to say, Emma, a year, maybe less. Do you want me to talk to Charles? I would be happy to explain the situation to him."

"No, Dr. Healy. I will tell him myself—in my own time. Thank you for being so straightforward with me. I couldn't handle this if I didn't know the truth."

Emma stood up and walked toward the door. The only thought in her mind right now was Julia. *I have to talk to Mama. She'll know what to do.*

Chapter 54

Emma put the phone back in its cradle. Her conversation with her mother had been brief. All she had to say to Julia was *I need to talk to you* and she knew her mother would be there as quickly as possible. This was not something you could discuss over the phone and Emma needed to feel the warmth of her mother's arms as well as her ability to listen.

She walked slowly into the kitchen and poured herself another cup of coffee. Then she went upstairs and got her journal and brought it with her to the kitchen. She selected a pen from the cup on the counter and held it thoughtfully against her cheek.

"Deus ibi est" she wrote. *God is always there. Father Nevins used to say that all the time. I pray he is there for me now as I have just had devastating news. My cancer is back, and I am going to die before the end of the year. I probably won't see Christmas again and maybe not even Thanksgiving. How hard that is to comprehend. Mama is on her way here so I can explain this to her in person. I need her wisdom when it comes to telling Charles. He won't understand because he won't allow himself to accept the truth of the situation. He will go into denial immediately and just be angry with God for putting me through this. She'll help me find the words; I know she will.*

And then there's Joan. She will be angry, too, at first and then totally devastated, We have become so close these last few years, I'm afraid she has become too dependant on me. She has never gotten along with Charles and he will become a burden to her after I am gone, if she allows it. Young Charles will suffer the worst because he will still be living at home with his father. What will happen to him, Lord? What recourse is there for him?

Before she could begin to consider an answer to her questions, the front door opened and Emma could hear her mother's pronounced footsteps in the hall. When Julia entered the kitchen Emma stood and ran to her immediately. The two women held each other close and the tears began to flow between them. Suddenly Julia held Emma away from her. Without releasing her hold on her daughter's shoulders, she looked deep into her eyes and her voice was firm and controlled.

"There is no time for tears. We will get through this, Emma. With God's help we will survive this and so will all those who love you—Charles and your children included. There is no need to tell Charles anything other than that the cancer has returned and you will have to submit to some heavier forms of medication which will not allow you to do everything you may want to do around the house. He and Charles, Jr. will have to help you. From here on in we will take it one day at a time."

Julia drew her daughter back into her arms and hugged her tight.

"Thank you, Mama," Emma sobbed, "but how did you know what I wanted to talk to you about? I never mentioned my cancer on the phone. You must know me better than I know myself. What would I ever do without you, Mama."

Julia smiled and shrugged. "You are my heart, dearest Emma. I feel what you feel and I could hear the words through the phone lines even though you did not speak them."

"God bless you, Mama. I needed to hear your wisdom and now I know I will be able to handle whatever comes. I'll tell Charles and Charles, Jr. tonight and I'll explain to Joan tomorrow when she comes over to visit with the children. It will be hard for her, especially now that she is pregnant again. I may not be around to help her this time. At least this baby is due in early November instead of December like all the girls. Will you say anything to Papa about my being sick again?"

"I think it is best to tell him, Emma, so he can get used to the idea. I may wait a day or two but then I will try to explain to him what is going on. He will start praying at once and God knows, we need all the prayers we can get."

Julia smiled and Emma felt herself relaxing in her mother's calming presence. "Are you alright, Mama? I don't like that cough you have developed lately."

"Don't worry about me, Emma. These old lungs are just getting worn out. I'm being punished for yelling at your Papa," she laughed.

The two women hugged again and then sat down at the kitchen table. Emma went to work filling the coffee pot and Julia set out some pastries from the small brown bag she had brought with her.

"I made these last night," she said, pointing to the cinnamon cakes in front of them. "You always loved them as a little girl."

Emma smiled and poured the steaming coffee into the cups. She selected one of the cakes and took a bite, licking her lips in total appreciation.

"They're as good as ever, Mama."

The afternoon passed quickly and soon it was time for Julia to leave. Emma hugged her mother again and thanked her for coming. "I'll call you tonight, Mama, after I've told Charles."

After Julia left Emma sat down once again at the kitchen table and picked up the journal. She opened it to where she had been writing earlier.

Mama was here and as always, she knew what I wanted to talk to her about. I feel much better about everything—just talking to her makes all the difference. I hope I can have that effect on Joan. I don't want her to worry about me. She's got more than enough on her plate right now.

Emma glanced at the clock and realized that Charles would be home at any minute.

I'd better give some thought to dinner before Charles comes home so will write again tomorrow, she scribbled quickly and closed the journal.

She heard the key in the lock and fear gripped her. *Dear God, please let him be sober. I can't talk to him about this if he's been drinking.* Emma was startled to hear two sets of footsteps in the hall. Both Charleses loomed in the doorway and were grinning at her.

"Hi Mom," said Charles, Jr. "Guess you're surprised to see Dad and me coming home together, aren't you?"

"Our son was at a meeting in my department today, Emma, so we were leaving for home at the same time. Quite a coincidence, don't you think?" said Charles. "How does it feel to have both your men home at the same time?"

Emma smiled, relief enveloping her like a warm blanket." It feels great," she responded. "I hope you two are hungry. I was just about to start dinner.

"Well then, there's time for a drink before dinner," said Charles. "Will you have your usual, Emma? And what about you son; will you join us this evening?"

Young Charles looked at his mother and then answered. "I'll just grab a beer from the fridge, Dad, but thanks for asking.

Charles nodded. "And what about you, Emma?"

"I'll have my usual, dear. I can sip it out here while I'm preparing dinner."

"One Manhattan coming up for the cook," teased Charles. He gave Emma a hug and headed into the dining room where he kept the liquor.

Emma breathed a sigh of relief and set about reheating the chicken *papricash* from yesterday. It was one of Charles's favorites and she wanted him in a good mood for their after-dinner talk. She tossed salad greens into a bowl and put them in the refrigerator to chill. She was making the batter for the dumplings when her husband returned with one Manhattan in hand.

"Here you are, darling. This should inspire the chef." He laughed and clinked Emma's glass as she raised it to her lips. "I'll just change my clothes and be right back down. That chicken smells delicious."

Dinner went extremely well. It was rare that the three of them had dinner together these days. Young Charles always seemed to have classes or dates with friends that precluded sharing the evening meal with his parents. The two men told Emma about their day and the meeting that had brought them both together in Charles's department. There was not a cross word between the two men, which was a rarity also.

Emma served the desert and coffee. She drew herself up to her full height and addressed both of her men together.

"I have something to tell you," she began. They both looked up from their plates and waited for Emma to speak.

"What is it, Mom?" asked Charles. "You sound so serious."

"I went to Dr. Healey today for my checkup." She paused and then continued. "He said my cancer is back—in another place this time."

"What do you mean back?" Charles exploded. "I thought they got it all last time."

"Please let me finish, Charles. It is in my intestines. I will have to undergo some new form of medication to treat it which will leave me pretty tired. I may not be able to do as much around the house as I have been and I may have to rest more during the day while I'm taking these treatments. I'm going to have to count on you two to help me around the house. I hope that won't be a problem. Joan has her hands full with the three girls and, as you know, is pregnant again so she can't do too much to help me. Mama will, of course, help out as much as she can but she's getting older now and can't be running back and forth from New Jersey every week. After all, she's got Papa to take care of."

Both men were silent and then young Charles spoke.

"I'm so sorry, Mom. I thought you were done with that terrible cancer. We'll do whatever you need us to do, you know that; won't we Dad?" He looked at his father, waiting for an affirmation. Charles just stared at Emma, total disbelief evident in his eyes.

"I thought this was all in the past," he said. "Dr. Healey said he got it all when he took your last breast. How can this be? How could it come back again? I don't understand."

"Please be calm, Charles. I can't answer those questions and I don't think Dr. Healey can either. He explained to me that the cancer must have been seeded there already. It just didn't show up until now. It's like grass seed that was planted and suddenly sprouts up. None of the x-rays showed it until now. I'll start the treatments right away. I already have an appointment for next week so he's not wasting any time."

Emma could feel the tears fighting to break loose but she controlled herself. If Charles suspected she was afraid, he would be afraid too and she was trying to avoid that.

Charles held his head in his hands. After several minutes, he sat back in his chair and raised his eyes to the ceiling. "Why us, God? Why us? Haven't we been through enough?"

"Dad, Dad," yelled his son. "It's not us—it's Mom. She's the one going through this. Can't we just pray for her to recover and stop worrying about ourselves?"

"Don't speak to me like that, Charles," his father shouted. "Don't you think I've suffered through this with your mother? Don't you think it's been hard on me too?"

"Stop this, you two," Emma interrupted. "We're all in this together and we'll get through it together. I just wanted you to know what we're facing and ask if I could count on your support. Let's not talk about it anymore. I haven't told Joan yet but I will call her tomorrow. Go on now, do whatever you were planning to do. I'm going to clean up the dishes and then I think I will go to bed early. I'm a bit tired. It's been a long day."

Charles got up from the table and walked toward the living room. In a few moments Emma could hear the sound of the TV announcing the football scores. Young Charles rose and gave his mother a hug. "I love you, Mom, and I'm here for you, he reminded her.

"God bless you, son. Your grandmother always told me that loving someone deeply gives you strength, but being loved by someone deeply gives you courage.

That's what your love means to me now. I'm not afraid, so you shouldn't be either."

She kissed him on the cheek and patted his hair like she used to.

Chapter 55

Emma began her treatments at once but there was little improvement in her recovery. She became more and more lethargic and the pain was becoming so intense that it kept her from sleeping most nights. By early June Dr. Healey insisted she be hospitalized. Charles drove her to Miseracordia Hospital in the Bronx where she would receive the compassionate care she so desperately needed. The nuns at Miseracordia were known throughout the medical community for their magnificent service. Joan accompanied him and tried to reassure him that it might not be forever, although she knew in her heart that she was lying.

Charles's first thought upon arriving home was concern for his welfare. "Who is going to take care of me?" he questioned. "I don't even know how to boil water," he added as if it were someone else's fault that he was so inept.

"You and Charles will manage, Daddy," offered Joan. "I'll try to help when I can but I can't be here to cook for you. I have three kids and a husband at home, remember. I'll try to come with you to the hospital as many nights as I can and we can take turns driving; okay?"

"I suppose so," grumbled Charles. "I don't know how I'm expected to handle the housework. Your brother better be prepared to fill in around here. After all, I'm a busy man, you know."

Joan shrugged and did not answer. She was determined not to get involved in an argument with her father, no matter what.

The months went by in a parade of discontent. Charles was constantly complaining and Charles, Jr. was threatening to move out. Joan was at her wits end. By the end of August Joan had developed bronchial pneumonia. She could not take antibiotics because of the baby so tried to doctor herself with lots of liquids and rest. The latter was almost impossible as she was going to the hospital to see Emma almost every night. Emma was now heavily sedated with morphine on a daily basis and frequently didn't even know her family was there. Her only concern most of the time was when she would get her next shot, as the pain was now excruciating.

Joan was hospitalized herself on September 1st and though she was not due until early November, she literally coughed her son loose on Labor Day, September 2nd.

The doctor's initial remark was, "You have killed your baby."

That's when she knew it was a boy and insisted that she would go into labor. The doctor had her marked up for a Caesarean Section but Joan was determined to have her son normally, like all the others. By midnight on the 1st she had willed herself into labor and an hour later she delivered a three pound baby boy. She named him Brett so there would not be two Alans in the house. She had seen enough of that growing up with two Charleses. The baby was officially Alan on his birth certificate but Brett is what everyone called him.

He was so tiny, but he had all his appendages and seemed to be perfectly healthy. The doctor who delivered him was amazed at the successful birth but wanted to keep him in the hospital for the first two weeks of his life to be sure there were no undetected problems and to get his birth weight up to five pounds. Joan had to remain hospitalized, too, until her lungs cleared and there was no trace of the pneumonia remaining. She could only see her son from behind glass as she was not allowed to enter the nursery area in her infected state.

"At least I can visit him every day," she said to her husband, "but I can't wait to hold him in my arms. I still can't believe we have a son."

Although she was recovering slowly, Joan was getting frantic. She was terrified that her mother would die before she could see her again. She also wanted her to know she had a son and with luck, she could get to meet him. Joan was released from the hospital after ten days and went right to Miseracordia that evening to see her mother. Emma was more awake than usual and showed evident joy at seeing her daughter and hearing her news. Joan was informed that she would not be allowed to bring the baby into the hospital but that she could show her mother pictures using a slide projector.

Alan was an excellent photographer. He went to the hospital the next day and took photos of Brett with his slide camera. He was now able to get a picture of Joan holding their son on one of his brief sojourns outside the incubator. He got them developed immediately and the next night they took the slides to the hospital. Charles, Jr. had borrowed a projector from a neighbor and so they were able to have a slide show for Emma right in her room. She was thrilled and Joan was so happy that her mother knew she had a son and at least got to see him, even if it was only slides on the wall of her room.

Charles continued to be more concerned for his own welfare than anyone else's. He was terrified of losing his wife and his antagonism was his way of hiding his potential grief. Joan knew this to be true but her patience was wearing thin. She tried to be there for her father as much as humanly possible but it was difficult with a family of her own to care for and a new baby still in the hospital.

She went to see Brett every day until they finally were able to bring him home on the twentieth of September. The tiny infant had finally attained the requisite five pounds and was ready to begin his life as a member of their family. Alan and Joan settled him into the alcove off of their bedroom and his sisters were finally able to meet their little brother. This was one time that Joan was glad her mother-in-law was living with them because she could feel free to leave her son in the evening long enough to visit her mother in the hospital a half hour away.

She drove to her father's house one evening in mid November to pick him up and take him to the hospital. Charles was already complaining of being tired and not having enjoyed his dinner which young Charles's girlfriend had kindly prepared for them. "She's always hanging around," he grumbled to Joan. "I can tell she's set her cap for Charles, but she's not good enough for him; I can tell you that."

"Don't start, Daddy," answered Joan. "Be glad someone is there to cook for you."

He was about to retort but thought better of it. He shrugged and moved closer to the door. He was silent for the rest of the ride to the hospital, and Joan was enjoying the peace and quiet. She dropped him off at the front door and proceeded to search for a parking space.

When Joan entered her mother's room she was immediately assailed by a sense of foreboding. Her father was already dozing in the chair next to Emma's bed. Emma's eyes were closed but as Joan approached the other side of the bed, her eyelids fluttered and she met her daughter's gaze head on.

"Joan, is that you?" she whispered.

"Yes, Mommy, it's me." Joan leaned over and kissed her mother's damp cheek and ran her fingers through the lifeless still-blond hair. *Not a white hair on her head,* she thought to herself, *and here I am already going white at thirty two. Even Julia is still blond. What is it about these Hungarian women?*

Joan glanced over at her father who was beginning to snore quietly. "Daddy and I are both here," she said. "Can I get you anything?"

Emma lowered her lids and then opened them again. "What time is it, dear? I should be getting my shot now. Where is the nurse?" She seemed to be getting agitated.

"Don't get upset, Mommy. I'll go find the nurse for you."

Joan went out into the hall and saw the Mother Superior at the nurse's station. She walked over to her and asked about Emma's medication.

"She just had her shot fifteen minutes ago, Joan. I can't authorize any more for another two hours at least. We gave your mother The Last Rites this morning and she wasn't even aware of it. I don't think it will be too much longer, my dear."

Joan looked at the nun in disbelief. "The Last Rites—you gave her the Last Rites?"

"Yes, my dear. Father Nevins performed them himself. He said it was time so I did not interfere. We did not want to alarm you but you must realize it has been twenty six weeks now that your dear mother has been with us. I don't see how she can hold on much longer.

"I understand, Sister, I was just surprised that's all. The truth is I wish God would take her and put her out of her misery. It's just that she's so young—only fifty six. I don't know what my father will do without her; I really don't. I myself can't imagine life without her in it.

Well, thank you, Sister. I'd better get back to my mother now."

Joan returned to Emma's room and noted that her father was now awake. He was holding Emma's hand and she was smiling at him. What a picture they make, Joan thought. They look for all the world like a pair of newlyweds.

"You just had your shot, Mommy, so it will be awhile before you can have another."

"Oh no," whimpered Emma. "I can't wait any longer. I must have it now, Joan. Please get it for me now."

Just then a nun in nursing habit entered the room. "I can't give you any morphine, Mrs. Carney, but I can give you something to relax you a little."

Emma smiled thankfully. The nun raised the sleeve of Emma's gown and inserted a needle full of liquid. "This will calm her down," she said to Joan. "It will hold her off a bit for the next shot of morphine. Call me if you need anything."

When Joan turned back to her mother, Emma's eyes were closed. She looked so peaceful. Charles rested his head on the back of his chair and then spoke.

"She won't wake up again, Joan. Why don't we just leave now? She'll never know the difference and I am so tired I can't keep my eyes open."

Joan looked at her father in disbelief. "But we just got here, Dad. How can we leave so soon? I think we should stay awhile. Mommy might wake up again. You never know."

"No she won't, Joan. She won't wake up till the next shot and then she'll be out again anyway. I need my sleep, Joan. I want to go home now."

"Please, Daddy, please can't we wait a little while? I just have a feeling we ought to stay. Can't you wait a little longer?"

"No, I can't. I want to go home now. I'm tired and I need to get to bed. Take me home now, Joan." He stood up and walked toward the door of Emma's room.

"Daddy, please," pleaded Joan but to no avail. When her father made up his mind, there was nothing you could do to change it. She leaned down and kissed her mother's cheek and patted her hand.

"See you tomorrow, Mommy," she whispered and joined her father at the door.

As they arrived at Charles's house, Joan noticed that the outside light was out. "Let me walk you to the door, Daddy. The bulb must have burned out and I don't want you to trip on the steps."

She took her father's arm and led him up the path the steps up to the front door. Charles opened the door with his key and as he pushed the door open, they heard the phone ringing. Joan rushed past her father to answer the phone. It was the Mother Superior on the line. "Your mother is with God, Joan. She left us about fifteen minutes ago."

Joan hung up the phone and faced her father. The tears and the rage all came at once.

"She's gone, Daddy. She died fifteen minutes ago—right after we left. I told you we should stay. I felt it, but no; you wouldn't listen. You had to go home right away because you were tired. All you care about is you. I didn't even get to say a proper goodbye. My mother is dead and I didn't say goodbye. How could you do that to me? How could you make me leave? How could you?"

The tirade went on until Joan was exhausted. She slumped on the bottom step and the tears came in profusion.

Charles stood there speechless. "I didn't know......I didn't mean.......how could I know.........what will become of me?"

At that last remark, Joan raised her head, wiped her eyes and stood up. "Frankly, Daddy, that's your problem, not mine. God help you and my poor brother who has to continue to live with you. Grandma Julia was right. You are a selfish, wretched man who didn't deserve a woman like my mother and I don't care if I ever speak to you again."

The door slammed as Joan left the home of her childhood for the very last time.

Epilogue

Emma's death turned everyone's life upside down. Although Joan did not want to spend any more time in her father's company, she had no choice. He was unable to cope with the simplest details, using profound grief as his excuse. The funeral arrangements were left entirely to Joan. She selected the coffin and made all the necessary arrangements with the funeral home and the cemetery. Charles hovered in the background for some of these arrangements but had nothing to contribute except his attendance. Young Charles tried to help his sister as much as he could, but was always afraid of displeasing his father so tread very gingerly in his presence.

Julia, usually so strong and stalwart, was consumed with grief. She simply could not believe that her beloved Emma was gone. George was not much better and Joan had little success in raising their spirits. It was a terrible time for Joan, but she held herself in check until after the funeral was over.

She almost lost it at the funeral parlor when she was called in to view the body before it was placed in the casket. She was appalled as she looked down at her once-beautiful mother to see her mouth covered in bright red lipstick.

"She looks like a harlot," Joan said to the funeral director.

She grabbed a piece of Kleenex from the box on the table and begun rubbing at her mother's mouth. Then she took a tube from her purse and began to color her mother's cold lips with a soft shade of pink.

"There," she said. "That's much better."

The director said nothing as he watched her tear-stained face. He led her from the room muttering apologies.

The wake was held for two days and the throngs of people who came to pay their respects seemed endless. Charles was oblivious to everything so the brunt of the greetings of family and friends became the responsibility of Joan and her brother. He was her rock and the only person who could keep her from falling apart.

Joan's determination not to return to the homestead of her youth wavered when her father called and demanded that she get all her mother's clothes out of the house immediately. Joan packed clothes, shoes and jewelry into suitcases from the attic and took them home without a word of argument. The next day her father called again.

"I want you to return the suitcases you used as well as mother's good jewelry. Be sure you include all the diamonds and the antique watch that belonged to my mother."

Joan was in shock. *What was she to do with all the clothes? Why did he need the suitcases right away? Was he going on a trip? Wasn't she to have anything of her mother's?*

She complied the next day. Charles thanked her but offered no explanations. He checked the jewelry carefully to make sure nothing was missing. Joan left without a word. She did not talk to her father again for several months. He called one evening to inform her that he was getting married, selling the house and moving to Florida.

"Married?" she exploded on the phone. "But mother hasn't even been dead a year. Who are you marrying for heaven sake?"

"Her name is Florence and she works in my office," Charles responded calmly. "She is a widow with no children. She is well traveled and intelligent and will take good care of me," he assured Joan.

"And what about my brother?" asked Joan.

"He's already planning on moving out," her father said. "You can see he left me no choice."

"So you're saying it's because of Charles that you're getting married?"

"Well, of course. The doctor says I cannot be left alone—my heart you know. I have to have someone with me at all times. This seems like the perfect solution. Don't you agree?"

Joan was speechless. Then she asked, "Can I please have something of my mother's from the house before you sell it? I have nothing to remember her by except a few pieces of costume jewelry."

"I'll discuss that with Florence and get back to you."

Charles called a few days later to inform Joan that Florence had left something for her in the garage. She could pick it up any time.

Alan drove Joan to the house that Saturday. Charles' car was gone but the garage door had been left unlocked. They went in to the garage and on an old kitchen chair was a small package with 'for Joan' on it. Joan opened the package and found a pair of sheets that her mother had carefully mended. This was the remembrance her father's bride had chosen to leave her. She could not believe her eyes. Alan did not know what to say to make her feel better. He looked around the cluttered garage and noticed a large garbage can with the cover removed. He looked inside and saw a pair of old silver candlesticks. He remembered that Joan had said they belonged to Charles' mother. He scooped them out and surreptitiously wrapped them in an old piece of cloth. They looked pretty worn but he would have them re-silvered for Joan as a surprise.

Alan presented the candlesticks to his wife as an anniversary gift the following year. Joan cherished them as her mother had and they held a prominent place in their home all their married life.

"Most of the shadows of this life are caused by standing in one's own sunshine."

—Ralph Waldo Emerson

978-0-595-38320-7
0-595-38320-3

Printed in the United States
44736LVS00005B/216